THINGS UNSAID

THINGS UNSAID

a novel

Diana Y. Paul

SHE WRITES PRESS

Published 2015
Printed in the United States of America
ISBN: 978-1-63152-812-5
Library of Congress Control Number: 2015939230

For information, address:
She Writes Press
1563 Solano Ave #546
Berkeley, CA 94707

She Writes Press is a division of SparkPoint Studio, LLC.

This book is a work of fiction. Names, characters, places, and incidents are the product of the author's imagination or are used fictitiously. Any resemblance to actual events, locales, or persons, living or dead, is coincidental.

For Doug, Maya, Keith, Collin, and Isabel

The heart has its reasons which reason cannot comprehend.

—Pascal

What wound did ever heal but by degrees?

—Iago to Othello

The bitterest tears shed over graves are for words left unsaid and deeds left undone.

—Harriet Beecher Stowe

CONTENTS

FAMILY MATTERS

After penetrating the chain-link fence and knocking over the soccer goalpost, her father's car had landed in the deserted grassy field. He had been very lucky.

"You could have hurt a child, Dad, maybe even killed one," Jules said, pinching the bridge of her nose, as they waited to speak to an officer at the Edmonds police station. She had been pleading with her parents to stop driving ever since her father jumped a curb and plowed into an elementary school playground.

Her father didn't flinch. "If I hit someone, I'll stop driving."

"Are you Julia Foster?" an officer asked, interrupting them. "The daughter of Robert and Aida Whitman?"

"Yes. Please call me Jules." She cleared her throat and tried again. "My parents called me because they couldn't reach my sister, Joanne Grant, who lives nearby. I'm just visiting from California for my mother's birthday."

"Well, ma'am, there's a serious problem with seniors driving around here," Sergeant Hernandez said, making eye contact. He was respectful. "Your parents claim they didn't hear their car damage a parked Prius. And neither one of them heard our siren or acknowledged our lights flashing. We had to pull up to your father and use a megaphone before he realized what had happened."

What *had* happened? A deep grinding, screeching, and scraping against the front passenger door. Then the dangling . . . and the glass. A broken mirror hanging, like an organ, on veins of red and blue wires. Her father must have pulled slowly out of the parking spot, oblivious

1

to the damage he had inflicted. That's what Jules pictured as having happened, judging from the looks of her parents' car.

Sergeant Hernandez continued: "A witness heard the sound of the impact, so she ran out of the grocery store. She witnessed their 1978 Oldsmobile sideswiping a parked car."

Jules's daughter, Zoë, called the outsize muscle car her father drove a "pimpmobile." It was larger than some people's apartments in San Francisco.

"We have to cite your father for careless driving, and he'll have to be tested by the DMV. That is, if he doesn't voluntarily relinquish his license." He turned to her father. "Dr. Whitman, can you hear me?" the robust-bellied police officer asked, his voice more a shout than a question. But there was tentativeness, too.

"Yeah, of course, I can. You think I'm deaf?"

"Sir, do you know you caused a lot of damage to a stationary vehicle?" He paused. "A nonmoving violation is rather common . . . among beginning drivers, the intoxicated . . . and seniors."

"Well, I'll have you know, I may be eighty-four years old, but I'm as healthy and alert as any of you." Jules could hear the annoyance, the undeniable anger, in her father's voice as he flailed his arms, gesturing to the other policemen in the room. No one looked up. "Just give me those papers," her father said, pushing his words out with great effort. He yanked the forms out of Sergeant Hernandez's hand and turned away.

Walking out of the station with her mother, watching her father's stiff gait ahead of her, Jules cringed. He used to have such a strong, almost military gait.

"Mother . . . Dad . . . you really need to talk about giving up your driver's licenses. I know it's hard. But you don't want to endanger others on the road." Jules felt burning acid roiling in her stomach, pains radiating towards her back between her shoulder blades.

"Jules, you know how I refuse to get into the car with him." Her mother fidgeted, her hand deep in her jacket pocket, the knuckles moving like marbles under the thin suede fabric. "I can't let him shop for groceries by himself though. He'll only buy junk food and everything I refuse to eat. You talk to your father. I've given up. He thinks you're taking away his manhood if you take his license. And I could care less about driving. I'll hire someone young and handsome who can drive me around like little 'Miss Daisy.' I'm ready. I'm more than ready," her mother said.

"And would it be so bad anyway, Dad?" Jules tried. "SafeHarbour has regular shuttle service and volunteers to drive you wherever and whenever you want. That's why you're paying so much to live there. It's a top-of-the-line assisted-living community. Besides, it's chauffeur service, Dad. Anyone's got to love that." She touched his shoulder, hoping to reassure him, lessen the blow. He shrugged her off and silently fumbled with his keys.

Jules grabbed them from him. "I'm driving. Sit back and enjoy the ride. You've both been through such an ordeal." She felt like the parent. *It's tough getting old,* she thought.

"I've driven a lot more than these cops," her father muttered. "Some day those assholes will wake up and suddenly realize they're old men, too. Inside, you feel forever twenty-one, but others are constantly telling you to give up. 'You're useless, old man.' "

"Dad, look at the beautiful place you and Mother are living in. It's like a resort."

"For $5,000 per month, it's a bargain. A damn bargain," he laughed. The kind of laugh where Jules didn't laugh back.

Driving back to SafeHarbour, the three of them stared ahead in silence, a silence in which Jules felt even the sounds of her swallowing were exaggerated. When they got there, her father walked into his study, a sheen of sweat on his forehead, looking pale and wan.

"Let's leave your father here in front of his damn computer," her mother snorted. She was noticeably invigorated. "The rest of the day will be for more important matters. More quality time to be with your mother." She shuffled out of the room. Jules following her, thinking about how they didn't have much time left.

"Why did you have to go and buy him that damn computer last Christmas anyway?" her mother asked. "At least when he used to read the *Wall Street Journal* I could hide it and pretend I forgot where it was. Maybe we wouldn't be in such a financial mess. I blame you, you know."

Jules stared down into her coffee cup, stomach tightening, and tried to clear her throat. Her mother stood up, struggling to reach over for her insulated cup on the coffee table. After taking a sip, her pale hand trembling slightly, she slumped back down, sinking into the saggy stuffed chair. Jules swabbed the spill with her napkin the way her eighty-year-old mother still applied makeup, soaking the face oil and powder into her skin, pale and bloodless, beige dust resting in the soft folds and pockets of her face. "Mother, we need to talk about SafeHarbour expenses," she said, circling the spoon around and around in her coffee. Her heart raced.

"Oh, why bother," her mother said, redirecting. "You never really wanted to come for my birthday. Or help me. Or help your sister. Admit it."

"No, I really do want to talk. Joanne needs help, too, I know." Debts had to be paid. *I can't just abandon them. Where would they go if they had to leave this residence?* But the bills were so expensive—they were being paid at a cost not only to her and Mike but to their daughter. Their credit cards were maxed out. Her income was unpredictable, and they couldn't live on Mike's salary alone. Zoë's college fund was now at risk.

"Your sister has to lead her own life. I know that." Her mother's voice sounded as if she were trying to convince herself. "I don't own Joanne's life anymore. But still . . ." Her four-foot-ten body, stretching taller, looked ready. *What a shape-shifter.* Her mother could switch positions on a dime. Jules tried once more.

"Mother, I want to help, to be a good daughter. But I don't want to be like you. I just want to do the right thing."

"Ha, why don't you want to be like me, I want to know! I'm your mother, and your father and I have done more than enough for you. Without us, there would be no Jules. You have absolutely nothing to complain about. We're great parents."

Her mother started pulling out all the compacts, pill containers, keys, and other junk from her enormous black alligator tote bag, dropping things on the floor and then picking them up again. Jules scooped up some of the paraphernalia, just as her mother must have done for her when she was a toddler, dropping food and bits of things while she teetered on her soft, almost boneless, feet. She had loved going through her mother's purse as a child, laughing as she opened up her wallet, looking at all the pretty cards.

Her mother tap-tapped a bit of powder on her nose and smiled as she glanced at herself in the mirror before clicking shut the pearl-encrusted designer compact. She slipped it back into its black velvet carrying case, carefully pulled the silk drawstrings shut, and offered it to Jules.

"Here, try some of this. It's perfectly good. This powder is a lifesaver. And at your age, it's a must." She yawned. "I feel a bit tired all of a sudden. Fatigue shows as you get older. Not good for a girl's complexion, you know."

Jules held out her hand for the velvet bag. She retrieved the compact and inspected it. The powder puff inside was dark brown and crusty, but the compact had a pretty blue stone inlaid in its surface—glamorous, like her mother once was. She wondered if her mother knew her diva days were over.

"And these debts are not my doing, darling. They're your father's. Family matters. We gave you life." Her mother laughed.

Why did she feel stuck helping them out? Surrendering to their demands? A misplaced notion of obligation, of duty, perhaps? A desire to convince herself that she was a better person than they were? *That's what a good daughter is supposed to do—love her mother even if her mother doesn't love her back.*

There was no way the numbers added up. Their monthly fees were almost $70,000 per year. With its faux Southern antebellum appearance, SafeHarbour's circular driveway simulated the plantation from *Gone with the Wind*. Or a stage setting for the classic Greta Garbo movie her mother was so fond of, *Grand Hotel*. SafeHarbour had once belonged to the Marriott Hotel corporation—that explained its tennis courts, swimming pools, exercise rooms, and expansive parklike gardens, amenities that the semiambulatory residents hardly ever used. So what, exactly, were her parents paying for? She thought about how they liked officiousness and recognition for being special and elite. It made Jules uncomfortable, like being around tenured professors who expected deference and obsequiousness.

She couldn't get Mike's words out of her head: *"Think of your family."* But she had two families. Which one came first? Her tenure battle at Stanford had ended in termination. Her book, *The Narcissistic Mother,* was at risk. It would be more difficult to find a publisher now that she had lost her university affiliation. The Palo Alto school system paid such low wages that she couldn't afford to take an unpaid leave to complete her book. But she was the eldest child. Mommy's little helper. She had always liked doing the right thing, feeling needed. Maybe it was attributable to her Catholic upbringing and her Buddhist sense of karma and obligation.

Her parents had chosen SafeHarbour in Mukilteo—"good meeting place" in the Snohomish tribal language—themselves. Mukilteo had turned out to be a better place for the white settlers than for the Native Americans who had been cheated out of their land. Still circling the wagons. Her mother said she felt cheated, too.

Her mother dangled an unfiltered cigarette from her mouth, stained teeth exposed, lip curled. "Anyway, you haven't been out here for years," she said.

"What are you talking about, Mother? I fly out from Carmel almost every year in October, for your birthday or for Father's Day. Don't you remember?" Was her mother's memory fading? Jules watched her rummage through her purse, taking everything out again. "Goddamn it. I can't even find a cigarette in this thing. Maybe what I need is a drink instead." Jules wondered if her mother really did forget where she placed things these days. As opposed to just pretending. This new mother frightened her even more than the one from her childhood.

Jules placed her tote bag on the floor next to the sofa. An hour's worth of photocopied material from the library peeked out the top. Information on bankruptcy, consolidating debt, and credit counseling she had found for this visit. She had also gone online and discovered support groups for children of aging parents.

From inside his study, her father's keyboard clicked slowly and methodically, like a military march for miniature plebes, required but tedious. She watched through the door as her father scanned a printout. She noticed a slight tremor in his right hand. *Parkinson's?* She edged into the study.

"Dad, we need to talk about your stock portfolio," she said, her voice sounding like a scared child's.

Her father, smiling, gave her a kiss. "You're my little researcher." He passed her an Excel spreadsheet with his investments, including cost basis and return on investment. She pored through the figures.

"You two eggheads," her mother interrupted, stepping abruptly into her father's small office. Jules looked down at the graphs. "We're going to be thrown out on the street, aren't we?" her mother asked, lips tight. "Unless our Jules helps us. Those brainy types—they always know the right thing to do."

Her father's smile disappeared. "Andrew and Joanne have to pitch in, too. But I have a plan—to buy penny stocks with our Social Security. My broker warns me to avoid penny stocks, but I know better. Besides, Jules and Mike will have college tuition for Zoë soon."

"Andrew has too many financial obligations of his own with three— or is it four?—kids," her mother said, frowning. "So does Joanne, with her two daughters. Jules has only one child to think about."

"Hmm. Uh, check the answering machine, Aida. I think Joanne called and left a message," her father suggested, ignoring her mother's comment.

"Guess she can't get enough of me. Thinking of my birthday." Her mother looked pleased.

"Yeah, yeah," her dad said. "Birthdays just remind us that our lives are shorter than the year before. I think I'll take a short nap. Sleep is practicing for death. Wake me up, if you can, in half an hour."

Jules watched as her bent-over father, so curved in that he looked like a giant prawn, dragged himself off to the master bedroom with his file folders. A malodorous trace followed behind him, musty and dusty like their dogwood curtains. Jules sighed. She had hoped that on this trip, for once, they could have a good time.

"I got your text, Jules," Mike said on the phone before dinner. "Our savings have almost run out. Soon we won't be able to pay our mortgage. To say nothing of Zoë's college fund. Those selfish sons of bitches!"

He always said things like this. Again and again. Jules didn't like feeling defensive, but she did. "I know I enable them. What I really want to do is scream at them. Make them remember to take their pills. Report them to DMV for refusing to turn in their driver's licenses. I feel like I may strangle my mother. But I *need* to help them. They're my parents. After all they have done for me, they can't be thrown out on the street. We can help Zoë later. Her whole life's ahead of her."

"After all they have done for you? Are you serious? Just listen to yourself! You have to let go," Mike said as her head throbbed. "Be realistic. *We* are what matters now. Choose: our future or theirs."

"Is it really possible to turn away from those who brought you into the world?" They had had this conversation—or was it an argument?—so many times. Normally they had it at night, in bed, and she would snuggle into Mike's warm back, feeling how the muscles in his upper shoulders—between the blades—always and inevitably tightened. Jules now imagined him clenching his teeth, jaw set, on the other end of the phone.

"You're stuck. It's time to get unstuck. Before it's too late. Too late for us. Too late for our daughter."

"Mike—"

"They can move in with Joanne," he pushed on. "Sell all that unnecessary bling-bling of your mother's, and stop acting like the sky's the limit. Remember what they have done."

Jules felt her ears clamp down, like she was listening to a foreign language she didn't quite understand and felt overwhelmed by.

"You see their aging as if it were ours. Admit it. But we don't have to have their future, unless you make it so."

Jules heard the exasperation in her husband's voice. *Am I stuck with my parents?* She shuddered. She wished Zoë and Mike were with her—as a buffer, like a downy-soft comforter.

Mike clicked off without saying good-bye.

BIRTHDAY CELEBRATION

"Shouldn't I be able to do what I want on my birthday?"
Jules hadn't slept well. She felt drained. Her younger sister,
Joanne, had spent hours planning the celebration for their mother's
eightieth birthday, but their brother, Andrew, had refused to fly out to
Washington. Too busy with his own family in Vermont.

"You know, your brother didn't forget," her mother said with a lightness and satisfaction in her voice that Jules felt was reserved only for
Andrew. " 'Happy Birthday,' he sang in his lovely baritone voice over
the phone. Gets that from yours truly, you know. He *is* my special boy."
She turned to Jules as if she needed her verification.

Her mother became visibly calmer just talking about Andrew. Jules
nodded. "Well, happy birthday to you, Mother," she muttered sleep-
ily, not fully awake yet, pecking her mother on the cheek. She sniffed
a mixture of single malt whiskey tinged with tobacco. A familiar
smell. Her mother stooped over and poured coffee from a stained and
chipped coffeemaker. It wasn't an espresso maker, just a plug-in pot
in the shape of a red drip coffeemaker, only boiling water for instant
coffee . . . *Pretend coffee,* Jules thought.

A caffeine jolt from Instant Folgers and Sugar Pops were how her
mother jump-started her day. Next came her cigarettes, more caffeine,
and pretty glasses. Jules's own drug of choice was her ongoing manuscript for her book. Her mother never understood that. Called her too
academic, as if it were an insult.

Her mother pushed the Our Lady of Sorrows coffee mug at her. The
Folgers looked muddy.

"Couldn't you pretend to enjoy visiting your parents?" her mother asked again, with what looked like a sincere expression on her face. "Nothing wrong with pretending; with keeping up appearances," she grumbled, staring into Jules's eyes as she puffed. "Pretending is what manners are all about."

But I am pretending. Pretending that we are a family.

Her mother's upper lip tightened. Vertical creases made her thin lips pucker and disappear around the cigarette they held. They contracted and expanded as she talked, almost dropping the embers. "You could be so pretty, you know."

Garnet-red lip marks circled the filter ends of at least a dozen cigarette stubs lying at odd angles in the glass ashtray. Traces of past generations of tobacco were scratched deep into the ashtray's bottom. Jules daughter, Zoë, when she was three, had been startled by those ruby-red lips, afraid they were bleeding. They were the same ruby-red color Jules had always associated with Dorothy's shoes from *The Wizard of Oz*. When she was a girl, her mom's red lips had seemed magical and beautiful.

The apartment door flew open, like the prophet Elijah at Passover swooping in.

"Let's light birthday candles! Stick them in a cupcake or something," her sister Joanne shouted as she rushed in to hug their mother, her two teenage daughters behind her. "Yoo-hoo, Jules, my favorite sister." Joanne smiled and hugged her. Jules felt lucky having a younger sister, felt her body soften just having her there.

"Even the sunshine's going to cooperate for your birthday, Mom. Why don't we have a birthday picnic out in the garden? It's such a lovely garden. And I brought some light snacks. We can spread out an old bedspread on the grass like old times at Lake Tamsin when we were little. I bet Sarah and Megan would love that, don't you think?" Joanne turned towards her daughters.

Sarah, silvery-blue glitter on her eyelids, wore a pale pink, ruffled organza dress; she looked like a little Christmas angel. "Grandma," she said, "you're the only beautiful one here."

Jules's mother smiled.

How does she know exactly what to say? Jules wondered. But her mother was different as a grandma, more like the mama she had had fun with when she was her nieces' age.

"I don't feel like it," her mother said, her smile quickly disappearing. "Who wants to celebrate being eighty years old, anyway?"

"Let's go to the mall after our picnic, Grandma," Megan begged. "Oh, please. Pretty please."

"Great! Fresh air and a picnic to celebrate, then!" Jules started to slip on her rain jacket, the wrong type of jacket for this sunshine. She remembered long walks to the Girl Scout center with her mother as their Brownie leader. All the Brownies had so much fun with her mother in those days. Jules had felt so proud. How all the Brownies loved her mother, who was a joyful whirlwind, then had let them decorate their hair like Christmas tree ornaments and then had them spin like gyroscopes. So much fun, glitter and sticky glue in their hair, little prisms of light bouncing off the walls like rainbows.

Zipping up her jacket very slowly, flipping the hood up, Jules heard her mother's tread behind her, and one foot sounded like it was dragging a bit. She wanted to hold her mother's arm to steady her. Hesitating, Jules turned to see Sarah and Megan each grab one of their grandma's elbows in delight before she had a chance.

Jules pressed the down button again as they waited for the elevator. Her nieces whispered and giggled beside her. Most of the residents were too immobile to use the elevator without assistance. Jules watched her mother, who was now sullen, still as a mannequin.

"Well, it's the birthday girl," the handsome, dark-haired doorman, no more than twenty-five, said in his warm, melodious voice—the kind you would hear from the cute lion or bear cub in an animated Pixar film—when they entered the lobby. Jules inspected his navy-blue blazer with its pseudo–family crest as he opened the front door for them.

Her mother's face relaxed, looking younger in a way that no face-lift could effect. "Oh, I didn't want anyone to know it's my birthday today," she said, face shiny and beaming, as she started walking more energetically. But by the time they reached the sidewalk, out of sight of the doorman, her simmering resentment and grievances had returned.

After spreading out an old bedspread in the garden behind SafeHarbour, the girls laid out tea sandwiches and drinks.

"You know, Julia"—how she hated it when her mother called her that—"until now we were the successful Dr. Bob Whitman and his socialite wife: yours truly. So you've never heard *me* talk about money. Only your father. Money, money, money." Her mother twisted repeatedly at a huge diamond ring, at least two carats—that was just a guess— whenever the word *money* was mentioned. The ring must have been purchased some time ago, though. After one of her parents' corrosive interchanges. She knew that groove in her mother's finger as if the ring had carved out a resting place in her own flesh.

"I didn't marry him for his money," her mother said.

But didn't you? Jules thought to herself. And on this visit all her parents had talked about was money.

"But this!" her mother continued. This was her way of making Jules feel guilty. But Buddhism had been a paradigm shift for her. Or so she hoped. All those years practicing meditation had soothed and comforted her. Yet Buddhists also had an intense sense of obligation: to avoid bad karma. So there was still a price to pay. She had swapped Catholic guilt for Buddhist obligation. *Damn both of them! Neither is going to get me out of this mess!*

Jules sucked in her breath. Clutching for calm, she made her voice quieter and tried again. "Didn't you worry about this before, Mother?" Her right eyelid twitched as she watched Joanne fidget with the paper napkins.

"Your father won't face his problems. You'll have to deal with him. He just pays the minimum interest due. He's always envied your position at Stanford. Or should I say *former* position at Stanford."

Jules flinched. Of course her mother would have to open old wounds.

"After all we sacrificed for you kids—everything we could give, mind you."

"You both need to downsize, and fast, Mother. With Joanne and Andrew we can come up with something, I'm sure. Can't we?" she asked, turning to Joanne. Her sister looked down and took a huge bite out of her tiny tea sandwich, silent. Was anyone else in the family able to see that an emergency intervention was called for? *Hello? Hello? Anyone seeing what I'm seeing?*

"You're the oldest," her mother said, ignoring her. "And I want you to know I really don't want anything done for my birthday." She patted Jules on the cheek, gently, as if she were a little girl again. "Save your money, sweetie. For more important things. I mean it. I just want to hang out today and have a nice visit with my number one daughter."

When the picnic was done, Megan stood on one side of her grandmother, towering over her, and Sarah planted herself on the other. The two teens smacked their lips loudly against their diminutive grandmother's cheeks. Jules's mother gently touched her face where their kisses had landed, looking at Jules, pausing for dramatic effect. Jules remembered her mother stroking her cheeks when she was a child. *When did that stop?*

They shopped until her mother said her blood sugar was low and her feet hurt. Just like her Grandma Paulina's disequilibrium—*debolezza* in Italian. They all knew to be careful when she was feeling this way.

"What about my two sweeties?" her mother said when they had gotten her safely home. "Going to give your favorite grandma a lot of honey for her birthday before you go home to dress up?" They leaped at her obediently, shopping bags in hand.

Before Joanne and the girls left, Jules bent over Sarah and Megan and kissed them good-bye. Whispering in Sarah's ear, Jules confided, "Now, Grandma has to be the center of attention. You know that. So let's try to make sure she is in a good mood tonight."

Sarah's eyes widened. "But Grandma's always in a good mood. Like this," she said, gesturing to her grandmother's cheerful face, and she flashed a toothy smile. Jules imagined two different women: her mother and her nieces' grandmother. Or perhaps her mother had stopped being a mother and had decided to devote all her energy to her second chance to love, this time as a grandmother.

When her granddaughters were out of sight, Jules's mother started fuming. She was a fig leaf—concealing her anger while leaving pretense exposed for everyone but her own family. "It's *my* birthday . . . but it doesn't feel like it at all. Go out to dinner tonight without me.

Forget about the old lady. I just want to be left alone!" she yelled. She started to get undressed, twisting, yanking, and then pulling off her new taupe cashmere sweater. A birthday sweater from her, for her. Very expensive looking. Jules felt herself sinking, as if she had been punched in the stomach. She reached out to her mother—now half-naked, with just a bra and panties on—and with all her upper-body strength, she hugged her, half wishing to push the air out of her mother's lungs so she couldn't scream anymore, maybe not even breathe. *You know, a strangling sort of embrace.*

Jules looked over her mother's shoulder at the beautiful, silver-framed photo prominently displayed on the credenza. A recent photo of Megan and Sarah. Megan reminded Jules of her sister at about the same age. Sarah, thirteen, was a different matter. Organized and careful. Zoë was four years older than Megan and would probably follow in her footsteps and be a psychologist. She used to love how Zoë always wanted to go to her office and watch through the one-way glass window as she tutored kids. *Like mother, like daughter.* Jules fought back tears, but felt their sting anyway.

"I'm not an old lady so don't treat me like one," her mother barked, shrugging her off.

The temperature had dropped to the low forties. Very cold for October, despite the sunshine they'd had earlier for their picnic. They were all meeting at the Crab Pot, chosen because of its spectacular views of the water. Joanne had made reservations weeks ago and had requested birthday balloons, singing, and a special cake. And they had preordered oysters Rockefeller, their father's favorite, as a way of including him in the celebration for the birthday girl.

Jules looked down into the water as they made their way to the restaurant entrance. It was almost pitch black, with no moon. Jules could faintly detect whitecaps in the dark night sea. A storm was coming.

"See that lighthouse over there?" Al asked, pointing in the direction of the light flashing in an arc over the bay. Jules had never liked Al, even less now that he was Joanne's "estranged" husband.

"Megan just won first prize in a sculpture contest for her interpretation of that lighthouse, combining the themes of water and air, using old deep-sea diving headgear and astronaut suits formed from aluminum foil. She called her sculpture *What Lies beneath the Surface?*"

Jules could hear the pride in Al's voice. For a moment, just a moment, she understood why Joanne had been attracted to him almost twenty years ago. But he was not the same person anymore. *Then again, neither are any of us,* she thought. *Maybe* he *can help pay for some of the bills.*

Clacking on the boardwalk planks, her mother was the first to speak, walking up behind her and Al: "I didn't even want to remember my birthday, you know. I wanted to stay home . . . alone."

"How *dare* you say that to us," Joanne said, overhearing their mother's whining, her voice rising unexpectedly as she caught up with them and they all walked into the Crab Pot.

"But Grandma, don't you love blowing out candles?" Sarah asked, reaching for her grandma's hand. "And you're so lucky to have so many candles—eighty. I wish I were you."

Her mother cupped Sarah's face and gently planted a kiss on her forehead. "You are the dearest grandchild anyone could have. If I had known grandchildren would be so much fun, I would have had them first." She grinned and turned to hug Megan, too. Jules guessed this was so Megan wouldn't be jealous. She winced.

"Why can't we have fun now? Just try, as if we were a real family," Joanne said. The same old script. Hanging her head low so no one else could see her smile unfolding, Jules held her breath.

"That sounds good," her father said unenthusiastically as waiters came in carrying balloons.

When dinner was done, and the birthday cake was brought in to loud singing from other customers in the restaurant, the girls were at their grandmother's side.

"You can do it, Grandma," Megan said. "Blow them out."

Leaning slowly towards her granddaughters, her mother tapped the top of her head against Sarah's, then rubbed Megan's cheeks. "Sweeties, after Julia leaves, we'll go to Seattle and do whatever you like. I'll give you some spending money. A girl has to have what she has to have, I always say."

Sarah wrinkled her brow. "But Grandma, Auntie just got here and you're already talking about when she's going to leave. And why are you talking as if Auntie Julie isn't here?"

Their grandma's eyebrows jerked up. "Well . . ." she began, sputtering, not quite losing her voice. "Go ahead. See if I care," she finally said to no one in particular, gazing unsteadily ahead. Then she turned to Jules, face-to-face, locking onto her eyes: "And remember what I said. You hear me? Don't do what your father did to his brothers." Her mother's voice sounded close to breaking.

Her father sank lower in the banquette, looking out at the water's view. "Now, Aida, we have three kids. It's too much for one of them to bail us out alone."

Joanne squirmed and looked at Al, who refused to meet her eyes. "Mom, I can take out a loan. Somehow. You've been the best mom ever. That's the least I can do. Jules shouldn't do this all alone. And Andrew needs to pitch in, too. I don't understand why he didn't even show up for this!"

Jules was astonished that Joanne looked genuinely perplexed at Andrew's absence. He never came to visit.

"You two really should move in with me and the girls," Joanne continued. "I don't know why you keep turning me down. We would be really cozy together. And we would have quality mommy-daughter time."

"That *would* be sensible, Mother. You can be that much closer to Sarah and Megan," Jules said, exhaling deeply.

"You . . . you got us into this mess," her mother said, glaring at their father. "And Julia, you have only one child. Joanne has two and Andrew has two—or is it three?—and is expecting another one. And sweet Joanne, don't take this the wrong way, you hear me? I couldn't think of anything I would like more than to live with my favorite child. No offense to you, Jules," she said as she turned to glance at her, as if she were joking. "But your place is just too small for your dad and me. I need more space, so I don't have to be in the same room with him. And my mother lived with us and I swore I wouldn't do that to my kids."

Wonderful Grandma Paulina, her mother's mother. Like mother, like daughter?

Jules liked to refer to her mother as "Grandma" in front of her nieces. It sounded safer and softer. Like her own grandma.

Grandma Paulina Longo, a Sicilian emigrant, immigrated to the Bronx as a young married woman. A huge gnocchi in a floral-printed housedress, no more than five feet tall but about two hundred pounds and diabetic. Jules's Grandma Paulina had named her first child after her favorite opera, *Aida,* a tragic tale of vengeance and fury.

"My mother stole my childhood right from under me, you know that!" her mother repeatedly told Jules and her siblings when they were teenagers. "It was the Depression and both my parents worked long hours. I was a glorified slave, that's what I was, taking care of my sister and brother, cooking and cleaning. No time to think about what *I* wanted."

Jules had brought Mike home to Akron on summer break, during a body-melting heat wave. It was her grandma's birthday. Reaching up with her pale, doughy hands to cradle Mike's face, her grandma had stared up into his blue eyes.

"Such a beautiful boy," her grandma had purred in her velvety Sicilian drawl. "Oh, so beautiful, and a wonderful boy to marry."

Mike had grinned.

Grandma had been very busy making her specialty dishes the day before. Jules's mother had said nothing, leaving the kitchen to Grandma's culinary magic. To show what a good daughter she was. She hadn't wanted to relinquish control at first.

"I'd like to cook for my own birthday," Grandma had said.

"Nah, Ma, I'm going to cook," her mother had yelled. "It's the least I can do to celebrate your birthday." She'd raised her arm, as if to strike her own mother—something Jules had seen her do many times before, to her and Joanne and Andrew—but at the very last second she had bitten her forearm, then lowered it as a welt formed, and tied her apron tighter.

"I should be able to have what I want for my own birthday, now shouldn't I?" Grandma had said, and everyone else had nodded. They were all hoping for a break from their mother's cooking or frozen TV dinners.

"Mother, why can't Grandma eat something else besides lamb chops?" Jules had asked later, casting a sympathetic glance at her grandmother. Soaked with the juices from the meat, the cutting board had a solitary gray raw chop resting on top of a fresh red stain.

"She's diabetic." Her mother's jaw clenched. She could see a little knob of bone where the mandible bulged below the earlobe. "She can't eat carbohydrates—white foods."

"Not even for her birthday?" Jules asked, hoping for a different answer.

"I'm not an all-night diner. Lincoln freed the slaves," her mother replied, voice higher, wringing her red-and-white dishtowel as if it were sopping wet. Then she bit her arm. Hard. Drew blood.

Jules thought of the animals that got caught in her father's traps when he and Andrew went hunting. Some bit off their own paws to survive. She glanced at Mike, who'd seen the whole thing. He looked stunned.

After pasta—for everyone except Grandma—Jules carried in a tiny pink box. Mike gave her a quick hug, encouraging her, as she slipped out a cupcake with pink icing and "Grandma" written on it. "Happy birthday to you, happy birthday to you," Jules sang, feeling giddy, as she brought it to the table with one lit candle on a paper plate borrowed from her friend Deirdre.

"What do you think you're doing, young lady?" her mother said, yanking the plate away. The candle sputtered and went out.

"I know she can't eat it, but I thought she could have the fun of blowing out the candle and watching us eat tiny mouthfuls," Jules said.

"What's all the fuss about, anyway?" her mother said, picking up the paper plate and dumping it in the trash can. "Birthdays are just a reminder you're getting old."

Jules could smell the faint Parmesan cheese residue on her grandmother's housecoat, which revealed her ample décolletage. A warm, motherly woman. The closeness felt good. No one else she knew looked at all like her Grandma. She belonged in some old movie as a background extra with Sophia Loren or some other Italian diva, stealing the scenes. Grandma was a plump, sumptuous cupcake.

Sarah blew out the stubs of the candles before they melted into the white icing, like miniature snowmen collapsing, melting into the letters that spelled out "Grandma." Giggling, she pulled a candle out and started sucking the icing off it.

After the Crab Pot celebration, Sarah and Megan wanted to walk to the boardwalk and look out over the water at the Mukilteo lighthouse. Jules looked back to see the girls shivering in their short-sleeve, satiny dresses. Typical kids, oblivious to the frigid weather in the name of fashion. They wandered off in another direction, near some souvenir shops. Jules was left alone with Al.

"You know, I think seeing how your mother gnaws away at your father would frighten anyone. All that marital flesh eating," he whispered, as if it were a secret.

Jules's mother crossed her arms tightly and leaned heavily against the railing, watching the movement of the waves in the dark. A dim light or two shone on the water for safety reasons. The chamber of commerce wouldn't want anyone to get hurt.

Jules had chanted to herself the Buddhist mantra of mindfulness and loving-kindness: "May you be happy, may you be healthy. May you be free from worry. May your life be filled with loving-kindness." She uttered this meditation in reverse order. Instead of friends and family first, acquaintances second, enemies third, and then the world of strangers last, Jules started with human beings she would never know. She chanted "May you be happy, may you be healthy, may you be free from worry" to those she disliked. She chanted "May your life be filled with loving-kindness" to acquaintances. Then she chanted all four wishes to her family. Why did she have to work hard placing her parents in the same category as strangers, let alone friends? Would helping her parents through this make her feel less like an outlier? Did anyone ever truly know their mother and father?

It was the same mantra she had silently chanted before on other festive occasions. *May you be happy*—her mother had wanted to be happy, hadn't she? Didn't everyone?

A DIVA ON TAPE

A ll she'd ever wanted to do was sing.
As a student nurse at Montefiore Hospital in the Bronx, Aida
would pass by her Uncle Gino's restaurant/dinner club on Gun Hill
Road after classes were over. Nothing fancy, but there was a little stage,
and she loved being on it. She was always hoping against hope that the
regular waitress-singer had called in sick so she could fill in.

"Hello, my singing princess," Uncle Gino had said that day, kissing
her with heavy tobacco breath, smelling of sweat. Aida knew that her
uncle was a dirty old man. She could put up with the groping, though.
For an audience. For a pathway to a singing career.

"Any chance I'll get to sing tonight?" she asked him. "I'm always
ready to do 'Someone to Watch Over Me.' " That was her torch song.

Uncle Gino shook his head, regret in his eyes. "Sorry, sweetheart.
Not tonight."

Aida always wore the black crepe dress, the one that made her look
like Elizabeth Taylor, when she sang at the club. Low-cut, sultry; stiletto heels to make her stand out even more. To be a nightclub singer
at a New York restaurant and bar—*that's* what she had really wanted,
she thought as she dragged herself home. Not to be some drudge
cleaning up blood and shit, taking temperatures, and looking at old,
sickly bodies ready to die. She was the best-looking nursing student at
Montefiore Hospital, after all. And even her name destined her for a
better life—a life of beauty and song, like the opera *Aida* but without
the tragedy. Her fiancé, Steve Seigel, a psychiatrist at Bellevue Hospital,
had said she could do whatever she wanted after marriage. He wasn't

good looking. He wasn't even the smartest psychiatrist at Bellevue. *I could do so much better,* she thought as she opened her front door.

The dorm phone rang and she picked up.

"Hello, this is Bob Whitman, calling for Nancy Sanders. Is she in?"

"Nope, she's out." Nancy was the head nurse and her nemesis, a prissy know-it-all, plain if not downright homely, with no fashion sense whatsoever. "Don't know when she'll be back." What was her instructor, Dr. Whitman, doing with that spinster? Was he her fiancé?

"Well, could you take a message for me? I was hoping to take her out for a drink and dinner."

Aida could hear the disappointment in his voice. He always blushed so easily in front of the students, and seemed shy. He wasn't as boring as some of her instructors. No great personality either, though. Yet he was rather handsome. For a doctor, that is.

"I'm not doing anything right now, if you want to go for a drink. That is, if I'll do?"

She heard a gulp at the other end of the phone. Shortly after that drink, they had both broken off their engagements and gotten married.

Aida remembered how excited Bob had been a week after the wedding. They were moving to Akron, Ohio.

"You'll love it," he told her. "Akron's offer to open a medical practice near the tire companies is too good to refuse. A great place to raise a family, too."

Of all places: Akron, Ohio. No nightlife. No nothing. Just dreary suburban doctors' wives sitting around all day with their brats, gossiping on the phone to each other and making perfect cakes and lunches for each other. Never, never.

Akron was in its heyday then—a rapidly growing city, a boomtown. So Aida shopped with the other doctors' wives after the kids were dropped off to school. She had an unlimited bank account, or so it seemed to her. That's the least her husband could do with all she had to put up with. And the automobiles. Two of the most expensive cars on the market sat in their garage, provided as gifts by the CEOs in appreciation for the medical services her husband provided to their factory workers. Aida knew that her parents had photographs of those cars plastered on their refrigerator, as evidence of their daughter's living the dream. She always drove the pink Cadillac.

Aida had pretended to like Akron. Their home—a white Dutch Colonial clapboard with green shutters, a screened-in porch, and a solarium surrounded by dogwoods—was the standout on the block. Perhaps that was her consolation prize. She was so proud of the dogwood trees framing the solarium that she'd had custom draperies embroidered with their blossoms. She never replaced them. They eventually faded until the dogwood blossoms were virtually obliterated, just weathered white blotches on washed-out blue linen. Those curtains now hung in their apartment at SafeHarbour.

That house had only one bathroom—huge, but impractical. Over the years, there were bathroom fights between Jules and her brother. One fight was so bad that when Andrew blocked the door, Jules threw up on the floor in front of her brother, some chunks spraying all over him. Aida never had been able to understand what Jules was thinking. So opaque. Not like Joanne. Andrew was somewhere in between, but a mother knows most of the time what her son is thinking.

That morning, before her little Julia's first big day in kindergarten, Aida had struggled to help her get dressed in her brand-new white starched blouse with a Peter Pan collar and navy-blue pleated skirt. How that kid hated to get dressed. The school uniform would be a blessing. No arguments or decisions about what to wear. Julia stiffly walked into the classroom with her, trying to hold her hand. It was so tiring, Aida kept dropping it: such a sweaty little hand, soft and spongy, almost boneless.

"Darling, you're a big girl now. No need to cling on to me. Teachers don't like that. Do you see anyone else holding on to their mommies?"

Her little girl looked around. Some of the little girls were already sitting at low round tables, looking at the art supplies in the center and picking out the best colors for themselves. Aida spotted another little girl, shorter than her daughter, clasping her mother's hand. Her mother was trying to let go, too, but the girl was holding on with both hands, walking sideways and bumping into other chairs and toys in the room.

"Hi," Julia said, walking up to the other little girl, tugging Aida with her. "I'm Julia." She didn't adopt that ridiculous nickname, "Jules," until she was a teenager. Her little girl did it to reject her good taste. Aida was certain of that.

"Hi, I'm Deirdre," the small child said, her light brown hair clipped back with two little Bambi deer barrettes. Deirdre smiled right up at her little Julia.

"Oh, your name sounds like a deer—is that why you have Bambi barrettes?" Julia asked.

Deirdre clapped her hands, jumping up and down, laughing and bouncing. Aida could see that Julia liked her already.

"You think I'm a deer like Bambi, because of my name? No one's ever said that to me before."

"Yep, and your hair's Bambi color." Julia touched Deirdre's hair, then reached for her hand and they walked off to sit down at a corner table, away from the other mothers and girls. They became best friends, and remained so until they were both married.

That birthday dinner last night had been an obligation. Family matters. Celebrations for her were now long gone. *Some quiet time would be nice,* Aida thought as she pulled out her tape recorder and her old tapes, some wrinkled and partly unwound, from where they were carefully stored in a shoebox under the bed. She had loved playing those old recordings before her kids came home from school. A familiar ritual. She had been red hot and in her glory back in the day. It didn't seem *that* long ago to her. Certainly not yesterday—not a flash ago. She had been so light hearted in those days. A pretty little thing. But now, she was only a diva on tape. Her signature song . . . how she loved the sound of her own voice. Singing was her meditation. It seemed like her kids had just left for Our Lady of Sorrows hours ago. Not almost forty years ago.

Aida had always tried to hide the shaker, cold and metallic, sweaty on the sides, before the kids got out of school.

"Mommy, where are you? Mommy, Mommy!"

Aida hated hearing Julia and Deirdre's feet clambering up the stairs. Every day, incessantly.

"I'm in here, darlings."

She saw her daughter look at her face, puzzled, perhaps a bit scared.

"What are you doing on the floor, Mommy?"

"Listening to my favorite song." She knew her daughter could see the tape recorder before her, her legs curled under her. Her muffled voice singing "Doin' What Comes Natur'lly."

"Oh," Jules muttered. "Me and Deirdre are hungry. Can we have ice cream?"—and then Aida couldn't make out what her daughter was trying to say after that. She felt a bit woozy, head spinning.

"What did you say?" she remembered asking, but her daughter looked blurry and kind of weird. She never could figure out how they were related. But her Jules did love to sing— just like her mama.

Singing with her friends at the annual talent show and theater productions at SafeHarbour—that's what she had to look forward to now. How times had changed! With their debts, they would be lucky to have money to pay for dry cleaning soon. But Jules knew what to do—and Aida could count on her daughter. Her sense of obligation. Her duty. There was time to sort all that out later.

All those birthdays over the years, and what gratitude had been shown? Birthdays, birthdays—just a marker for the passage of time.

SHADOW DAD

He had deserved better, so much better. Looking down at the beginnings of a potbelly, cultivated for over two decades now, Bob Whitman slumped over his chrome and red Formica kitchen table, hearing the crunch of the plastic seat cover as he shifted his weight. That kitchenette table and chairs reminded him of the diners in LA, the ones where he could only peek in the windows, watching diners eat hot turkey sandwiches on Wonder bread, the white gooey bread all soggy and covered with rich light brown gravy the color of candy caramels. When he first had the money to eat in a diner—in the Bronx, when he was a hospital resident—he had thought he had died and gone to heaven. Now, he wasn't the moneymaking machine he had been for his family. The sacrifices he had made. If they only knew. Looking around the table at his teenage kids and wife in those days, no one ever made eye contact. Not even his wife. Especially not her.

Everyone should follow his passion. That was his mantra. Money hadn't been an obsession. It had been his passion. There *was* a difference.

And now what did he have to show for a lifetime of hard work? Eighty-four years of life, reduced to this.

Bob sat at the computer, tapping rhythmically on the calculator side of the keyboard. The numbers just didn't add up. Scrolling down through the pie charts from Fidelity Investments, the right-hand column, "Change Since Purchase," was all in red. How had all his stocks gone south? Two thousand and eight was the worst year on record for him. The Great Recession had become the Great Depression, and he certainly felt depressed. His wife's birthday dinner at the Crab Pot hadn't been worth celebrating either.

He hoped Jules could help. Aida was a liability: "Getting and spending, we lay waste our powers; Little we see in Nature that is ours." Bob had little that he could call his own.

It wasn't easy to admit that he had become a doctor for the lifestyle—not to heal others. His mother had died while giving birth to his youngest brother in a ramshackle hovel near the Los Angeles oilrigs of the 1930s. He was only three. His drunk of a father mostly ignored him and his three other brothers, so the baby brother was sent to live with an aunt. Bob became the youngest who still lived at home, with his older brother Wilson watching over him. His father didn't waste any time getting a housekeeper/stepmother who dressed him up in starched pastel-pink pinafores with lacy hems and hair bows, a stale memory. Soon all his friends called him "Barbie," and that was way before Barbie dolls. His brothers had trouble saying "Bobby," and the dreaded nickname stuck. Ever since, he had never been very comfortable around girls and then women. Only guys.

After their father died from an alcohol binge, Bob's brothers took out huge loans to pay for his medical school tuition at UCLA, even though they themselves were living from paycheck to paycheck. Bob promised to pay them back by covering the tuition of any nephew who was accepted into a medical program. Charlie, his brother Wilson's son, had only been an infant at the time, so no one knew, of course, if he would have to make good on his promise.

At Montefiore Hospital he became engaged to Nancy Sanders—not good looking by anyone's standards, not even by a close girlfriend's generous and kind opinion, but she was refined and came from a good family. So he would be happy enough with her. Besides, she was the head nurse, and studious. She was good company. Not too quiet, not too noisy. Like Goldilocks. And not dumb, like some of the others. She would be a fine mother for his children. With his intellect and her slightly lesser one, their kids wouldn't be just average in the smarts department.

How could he ever forget that phone call? His fate. Dismissing his class at the sound of the bell, he had been bone tired, too tired to go back to his apartment for a can of warmed-over Campbell's soup. Massaging the bone at the nape of his neck, his temples tender, but not exactly painful, he had cranked his neck back and forth, left to right, listening to it crack. From bending over cadavers in the medical examination hall—probably from showing the nurses the various vertebrae of the spine. He did have a big head.

"Hello, this is Bob Whitman, calling for Nancy Sanders. Is she in?" It was so irritating having to identify himself. All the nurses in that dorm were either in his lecture class or his seminar and he didn't like their knowing his business. Especially not his dating life. Nancy was discreet and he appreciated that. She was gentle and soft spoken, the ideal woman for him.

"Nope, don't know when she'll be back." Whose voice was that? He thought he recognized her theatrical, almost-singing voice—but it had an alarming association for him. What was it, exactly?

Of course. It had to be Aida Longo, the one all the other residents laughed about. He never could quite figure out why. Perhaps because she was something of a drama queen. She did resemble Elizabeth Taylor a bit. Was an attention getter. And her voice always seemed several decibels too high whenever he called on her in class. She never knew the answer. He figured she just liked to raise her hand. Aida would make anyone look good escorting her. Nancy—not so much. Bob felt his face get inflamed and hot.

Within two months of their marriage, he and Aida had purchased a huge white Dutch Colonial on a West Akron hillside, the "good side" of town: Crestview Avenue. Elms and oak trees framed stately homes, set back to look down on those who drove by in envy. Each home had a long, steep driveway that showcased the latest models of luxury cars.

The house was built in 1927—the same year Dr. Whitman was born, as he liked to boast. A good year for coming into the world. An omen for their future happiness. He hoped so, anyway. He felt mostly settled down by then. Except for the mountain of bills and the huge mortgage—but he trusted that they would be paid off in time. Their future was their own to construct. And yet.

Aida had volunteered to help him move into his new office. She bought magazines, placed a few ashtrays on side tables, and put up a bulletin board with health tips sent to him by the American Medical Association. With his shiny new x-ray machine, his antique black-walnut desk that telegraphed his power and status, and his black-leather examining table, complete with the highest-quality stainless steel stirrups, he felt complete. Then, she told him.

"Oh, sweetheart. You know, I haven't been feeling myself lately. And now my period's late."

Elated, Bob went in to hug her.

Dodging him, blocking him with her right shoulder like a defensive back, Aida said, "It's too early to start a family. Way too early. And we haven't even settled in yet, Barbie."

Bob hated her adoption of his family nickname, especially when she said it in that false, saccharine voice of hers. "You have your practice to think about. It's not the right time."

Of course, his wife had been right, he now admitted reluctantly. Neither of them had talked about starting a family, and they needed to save more money. But her words had felt like a slap. They could have managed, if they both had wanted to.

But in that moment, he could see in his wife's face just how unfit she would be as a mother. She bit her arm hard. Bright red teeth marks flared up on her forearm, alarming him.

"An abortion's the *only* option," Aida said. "A baby now would ruin any chance for happiness."

And so he had given her a dressing gown, had her slip her feet in the stirrups—she was the first patient to christen them—and performed the procedure.

Aida rested as he moved brand-new equipment into his office. Lots of new vinyl furniture—tough, so kids couldn't ruin it. But their own kids wouldn't come until later.

Sometimes, over the years, Bob had felt like a shadow dad, a ghost of a dad, an outlier in his own home. Like his own father had been. Hardly ever saw them, and now his middle-aged son and daughters had moved on with their own lives and families. Raising kids had not been heart healthy. No one ever says that.

What he'd really wanted was to be a writer, an author of a how-to book: *Beat the Wife and Save the Marriage*. He kept this to himself, or at least the title. Never knew when someone would steal his idea before he found the time to write. But he never started the first paragraph. Too tired and too angry, he guessed. Just never found the right moment to begin. He had thought there would be time after he had more financial security. There never was enough time. There never was enough money either. What had happened to their marriage, anyway?

All those decrepit virgins he had forced himself to visit. For over thirty years he had driven to the convent. The promised Sunday-morning house call. Our Lady of Sorrows had once been the O'Neill family estate. Devout Catholics with too much money, the O'Neills were also founders of one of the four major tire companies. They donated their Gothic stone mansion for a girls' school focusing on etiquette and good posture—rather ironic for the sixties. The convent halls, though imposing and haunting, were somehow pinched, starved in decor with their dusty-heavy curtains—probably relics from the O'Neills's days there—and the rows of statues of Christ and the Virgin Mary. Only the statue of the Infant of Prague had fabric; glistening and regal, the mantle, which baby Jesus wore upon his shoulders, almost matched the draperies.

Being there was like viewing the "picture of Dorian Gray." The white wimples the nuns wore—like chin straps, bandaging the entire border of their faces—were so tight they left deep creases that cut into their skin, red and raw. And when they uncinched the wimple, my God . . . their faces collapsed! Frightening. Instead of forty-five, they looked seventy-five. The wimple was like a religious form of facelift. Still, he never passed the obligation on to another doctor. Bob knew his obligations. He supposed he did care about the discount on his daughters' tuition, too. December, though—flu season—that was the worst month.

In those days he only had Sunday afternoons off, after his hospital and convent rounds, all in pursuit of greater wealth. How he had liked to take his Cadillac out for a spin. The car was his consolation prize.

Even when enjoying boomtown status as the "rubber capital" of the world, Akron was no joy ride.

Bob wasn't sure his wife and kids really liked going to Lake Tamsin, a gigantic mud hole that smelled a little bit like their toilet. The summer before, one of the Kofer boys had drowned there after diving off the platform and hitting his head. The lifeguards couldn't find him in all the sludge and muck. He must still be down there somewhere. The ghost of Kris Kofer—the son of one of those colored families who wanted to be there, too. They should swim elsewhere. No one gets what he wants.

So many southerners and West Virginians had migrated to the tire companies for employment. He knew how they thought: the majority of his patients, just normal people like everyone else he knew. Just because Akron had the largest chapter of the Ku Klux Klan in Summit County and had the Wooster Avenue Riots of 1968 didn't mean there was no place for the coloreds. Colored people were making too many demands in those days, and his daughter Jules was so upset with his opinions.

"Daddy"—he couldn't figure out why that word coming from his daughter seemed hollow, without any affection, sort of tinny to his ear—"have you been reading what's happening in the South?"

His wife smoothed out the bedspread to lay out their picnic.

He thought he sounded like a Sunday school preacher. "There's nothing but that goddamn Martin Luther King in the headlines." The beer bottle sloshed and dribbled near his knee. "Who does he think he is? Nothing's going to change! He's going to be killed. Mark my word." He could count on holding Jules's interest. She was the only one of his three kids to read the newspaper, *Time* magazine, anything with print on it about college students who were marching and protesting in the streets. Jules was intellectual, something of a bluestocking. Too bad it wasn't his son who had the intellectual smarts. Wasted on a girl.

"I just read that police are using tear gas and dogs. Fire hoses powerful enough to knock the protesters down. But they just stand there and take it until they get hurt. That can't be fair, can it?" Jules asked.

"Nah . . . Billy clubs and guns, now *that* would hurt."

Jules looked worried as he leaned back in his chair, pleased with himself. "You're kidding . . . aren't you? There are photos of people knocked off their feet by the force of those hoses."

"What do you expect, huh? It's water, for God's sake." His voice rose. "How can water hurt?"

No one said anything. His wife moved just a bit closer to him to respond. What could she possibly have to say about important matters?

"But the colored are God's children, too. And don't say anything but 'colored' or 'Negro.' It's too low class," Aida said, turning towards their kids. He thought that was an affectation. He knew she was more concerned about class than mean-spiritedness.

Confused, stumbling into a response, his older daughter seemed as if it took all her effort to talk back to him. The confidence of a high school freshman—stammering, blushing, fidgeting—was ridiculous. Fake, signifying nothing. "The nuns say the same thing. 'We're all God's children.' But they don't like the marches either. Sister de Montfort told us their reward would be in heaven. But why should only Negroes have to wait until after death for their reward?"

Bob's face felt boiled, swollen, sweaty, and lobsterish. "We all don't get what we want. That's just the way it is. Everyone should just shut up and take it. All this 'I Have a Dream' nonsense. It is what it is." He had felt out of breath. Always did with Jules.

Remembering Lake Tamsin and still recovering from his wife's eightieth birthday party, Bob felt tired, more tired than after those long days making hospital rounds, visiting nuns, and even making house calls to patients rendered immobile by old age. His family always had done that to him: exhaustion. How could anyone be generous under those circumstances? As a kid, he had learned fast. Helping his father pick tomatoes from the time he could walk, harvesting them with a flashlight, Bob and his brothers had looked for the rotten ones they sold to Dole and Hunt's for canning. They got more money for those than for the perfect-size ones. Taught him a lesson—the prettiest weren't always the best deal. You could camouflage almost anything and make it palatable.

His stock portfolio could wait. He propped the pillow under his head and turned off the lamp, hoping that Aida hadn't spotted the light from under the door. A few minutes later, as the sheets on his side of the bed cooled his hot body, he felt her slide in under the light sheet. He always felt seething, a restless turmoil inside. The turmoil was ugly, nasty. He no longer could tolerate even the slightest body contact from Aida. They hadn't had sex since Joanne was born.

"Don't pretend. You're not asleep. Wouldn't want to soil my new pink negligee anyway."

He hated all the pink nightgowns: see-through and transparent. Made of gauze, like the surgical kind. The opposite of beautiful. And pink was his least favorite color—reminded him of the bows his step-mother pinned above his ears. Why hadn't he listened to the residents at Montefiore Hospital who had warned him—I eat-a, you eat-a, we'll all eat-a. He hadn't believed what they had said about Aida. He had ignored the nuggets of truth. He always had understood what men wanted more. Aida's snoring could wake up the dead. He sobbed into his pillow, a child's kind of sob.

"Bob, this is Alice calling from LA."

Oh, his sister-in-law was a good woman. His brother was a luckier man than he had been. Alice reminded him of his former fiancée, Nancy, except that Alice had also been something of a flirt. That had been his downfall. Just a game, couldn't resist—and that's how he'd ended up marrying Aida. He was still recovering from her "birthday blast" two days before.

"Oh, Barbie. Such bad news, I'm afraid."

While Alice was trying to speak, Bob knew what the next words would be.

"Wilson has suffered a massive stroke, Barbie. Can you fly out here as soon as possible?"

How could he refuse his ninety-year-old brother, the head of what was left of their clan? Almost thirty years ago, when it came time for Wilson to collect on Bob's promise for his son Charlie, he'd dutifully handed over $10,000, the exact amount that his tuition had been in the late 1940s. Bob was pleased he could honor his promise and still have enough for his own kids. But his brothers seemed ungrateful, even outraged, and he didn't understand why. Did they think he owed them interest on the loan—or perhaps the 1980s equivalent, somewhere in the range of $100,000? Only a fool would promise that—a tenfold increase on the original loan—and he was no fool.

Charlie applied for financial aid and a student loan and eventually became a renowned neurologist at UCLA medical school. And one of their other brothers also helped Wilson pay back his son's loans. So everyone should be happy, shouldn't they? No great loss to anyone. Besides, by his own mental calculus, he had paid his debt in full. And he was good with figures.

"Wilson Whitman, please. He should be in ICU. I'm a doctor—Dr. Bob Whitman. There isn't much time. I need to see him before it's too late," he said to the nurse at reception.

"I'm sorry, Dr. Whitman. As you know, very few visitors are allowed in ICU. I'm afraid your name's not on the list."

"But that's impossible. Some kind of mistake, I'm sure of it." He turned to see Alice beside him, reaching out to touch his arm.

"Alice, would you please explain to her who I am?"

"Oh, there's been a mistake—this is my brother-in-law. Please put his name on immediately. We have to rush upstairs." Her cheeks were tinged pink. "Your brothers are already with him."

Wilson, tethered to a ventilator, blood pressure monitors, and IV drip, looked shriveled. How many times had Bob seen identical steel medical equipment? But not attached to his brother. Where the oxygen tube had pressed against it, a small boil, filled with pus, had formed on Wilson's lower lip.

"Who's that? Who's that?" Wilson rasped, agitated, picking at the sheets.

"Sweetie," Alice said, tears near the outer corners of her eyes, not sliding down. "It's Barbie. He's come to see you, darling."

"No, no. Not him." Wilson's mouth twisted. Bob shifted his weight from one foot to the other, wanting to touch him, at least to move the tube so it wouldn't irritate his lip.

Wilson died without another word for his youngest brother. Bob remained composed and quiet. One brother down, only two besides himself remained standing.

"Who makes more money, Dad? You or Uncle Wilson?" Jules had asked him this question way too often, usually when they were discussing allowances. His older daughter loved to talk about his brother just to make him feel bad, he was almost sure of it. Wilson had earned more money than he had—quite a bit more in fact—in real estate development in the Santa Barbara and Orange County areas. And this had always rankled him. After all, Wilson had started with practically nothing—just a sporting goods store on Centinela Avenue in LA. Wilson had been a small tomato farmer, and he and his brothers had run the sporting goods store together. But his farmland in Anaheim had proved extremely attractive to the Walt Disney corporation, who bought it at a premium in the 1950s. After that, Wilson never had to farm again. So he bought strip malls and apartment buildings in his spare time instead. And he had lots of spare time with his beautiful wife, Alice. She was intelligent, too. Worked hard and quietly. They raised two sons—a doctor and an engineer, honorable professions—and they did everything together. Wilson almost unintentionally developed into a real estate mogul.

"Spends way too much on his kids and grandkids, if you ask me. What a waste. Save for your own future, not theirs," Bob told his daughter, playing with his sideburns. Always the same thing with his kids. Money, money, money.

"Well, you're always arguing about what Mother spends on clothes and shoes, aren't you? Uncle Wilson and Aunt Alice never do that. At least I've never seen them argue."

"You never know what really happens in families, now do you? Anyway, I'm not interested in comparing myself with others, and neither should you. End of story." Talking about Wilson always and forever put him in a bad mood, though he didn't know why. And now he was dead.

Some people did not understand the meaning of true obligation. Of debt. But in the end, his older daughter would come through. Blood is thicker than water—for better and for worse. Eighty-four years old and reduced to this. Why had his two daughters even bothered to celebrate his wife's birthday anyway? Out of a sense of guilt? Certainly Aida hadn't appreciated it.

BAILOUT

"You have to move from the penthouse to an efficiency," Jules said, filled with dread. She could hardly wait to fly home the next day. She hated this. Obligations. Having to talk about this with her parents two days after her mother's birthday. So much for celebration. But this had to be faced head-on.

"What a step down that would be. For people like us, mind you. In our so-called golden years. We have no room even here. How can your father and I live in one room, darling, without killing each other?" Her mother's voice cracked. "Just because you insist we start saving rent," she continued. "What's the big deal, anyway? Two thousand dollars' savings per month. Chicken feed, when you're in our position."

Her mother had always been self-centered, but she had been glamorous, too, a wonder to behold, for little girls who dreamt of castles and princesses.

"But you will be in better shape financially. Your expenses will be reduced by nearly $25,000 per year," Jules said. "And we have a small equity loan we could share, so if you give me power of attorney to supervise your expenses, you should be fine." She rubbed her sore and stiff neck, arching her back, and cracking the vertebrae. This was enough, but when was enough ever enough for her parents?

"Okay, okay, don't need to be so snippy, Julia."

Was she being "snippy"? Jules didn't think so.

"You always seem like you're in a bad mood whenever you're here. You used to be so much fun as a little girl, so full of life. We'd laugh until we cried. Remember? Your father's a proud man—and a know-it-all.

We have to be in control of writing the checks, don't you see? Moving into a SafeHarbour efficiency unit? A tiny hovel on the first floor, with no view?"

She could see her father watching his ticker tape on his computer—studying his stocks in the next room. He was even more sullen after returning from seeing his dying brother, Wilson. And now his investments had tanked in the most disastrous stock market climate ever—in her life, anyway. But her father liked to buy on margin.

"Mother, he's not still speculating after all that Mike and I have told him, is he?"

"You just don't get it, do you, Jules?" Maybe she didn't. Maybe they were playing her. Maybe she really didn't have a clue. "Your father thinks he knows more than his stockbroker, who pleaded with him not to buy penny stocks to try to recoup his financial losses. When our stocks plummeted to below $10,000! So your father started using our Social Security checks to buy more penny stocks to cover previous losses. There is no more credit line. It's been erased. Nada."

Jules couldn't breathe. She stopped being able to hear what came next.

What was Mike going to say when she told him? How was it even possible to lose so much money in a matter of months, with nothing for SafeHarbour rent and medical care? She didn't want her parents to be thrown out on the street, but they weren't helping matters.

"As I was saying, to my number one daughter, I don't understand why you and Mike are so conservative in investing. That's what your father is always telling me. He likes to think you're not using real money when you buy on margin."

Why did her dad think that way, as if borrowed money was Monopoly money? As if the money they were borrowing for her parents' debts was Monopoly money, too? Maybe she was the one with a cognitive disorder.

Mike was a civil servant for the government, in the Department of Health and Social Services. His classmates in law school believed the average investor could never beat the stock market. Given that assessment, Mike and Jules had set up a college fund for Zoë that was managed by professionals at a discounted management fee. Soon Zoë would need those funds. They were almost certain their daughter would also receive some financial aid with her academic record and their financial documentation.

Mike worked hard taking shit from a sadistic boss in a thankless job. A Good Team Player: that's what everyone at the office called Mike. Code for Kiss of Death. He was just high enough in the food chain to have a small coterie of junior hearing officers to supervise but low enough to have no real power. Still, he tried his best to see her perspective: that her parents depended upon her. The dutiful daughter. Not someone who reneged on obligations the way her father had. But Mike could lose patience with her. Geez, even she was losing patience with herself.

"I just don't know what else we can do, Mother. We'll all be ruined if you don't change your lifestyle."

"Now, now, Jules. I'm not worried. You'll figure something out. Other responsible adult children must face their parents' needs, too, mustn't they?"

What was going to happen to all of them? There were consequences, sometimes irreversible. How was she going to pay for her parents' assisted living bills now? Certainly not without cooperation from her sister, Joanne, or her brother. Was it even possible for Joanne to be approved for a loan? And Andrew had never chipped in for one god-damn Christmas gift, although he was in better financial condition than Joanne. Dentists had a good income; why was he so cheap? What had their parents done to him that was so unforgivable? She had to think of Mike and Zoë—their dreams, their future. What happened to *The Narcissistic Mother,* the book she wanted to publish? Jules was supposed to be the expert. Sometimes she felt like a fraud.

"Oh, Julia . . . We're your family! Maybe we aren't as close as we used to be. But that's inevitable as you move away, isn't it? But you were always the one with the long, unforgiving memory. An unreliable memory, if I may say so myself. A memory of a memory of your last memory. Always holding a grudge. Even as a little kid. No lightness in your nature. You just can't move on, can you dear?"

Jules listened to her mother's words. How could all this be of her own construction? How could she choose between her parents and Mike and Zoë?

"I'm just glamorous, you know, a diva meant to be on stage," her mother went on, a cracked vinyl, skipping tunes until the needle landed on her. "You were so tongue-tied in high school. Except when you sang in the choir. That beautiful vibrato I had taught you. How we loved to sing together! Those were the good old days! Then you changed. If I hadn't stepped in to entertain your few-and-far-between boyfriends, you wouldn't have had any. They knew a red-hot mama when they saw one, that's for sure. I rescued you. I gave you joy—joie de vivre."

Is that what her mother called it—"rescue," "joy"? Jules's heart pounded faster, until the pressure in her chest traveled upwards and became a throbbing headache in her skull. *That petal-pink nightie.* Her mother had called it Valentine's Day pink.

"Well, of course you may speak to my gorgeous daughter," her mother had said, two feet from where Jules was standing. "It's for you, darling. A boy."

The night John had picked her up for the Valentine's Day dance, her mother must have been listening upstairs, just waiting for him. Having her evening manhattan. Dashing to put on the first dress she could slip over her head with a minimum of fuss, Jules still couldn't outrun her mother down the stairs.

John stood there in the hallway, so tall and strong, looking down at his dress shoes, all polished. An odd look for a teenager.

Her mother's outline shone through like the filament in a lightbulb. Naked. In a pink, transparent nightgown. "Now, you'll take good care of my daughter, won't you? She doesn't go out on many dates, you know. Wants to be a psychologist or some kind of scientist. Who knows why?" she said, standing so close to John that he stepped back into the wall. He was holding a corsage near his thigh, clenching it so tightly that he was crushing it and coloring the soft pussy willow–gray carpet with the flowers' pastel-pink petals.

Jules had grabbed John's arm to escape, but her mother caught her by the back of the neck, laughing, as she looked not at her but straight into John's eyes. "You never know with Julia. If she is even wearing underwear." Still laughing, she turned to Jules. "Don't forget to tuck in those dress labels. Yours is sticking up in the back. What an impression that makes on a young man." She patted the label and tucked it under. "You do look beautiful, though."

Jules thought she detected a glistening in her mother's eyes.

"And mind you, John, my daughter sings like an angel. And she can be a lot of fun."

"Are you listening to me, dear?" her mother asked, breaking into Jules's thoughts. "We'll move. Do you hear me? We'll move . . . but we are too far in debt. We'll end up on the street, homeless, if you and your brother and sister don't help us. Dribbles and drabbles of money are not enough now. The collectors are after us. We're in desperate circumstances! Forget about the little things now. Every family has some little commotion here and there."

But Jules couldn't. Neither could Andrew and Joanne, apparently. She remembered how her younger sister would lock her bedroom door and refuse to speak to their mom when her boyfriends came to the door and she greeted them in a nightgown, just like she had with John. And there was another scenario entirely for her brother's girlfriends. No girl was ever good enough for their mother's one and only son. The Narcissistic Mother.

What would happen to Zoë's college tuition? To Mike and her? She couldn't imagine how they would react. A betrayal? A renunciation of their love? Could her book raise income? She still had the literary agent's business card somewhere. Ginger Pressman, an independent agent in Palo Alto. She and Mike had sat next to her at the parents' reception last June when Zoë was invited to hear a Stanford University presentation for prospective future freshman. Who knows? Maybe Ginger would remember her. Never say never. She had to believe that.

How many stamped postcards with a bland, general rejection note had she received? Boilerplate. Nothing personal. The manuscript didn't fit the publisher's profile. *The Narcissistic Mother* was now in its thirteenth year of research, notes, and spinning around in circles. Ever since Jules was denied tenure, she had kept on writing. But she was growing sick of it. She had a college-age daughter now who needed her attention. Her daughter's dream choice was Stanford. Everyone deserved to have dreams. But in order to make her daughter's dreams a reality, Jules needed to change. Now. And fast. And her parents had to change, too, or they all would be destroyed.

FOREST LODGE

Andrew had sung happy birthday to his mother to appease her, knowing so little did so much. There had been no time to see any of them for so many years. Why had she expected anything different this year? But his dad would understand. He always did.

There was no way he was depleting his own family's savings to help them. Enough was enough. He hoped he never had to actually be there in person for one of the family celebrations. Unless Jules came to her senses. That could happen, couldn't it? But he hoped not. Would his parents actually end up in public housing without his sisters' support? Destitute? How much more could Jules take?

Time moved in reverse. Moving backwards always made him feel sick. He went back to years and years ago, when he left for Forest Lodge—the night of the car accident, right after the first heavy snowfall. Forest Lodge, an old-fashioned turn-of-the century converted log cabin, housed an outdoor skating rink and could fit snugly into a Norman Rockwell painting. Postwar suburban housing developments, where most of his friends lived, encircled the lodge. On cold winter nights like that night, he could count on all his friends being there, eating hot dogs and checking out the girls before going out on the ice to slide and glide in front of them.

He was a sophomore at Hoban High at the time. License still warm in his hand from passing his driver's test, Andrew had wanted to take out the Bermuda-pink Thunderbird with its porthole window. His father had special-ordered the sports car and it was only one week old. No one in Akron, that he knew of, had such a car. Not even the O'Neills.

They had boring, fussy cars—old people cars. But the Thunderbird . . . all the girls would see him driving it and want his number. And then maybe he wouldn't be so bored. Akron was for old people—never anything to do.

"Trust me, Dad. I'll take real good care of your new car," Andrew pleaded. He hated how his voice sounded—unnaturally high, childish, even girlish. Ever since the priests at the Church of the Holy Innocents school had forced him to wear a pink hair bow for a week as punishment for chasing a ball onto the girls' side of the playground, he worked extra hard to make sure nothing about him was girlie. His dad sympathized with him, at least. Like father, like son. After all, his dad told him he had been forced to wear pink hair bows as a kid, too. Little Barbie.

"My car still smells new. Why can't you take Mommy's?" His father always called their mom 'Mommy,' except when other people were around, in which case he called her "Mother." His best friend's dad did the same thing. Always felt a bit weird. Like his father hadn't grown up yet. Andrew hoped he would be a doctor. Or a dentist, if he couldn't get into medical school. But he would never call his wife—assuming he got married—"Mommy."

Andrew knew his father would be proud of his driving skills. They had practiced in empty parking lots all summer. He knew how to be like his father: a good driver. He sensed he asked for too much sometimes. This might be one of those times. Jules had never gotten to drive their father's new car. But his father always claimed boys could do lots of things better than girls . . . like driving.

"Well . . ." his father said.

"I don't know why I don't get to drive Daddy's T-bird first," Jules protested. "I've had my license for over a year!" She gave Andrew a pleading look. "Can I at least come with you?"

Never disappoints, Andrew thought, shooting a glare at her. He could always count on his sister to tag along. But she could be a passenger, if that would help him get what he wanted. He could put up with almost anything if he could get the hell out of that stifling house. Nothing could be more pitiful than staying at home with the old folks.

His father was relenting. As usual.

"Come on, Dad. Where are the keys?" Andrew asked, all hulked up like a quarterback in his dark quilted ski jacket. "We want to get out of here." It was a done deal, he knew it. The T-bird was his for the night. Free at last.

His father reached into his pocket and threw the keys hard. *Nice, Dad.* Andrew just shrugged without blinking, catching the keys square and solid in his fist. His dad always seemed angry at him—at everyone in the family, actually, and he didn't know why. Outsiders thought his dad was mild mannered. Andrew knew better. Still, he wanted to be more like his dad. Guys had a special way of bonding.

He ran out of the kitchen and Jules, grabbing her jacket, ran after him. *She better not hang on after we get there,* he thought. Just at the flashpoint of changing his mind and leaving her behind, he decided he needed to escape fast before their father changed his mind. So he didn't stop her from getting in the passenger seat. But he wanted to.

As soon as they were well out of sight of the house, Andrew accelerated with a vengeance. Skidding block after block downhill towards Forest Lodge, swerving from one side to the other on Crestview Avenue, the T-bird spun around and around down the street, almost doing 360s. Andrew kept on flooring the engine. It was like flying. There wasn't another car or person in sight—he was so lucky sometimes! He imagined he was a driver in the Indy 500, feeling the freedom of life and all the fun he would have once he left Akron for college. He was counting the days to high school graduation. Two more years. Only two more years.

Black ice. He panicked and froze. Before he realized it, his sister had grabbed the wheel. As they struggled, fighting over the steering wheel, the car started skating out of control towards the lodge, towards the housing development surrounding the rink. After jumping the curb and plunging into a snow bank, a huge, twisted oak brought the T-bird to an abrupt halt.

The porthole was covered. Andrew couldn't see out of the front window either. Shakily, his heart feeling like it was pulsating through every vein in his body, he muscled the door as far open as he could, squeezed out, and trudged through snow to the front of the house. The owner was already standing there, front porch lights on, startled to see the cockeyed T-bird. Andrew didn't look back to see if his sister was okay. The homeowner waved him inside without a word and gestured to the hallway phone. Andrew called home.

"Hi, Dad?" Andrew cleared his throat. "You have to come get us."

Silence. Andrew could hear a deep, threatening sigh on the other end. "What have you done now?" Their father's voice was hard.

"We had a little accident," Andrew gulped. He looked up; Jules was standing near the front door, waiting.

His father hung up without another word. Andrew and Jules waited there in the house, fidgeting. Ten minutes later, their father arrived in his silver Buick Riviera, his second most favorite car, and said something, probably an apology of sorts, to the homeowner. Andrew saw him write his telephone number on a sheet from his prescription notepad. Then he grabbed Andrew's elbow and twisted him out the front door. Jules followed. Andrew wished he could be anywhere else.

Chesterfield dangling from her lip, his mother stood up from the kitchen table as they walked through the kitchen door. She spit out something—he didn't know what—but the cigarette didn't eject. Then she laid into him. "Goddamn it. Driving crazy in this weather. Now that fucking car's going to cost a fortune to fix. You think money just grows on trees around here." Their mother looked so full of rage that she could bite a chunk out of her own arm. He recalled her saying she had actually done that once so she wouldn't hit Jules.

Andrew looked down at the melting snow still on his shoes, the blood-red linoleum all wet and slippery like the afterbirth from a newborn baby.

"It wasn't my fault, all right?" Trying to head off the inevitable. "I hit an ice chunk. Could've happened to anyone."

"Well, but it didn't, did it?" His mother's voice was whiskey hoarse. "It's a privilege to drive his new car. Now your father's afraid of the damage to that guy's yard. Maybe even a lawsuit. More money wasted on you."

Andrew nervously fingered his black-and-blue ski jacket while their father stood quietly in the kitchen behind Jules, waiting for his mother to finish. He was *too* quiet. Then his father moved towards Andrew, dangerously close, and Andrew's back petrified. He looked over his shoulder, then down at his boots. He knew what was coming.

He felt a crack as his arm was torqued, wrenched into an ugly angle. His father dragged him upstairs. Shoulders hunched, head down, he lost his breath. Then numbness. As the belt slap-slapped against his back and head, he curled like a fetus, trying to avoid the hook of the belt hitting his eyes. All he remembered after that: the toilet flushing, over and over again. And blood washing down the drain, swirling in the toilet bowl.

A couple of hours later, in his boxers, bare legs showing, Andrew limped towards the couch in the solarium. His mother and sisters seemed to have ignored what had been going on upstairs. His little sister, Joanne, he could understand. She was too young, and she was busy watching TV. But Jules knew. She knew, all right.

His mother came to his side and kissed his cheek. "Does that make your owwie better?" she asked, looking down at his legs: red welts with little white dashes where the stitching on the sides of his father's belt were embossed. He raised his right leg so she could have a closer look. She bent down and kissed him on the leg, too. Andrew let her do it, but she made him uncomfortable: too much contact. He was the sun that rose and set for their mother. She often told him so, even in front of his friends.

His very first childhood memory: his mother's kisses. The ones in the wrong places.

His father had ordered a rubberized, electrically charged sheet as a deterrent to bed-wetting. To make him a man. He was getting ready to enter kindergarten, and bed wetters weren't allowed. The school principal had said that naptime would be ruined for the other children if anyone peed. So right before kindergarten started, he remembered waking up in the middle of the night, zapped with electrical current, his pajamas soaked through. Smelling like pee.

Crying and screaming "Mommy, Mommy," he would run to his mother, who would be waiting in the bathroom. Stripping him naked, she would hug him and stand him on the toilet seat, kneeling in front of him, washing his body with a cool washcloth. Andrew remembered her saying, "Now, now, Andrew. You're a big boy. Your daddy wants you to go to kindergarten, so we bought that special bedsheet just for you. It's to wake you up in the middle of the night when you do pee-pee. You can't go to school if you wet your bed, you know. Big boys don't do that kind of thing. And Daddy and Mommy want you to understand that. We love you very much and want you to make us proud of you." And then she kissed his penis.

It surprised him. Who kisses where your pee-pee comes from? He remembered understanding that much, even at five years old. But before he could say anything, he saw his father peeking through the cracked-open bathroom door. He still remembered that one dark eye tilted at him.

He was the only son, and it came with a price.

"You know, I never liked chicken when I was growing up," his father would start off. "The slaughter of chickens would turn and churn in my stomach when I was a kid. Those bloodied chickens squawking with their heads cut off—gushing blood from open wounds, running in circles. They'd stink so badly. My father shoved it down my throat. Shouted that we had to eat whatever was in front of us. We couldn't afford anything else. One of those chickens had been my pet. Used to sleep with it. I never ate chicken after I left home."

Andrew ended up hating chicken just like his father.

But when he was maybe about ten years old, he'd tried an experiment. He'd chopped chicken into squares, skewered them, and slathered them with loads of spicy jerk sauce. The taste of smoky barbecue and the crispiness ringing the meat had been irresistible to his dad. After his father had eaten at least four kebabs, Andrew couldn't control himself any longer. Smirking, he said, "Hmm, Dad, how'd you like those kebabs? They were really good now, weren't they? They didn't have any nasty smell or dirty taste, now did they—did they?"

His father stared at him, the beginnings of suspicion in his eyes.

Andrew couldn't keep it to himself any longer. "You ate chicken," he blurted out, gloating. "You ate chicken!"

His father stood up immediately and said something in an unnaturally low, soft voice that Andrew couldn't quite make out. And then it happened. He retched on top of the platter with the remaining kebabs.

And he retched some more, throwing up everything, as everyone else jumped away from the table. Until there was nothing but piss-colored water with little pimple-size lumps. But even then he kept retching. And he never forgot—or entirely forgave Andrew for what he'd done.

As the only son of a doctor, Andrew had exalted status. Some medical field would have to be his career "choice." The arguments for this were constant and repetitive.

"You know, your sisters will marry well, to a good provider, and raise a family," his father always said. "That's all they have to do. Like your mother. But you—I expect lots more from you."

And Andrew didn't want to disappoint.

"Well, you just remember—there are expectations you have to live up to. Your father is an important man in this city. Everyone knows me. Now, if my father had been more than a farmer, I probably would have followed in his footsteps. But I had other dreams . . . to be much more. A success. To have the life that only money can buy. And, of course"—this part seemed like an afterthought to Andrew—"a good wife and mother, and three wonderful kids."

That wasn't quite believable to Andrew's ears. He wanted to believe it. But his father just looked sad.

How Andrew envied his sisters. They didn't have to worry about what their father thought of them. They wouldn't need to work. Their husbands would do all the heavy lifting. He wished sometimes that he had been born a girl—with a pink bow in his hair. He knew Jules wanted to have a profession. It wasn't typically female, but she had been like that since kindergarten. Studying famous women in history, winning academic awards, even the National Latin Society, whatever that was. She should just relax. She would have it easy. Like their mother. But Andrew—he had to prove he was worthy.

"No son of mine is going into something so worthless, to say nothing of mindless," his father would say of race car driving and motorcycle competitions. "Racing cars and driving motorcycles are for ne'er-do-wells. Do you want to make me proud or not?"

He *would* make his father proud of him. And, much to his surprise, he had begun to love studying the intricacies of the cardiovascular system. For the first time, he'd started to feel respected, aglow with medical jargon about this or that ventricular cavity and arterial defect. That was the way to his father's heart. Dissecting animals helped reinforce learning about anatomy, too. He always aced biology exams. He had a collection in their attic: translucent, pinkish fetal forms with veiny, glossy legs splayed, strapped, and nailed to a board. Cats, dogs, birds, even a squirrel. He liked the squirrel tailbones best. Fine, delicate, easily broken.

After the car accident, Andrew had spent the summer lifeguarding at the country club pool, wanting to save money just like his dad. That was the summer before he was sent away to George Washington Military Academy. His parents had talked to the board members, promising that he would follow the rules. No big deal, until Woolworth's.

"Can't Buy Me Love." The song was number one on the charts, and his friends wanted to get the single. Andrew had had his name on the waiting list for weeks but still hadn't gotten his copy. He volunteered to go buy the record for them.

He walked into Woolworth's and nonchalantly wandered over to the right side of the store, where the Top Ten Hits section was located, and started flipping alphabetically through the singles in their paper sleeves, looking over his shoulder. Rows and rows of records, and yet only one of the singles he was looking for was left. On the envelope, clear and bold, was the warning: "Display Copy Only. Do Not Remove."

He looked around, down the aisles. The store was packed. Probably because it was so hot and the air-conditioning was on full blast. Everyone hung out at the mall on blistering July days like this one. But he didn't see anyone working the floor. He bent way over the row of singles. Easy to slip the envelope into his baggy T-shirt.

He was almost to the door when a heavily muscled man, about six foot four, stepped in front of him, blocking him from the exit. Towering over him, he tapped Andrew's chest. "Buddy, come back into the store, please," he said as Andrew felt his fingers set off a paper crinkle sound under his T-shirt.

Red—his face turned so red. The guard escorted him upstairs to the small office on the second floor, directly across from the wall where the records were displayed. An unobstructed vantage point for seeing what he had done.

"Hey, junior"—Andrew had never been called "junior" before—"we have a zero tolerance for theft." The manager, a small, round-bellied guy of what Andrew considered to be "normal" adult age, perhaps thirty, forty, turned over the single that was now in front of him. "You're a shoplifter, plain and simple. And I believe the punishment they give you teenage thugs these days is nothing, as far as I'm concerned. The consequences should be harsh." He picked up the 45 and looked closely at the label. "'Can't Buy Me Love,' huh? Sounds like you can't buy anything."

Andrew wanted to bolt. The guard stood by the door, no expression on his massive bulldog face.

"Look, I can explain," he said. "My name was on the waiting list for this Beatles tune. I can pay. I only borrowed it, until my copy came in. Just didn't want to wait, you see. We're having a party and all. To celebrate before school starts. Give me a break, won't you?"

The shop manager looked unconvinced, impassive. His dirty blond, greasy hair was long and clung to the back of his neck in the humidity.

"What's your name, junior? Better yet, you can tell it to the police downtown. See if they believe your sob story."

Andrew stared at the guy's sweaty armpits. He worried that he was sweating as much as the manager. "Andrew Whitman, sir. I go to Hoban High School." Maybe that would impress him. He wasn't just some thief from the bad section of Akron. He went to a private school. His dad said that got you breaks in life.

"Whitman, did you say? Whitman? Are you related to Dr. Bob Whitman?"

Oh my God, thought Andrew. *My father knows the manager of Woolworth's.* What would happen to him now? "Please don't tell him, sir."

The manager called his father, and, as a satisfied patient, he agreed not to file a complaint.

Walking into the assembly hall the first day of orientation, Andrew had noticed "Dr. and Mrs. Robert Whitman—for their generous donation" engraved on a plaque right next to the front door. He knew his father loved that George Washington Military Academy was exclusive, loved the snob appeal implied in their flyers. What his father didn't know was that erstwhile shoplifters, drug "experimenters," exam cheats, and other delinquents who had narrowly avoided juvie hall were all George Washington military cadets, there because of their parents' money.

The campus *was* beautiful. Lush landscaping and expensively manicured, red-and-white brick buildings as upright, perfect, and uniform in appearance as the cadets. The teachers were intimidating and handsome at the same time in their military uniforms. They paraded in front of the parents at the beginning of the semester, marching in step up to the auditorium stage for their presentations, exuding a cool, polite air.

"All right, plebes," Captain Grissim shouted after the parents left. Grissim was his barracks commander and the captain of the lacrosse team. Tall, blond, Germanic bone structure, his face never smiled. He was movie-star handsome. "No mercy or second chances will be shown for failing to make a military-standard bed. The test is quite simple. You pass inspection when the quarter I throw on the bed bounces without making a dent. If you pass, you move on to learning how to shoot. If you don't pass, your choice is to do one hundred push-ups and then try again the next morning, or request permission to leave George Washington Military Academy permanently. And how would your fathers feel about that one? Huh? Not your mothers. Your fathers. So there really is no choice."

Andrew watched the other plebes perform. He could hear faint throw-up sounds in the bathroom. He assumed they were the two cadets who hadn't passed. Now it was his turn.

"Next. Whitman. Come on, we don't have all day. You're the last one and I want to go to the rifle range after this." Andrew's hands shook, trembling as if he had Parkinson's like his grandfather, and he saw Grissim notice. How could he stop his vibrating, agitated movements so the older cadet would not suspect he had absolutely no confidence in passing? Grissim smiled stiffly. His parents must have spent a small fortune on his teeth. They were so perfect they looked fake.

"I'm not sure I did it right." Andrew said in that same falsetto, high-pitched voice he used with his father before a beating.

"If you didn't, you get to do one hundred push-ups in the shower. That is, after you wash down all the throw-up from those other two losers who are leaving the latrine as I speak."

Later—after washing down the vomit in the shower and performing one hundred push-ups while Grissim watched—Andrew learned how to pass bed inspection. The following morning, when the quarter bounced off the bed, Andrew saw an indentation in the bed covers, but Grissim insisted he had passed, flashing those beautiful pearly whites. Andrew could never stop staring at them. Or at Grissim.

That afternoon, Grissim taught him how to shoot, both indoors and out on the immense range. The paper targets were rough outlines of a male body—the kind you see on the floor at a crime scene—but with red circles for aiming at the brain and heart.

Family celebrations at SafeHarbour? Really? Who were his parents kidding? The last celebrations he had no choice but to attend were Thanksgiving and Christmas, when GWMA was closed. That first Thanksgiving was the beginning of breaking away.

The Akron-Cleveland airport was suffocatingly crowded. His parents and sisters spotted him right away by his signature GWMA helmet. It always was an attention getter, an odd, archaic sort of thing —a *pickelhaube* Prussian spiked helmet, more a weapon than a type of headgear. He spotted them. That was his family, all right. They didn't know how to act—even pretend to act—like normal people. He lowered his head and walked towards them. As if he were a bull facing opponents in a bullfight, horns pointed at the vulnerable center of the toreador. He was a bit self-conscious of the slight double chin this posture created, incongruous on the face of any average-weight teenager. He was slimmer than he had ever been, but military posture required emotional control of one's face.

"Hi," he mumbled as his mother reached up to graze his face with that topaz-and-diamond encrusted ring she had promised to Joanne someday. Lipstick exactly defined in two fire-engine red lips was stamped several times on his face. He didn't have to look in the mirror to verify that. He just knew it. He glanced at Jules and Joanne; they saw him cringe, and they looked at each other, smirking in collusion. Maybe that was why he had been sent away: to get away from the female influence in his household. Or was it just to get him away from his mother?

Andrew reached down and expertly threw his giant duffel, GWMA emblazoned in navy-blue and gold lettering, over his shoulder without disturbing his helmet. In the car on the drive home, he carefully placed his *pickelhaube* next to him while he told tales of his first two months at George Washington Military Academy—the great guys there, the sneaking into town to drink, missing curfew. He loved being the center of attention, watching his sisters sponge up the stories, thirsty for adventure and something new in their boring lives.

All the stuff that their father thought he wouldn't be able to do in military school was exactly what Andrew liked to do.

Their father's hands, white knuckled on the steering wheel, looked cadaverous—all the veins wormy and popping up. He was silent. Uncomfortably silent. Andrew's mother turned around in her seat and reached far over to stroke his head, her red-polished fingernails curled under like claws. Her eyes luxuriated on his face, that type of eye contact he hated.

"Good thing you got lucky, hon—with the lower bunk and all," she said when he told them of Grissim's bunk test. Her right hand, adorned with that cockroach-size ring, stroked his cheek, just missing his eye.

"So I'm spending all this money on you, and for what?" his father grumbled. "That school's supposed to make a man out of my son. What a waste."

Still, his parents seemed relieved to find that it was only alcohol he was experimenting with. They didn't know about the dope and other recreational drugs. Shoplifting was in the distant past. He had found his religion: adoration for a new trinity—the military, guns, and authority. Guy things.

"Hmm," his father broke in during one of his stories, "you mention Grissim an awful lot!"

"Like I was saying, Dad, the teachers are awesome. Learning a lot." Andrew ignored what his father had said. His own voice sounded hollow, parrotlike, to his ears. Turning around, perhaps to look for a sign of truth in his face regarding what his father said, his mother smiled. But Andrew was in control of his face.

"I never had any doubts about you, sweetheart. And you need a few years' break before all the girls start chasing you in college. They won't be able to keep their hands off of you."

Like you, Andrew thought, ignoring her. He looked at Jules and Joanne and grinned like the Joker in Batman. There was no way that anyone in his family would think there was something "off" about his smile. They didn't get him. Never did. Never would.

"Hope George Washington isn't some kinda glorified gay camp."

"Dad, you keep telling me that GWMA's for the best of men: courage, discipline, integrity. Isn't that why you sent me there?" Andrew thought way back to that electric rubber sheet. A tool so he wouldn't be a bed wetter—someone who could turn gay.

"Yeah, yeah, sure," his father said. "Didn't want you getting into even more trouble." He sighed, looking worn out by time.

"Dad, listen. I feel at home. They're my brothers—the brothers I never had. My family away from home." He hoped he had put his father's mind at ease, so he could return to GWMA.

The envelope lay on his desk. His wife, Abigail, always placed his mail carefully there, each envelope discretely sliced open, staggered—one envelope layered halfway beneath the previous one—so that each return address was neatly revealed. His wife was very precise and dependable. He loved that about her.

He opened the announcement: Uncle Wilson's memorial service. No time to fly out to Santa Monica for the requiem. Besides, there was no love lost between them, and the flight would cost money. Uncle Wilson had always favored Jules, especially when they were teenagers. She could go and represent all of them. Besides, he sided with their dad—obligations only went so far. Andrew and his dad were very close. First Forest Lodge. Then Woolworth's. His father never forgot to remind him how mortified he had been to have a thief for a son. But not anymore. Like father, like son. He knew how to celebrate.

TETHERED OR TENURED?

"Darling, we're falling apart, and I don't know what to do." Jules wanted to avoid an argument. Usually it was Mike who inched over to her side in bed, saying he wanted to warm up the sheets so she would be more comfortable. But tonight he was the one who seemed cold. Neither of them had brought up the subject of her parents since she had returned from SafeHarbour. It had been almost a week now.

Mike adjusted his dream machine, a contraption for alleviating the worst symptoms of sleep apnea. Sometimes he had anxiety attacks or would wander around the house, hoping to head off another fitful night's sleep. Jules slept like the dead. Mike said it seemed like she lost consciousness before her head hit the pillow. She knew it was because Mike's warmth near her was so reassuring. Did she take him for granted? But wasn't she sparing him from the ugliness of family conflict? She hoped she was doing the right thing.

"I know you must have had an awful time with your mother," Mike muttered. "And Zoë and I fended okay for ourselves. As usual. I told her that it was like one of your business trips. A duty, something you couldn't avoid. But she cried. Said she's always picked last . . . just like in gym class. Only her best friend Deidre chooses her first for a sports team. And then everyone else badgers her friend for picking such a loser. Do you hear what I'm saying? Zoë thinks you're choosing her last."

That was the truth. Jules had failed them over and over again, always in the name of some other priority that seemed right at the time, but

59

now she knew better. What did other people do who didn't love their parents anymore, but wanted to, or at least wanted to help them at the end of life? She had once felt love for her own mother, too. Didn't every child . . . at the beginning? Now Jules wanted more time with Zoë. It seemed like it would have to wait until after her parents no longer needed her. But being a mother was forever, wasn't it? And so was being a daughter?

Mike turned off the light and they lay there in silence, not touching. Exhausted, Jules finally fell asleep, tears sliding down her pillow. Night terrors woke her up as she drifted back to an unforgivable time, to almost the very beginning of Zoë's life. She and Mike had yearned for a baby. They'd read books together about healthy pregnancy and parenthood—this was at a time when the Internet wasn't a serious research tool—and Jules had hoped she could be a good mother. She'd pictured the tiny, intimate inner world inside of her where her baby would grow: its cells, brain, each emotion a bud. Floating and morphing, her baby wouldn't drown, would she? There would be a loving connection between her and her baby, from heart to mind, in each cell. She certainly hoped so, anyway.

But then she started as an adjunct professor in the psychology department at Stanford when Zoë was a six-month-old baby. Almost eighteen years ago now. Women professors were still a rare sighting then. At almost forty years old, she had become a middle-aged "junior" faculty member and a middle-aged mom. Two dreams come true.

Jules needed a book under contract for her tenure review. Then she could concentrate on nurturing Mike and Zoë. Dr. Schlepp (even his name sounded like a bad joke) had told her not to worry. He was a lecherous, seventy-something psychiatrist of some fame and notoriety. Balding, resembling a rapacious Rasputin or sinister Spinoza, Schlepp had a thin goatee and the kind of lean, muscular body mass that only the old obsessed over as a way to control the only facet of aging they could: weight. He fancied that women found him hot. In his spare time, when he was not seducing clueless female students or writing novels loosely disguising his sexual exploits and those confessed by his nubile patients, he was on a strict Atkins diet, working out at the gym. Schlepp's groping and leering were the price she had to pay for tenure.

He claimed that he had an open marriage. No one bothered confirming that with Mrs. Schlepp.

She had to tighten her guts to control herself. For five long years she exhaled, thinking of her Zen meditation practice. *No mistakes now, she told herself. Just a little more time. That's all.* The carrot dangling in front of her—tenure—was worth it. Or so she thought.

"Your baby is so pretty—just like her pretty mommy," Schlepp said one day. "You know I'm your biggest supporter on the tenure board and only my vote really counts with the dean. So you need to play nice." His lips looked sticky and gooey.

I need to play smart.

Schlepp laughed, the look on his face indicating he could push as hard as he wanted. *How he must love that feeling,* Jules thought, her stomach queasy.

"Come on, one little kiss, no tongue, okay? It's no skin off your ass. Besides, you should be happy that I'm your number one fan. That husband of yours will be no wiser." He chuckled as she stiffened. The first of many of his displays of power. Over and over again, the idea of Schlepp's death had consumed her. Between lectures. Sitting on the toilet. In her dreams. For him to live only as long as Jules needed him, then no more—that's what she wanted. But that was her secret; not even her husband knew.

Jules remembered her three-year old Zoë, only months before the scheduled Holy Tenure Committee review. She was picking her up from the campus day-care center, called My Second Home—and to Zoë it was. The building was specifically built to look like a suburban home, with a huge yard that included jungle gyms, a tree house, and sandboxes. My Second Home had a long waiting list, and graduate students had priority over faculty, and faculty over administration and staff. When Zoë was accepted for one of the few coveted openings, Jules had been as excited as if her daughter had just been accepted to Harvard. No, *more* excited. As if she had beaten the odds and won the state lottery.

On this day in particular, Zoë was waiting by the gate when Jules arrived. So little and vulnerable. Her little girl was the last child to be picked up . . . again. Zoë's face lit up at the sight of Jules. She jumped into the front passenger seat in their yellow Honda Civic station wagon, her incredibly soft, sweet smile illuminating her heart-shaped little face, and looked up adoringly at her mother. Jules felt reenergized, ready for a treat, as if she were tasting some Belgian truffle.

"Mama, I wish I were your sun." Zoë's singular, baby-sounding voice lowered Jules's blood pressure, releasing endorphins.

Did she say "son" or "sun"? Jules wasn't sure. Did her little girl think she wanted a boy? That wasn't true. She had wanted a girl more than anything. Not like her own mother, who had danced around Andrew— his whole life. When Jules was pregnant, she had known the being inside her was going to be a girl. She'd had no doubts whatsoever.

"Zoë, why would you want that?" Jules asked.

"So I could shine for you."

Her little princess, the daughter of her dreams. Such a good heart. She looked so small and precious.

"You make me glow every day, sweetheart. More than the sun, the moon, and all the stars," she said. Zoë needed her attention now, and Jules wanted to listen. She didn't want to be distracted by the lecture she had to give tomorrow. The manic footnoting and minutiae of academia could wait now. Balance, all about balance. She shuddered at the thought of Schlepp and tried to flush the thought away.

Zoë wiggled, squirming delightedly in her seat belt like a kitten. "See my picture? I made it just for you, Mommy," she said, holding up a tempera-painted, primary-colored building and bright blue sky with a smiley-face sun.

"Yes, my sunshine. Your picture is beautiful." Jules heard her own mother's voice inside her head, asking, "What did you say, darling?" and then walking out of the room before she could answer. She feared turning into her mother or her mother's ghost. She wanted more time to paint with Zoë, to make gingerbread houses, to laugh and read with her. Before it was too late. But without her job at Stanford she could end up the type of stay-at-home mom her mother had been: a diva without an audience.

How many times had she disappointed her daughter? Too many to count. She felt guilty. She believed their lives would change for the better once she had tenure. Family would take top priority. She would make more time for Mike and Zoë. "Zoë" meant "life," and she and Mike had named her that for a reason. Zoë was one of Jules's lifelines. Mike was the other. They knew that, didn't they? She was just waiting for the time to come when she would show them.

But tenure never came.

"Don't go yet . . . please?" Schlepp had pleaded with Jules when she headed for the kitchen to get Mike. That night—January 8, 1998, a party hosted by Schlepp—was etched in her skull. Almost thirteen years ago now. She should have realized that Mike had changed after that. That he wasn't the same. She hadn't wanted to see.

"I just poured you another glass of sangria, since you love Betsy's recipe so much." He tugged on the silky sleeve of her cobalt-blue dress. Her favorite blue—one her mother thought drained her of color.

"It's late. The party's over," Jules said, taking a sip from the glass he handed her.

"Your tenure's a cinch. No one's going to vote you down. Not when I'm endorsing you. We can talk tomorrow in your office about all the details. If you're that worried, that is." He swayed, listing left.

"Mike! Mike! Where are you?" she called out towards the kitchen. No response. The house was more like a cave—too damn huge! *What is taking him so long?* she wondered. She suddenly felt woozy, drowsy, and she stumbled over to the sofa, which caught her fall.

Where was Mike? Schlepp was sliding his hand under her dress, but she couldn't push back. Her hands felt rubbery and detached from her wrists. She couldn't quite sit up either. The last thing she remembered was Mike coming into the room to pick her up off the couch. She remembered tripping, losing her balance, as she went out the front door, leaning heavily on his shoulder. She remembered that his body felt upset.

The next day, when Jules walked through the door after work, it was 7:30 p.m. and Mike hadn't come home yet. *Probably still pissed over what happened last night.* But seven thirty wasn't that late, she reassured herself.

She saw the answering machine's red light flash twice: two calls. She expected one would be from Mike; he always called to let her know when to expect him for dinner. *Perhaps he had a last-minute client emergency,* she thought, trying to talk herself out of worrying.

"Hi Jules, this is Ann Price from the department," the voice on the first message said. "I'm so sorry to have to disturb your evening. Something terrible has happened. Please call me back."

What could be so terrible? Was it something about Schlepp? What a pain in the ass he was. Jules knew Ann was no friend of the chairman's either. But her voice sounded shaken, thin, on the message.

Jules breathed in shallowly, evenly, distractedly, as she called Ann back. "Got your message. What's up?"

"Dr. Schlepp has died suddenly of an apparent heart attack. In his office. I called 911. I had forgotten my medicine for my nerves—so I had to go back to the office. The police and ambulance both came. Taped off the office with yellow-and-black tape, skulls and crossbones. Macabre, I know. There's going to be an investigation. It seems that he fell hard, and the office is a bloody mess. Sorry, don't know how else to put it. That's clumsy of me, I know."

"Whoa! Sorry to hear that awful, awful news," Jules said. Did her voice sound sincere? She hoped so. Maybe Ann would think she was just tired, or shocked. "Let me know what I can do," she said. She thought of how she had dreamed of his death.

"Some of Professor Schlepp's female students have filed sexual harassment charges with the dean recently, so the police have to rule out foul play." Ann had wanted to file a complaint, too, but was afraid she'd lose her job. Jules knew about Schlepp's garage apartment. Students had come to her in tears describing how they had been pinned down as part of their "therapy."

There was no way a university like Stanford would allow sexual harassment charges to be brought out in the open. That was not going to happen. They would be swept under the rug, like so much else in life. Never brought to the surface.

None of Jules's colleagues knew Schlepp had promised that her tenure would be a mere formality. There were no witnesses. *"No big deal,"* he had said, practically drooling on her.

Jules pressed the answering machine message button again after hanging up with Ann.

"Hi, sweetie pie. This is your mother. You really should call me more often, you know. I feel like you're a stranger sometimes. There's so much to tell you about what's happening here at SafeHarbour. The talent show I'm singing in. You know, we aren't getting any younger. And my birthday's coming up. Call me before it gets too late."

It was too late. She would call her mother tomorrow.

The sound of the RAV4 in the driveway woke her up. Or maybe it was the high beams that always shot through the living room windows whenever someone pulled in. Mike was loud, stumbling in and then down the two steps from the front door to the living room. Jules hadn't realized she had fallen asleep watching late-night television. One of those comic monologues that wasn't so funny. It was almost one a.m.

Nuzzling for a kiss, Mike's breath smelled like bourbon. His favorite. She muttered, hoping her speech wasn't as slurred as his: "Where have you been tonight? I was worried, and stayed up waiting. You could have called."

"I did. But you must have slept through the call. Just went out with some of the guys after a long hassle over some compliance issue. To discharge stress. You know. Did you miss me?"

Jules rolled over, too tired to answer.

"Hey, hon, what's wrong? Is it that asshole Schlepp again? We shouldn't let his ghost be in our bed, you know what I mean?"

"That isn't even funny. The man's dead," Jules said.

Mike's face remained as impassive as a Buddha's. Not like him at all. Not when Schlepp's name was mentioned, that was for certain. Maybe because he'd had too much to drink, Jules thought. Now she was wide awake.

"Don't you want to know more about it?" she asked, touching his arm.

"I don't give a damn about the old geezer. How about me?" Mike's voice was slurred, thick, unappealing.

Jules got up from the couch and went to the bathroom to pee. She wasn't in the mood. Too much to think about tomorrow.

"At least now we don't have to go mad worrying about whether he's going to deliver on his promise, groping you and getting erections whenever he feels like it!" Mike shouted from the bedroom. Jules heard him throw his clothes and belt on the floor. She waited in the bathroom until it was quiet. Then she made her way to bed and slid in beside Mike. He had already passed out.

~

Jules's office in the Palo Alto School District Administrative Building was actually a cubicle, shared with three other part-time psychologists. Jules, initially upset to no longer be an academic, was somewhat surprised that she loved her new job. Her desk overflowed with diagnostic tests for kids who had difficulty learning how to read or do math. There were no file cabinets to store anything in her cubicle, so every night she had to stuff all the tests into her well-worn black leather briefcase for reviewing at home. Sometimes the papers got crumpled, or fell out of the file folders. She knew she was dispensable to the administration.

Palo Alto was considered the holy grail for education assignments, although she knew that was more myth than reality. One parent actually told her that children in their school were the most beautiful in the county, perhaps the state. Looking at his affable, middle-aged face, she thought he was joking at first. His expression didn't waver. He was serious. Still, the parents were always attentive and engaged—perhaps overly so, but at least she knew that when she tested children for learning disabilities in this district, follow-up support was guaranteed. None of the parents wanted their children to fall behind, not in this school system that some parents would sell their mother to get their kids into.

They had bought a fixer-upper when they first moved to Palo Alto with a small life insurance policy Mike had inherited from his parents. It never was fixed up, and they struggled every month to meet the payment.

What stupid mistakes she had made. Mistake after mistake. She was a practicing Zen Buddhist, and though she was often grateful she had adopted Buddhism, her Zen practice didn't seem to help now. She felt broken and stupid. Ahimsa—noninjury and compassion for sentient beings—was one of the essential tenets of Buddhism. But all she seemed to do was harm others, the ones she most loved. It had to stop. Jules was supposedly an expert in the psychology of parenting. But her publish-or-perish book, *The Narcissistic Mother,* was still unfinished. It was a cliché that psychologists gravitated to specialize in neuroses and other mental disorders they were struggling with themselves. But in Jules's case, the cliché was true. She knew nothing about motherhood. And she had regrets. As a mother. Terrible, terrible regrets. She felt ashamed, felt that her abandonment of her daughter—and Mike— was unforgivable.

Motherhood could be dangerous. Of that she was certain. Not everyone should be a parent. Her own mother was a good example. But perhaps motherhood had been forced on her mother; maybe she didn't believe she had any other choice. It was a different time then. Besides, Jules wasn't one to talk. She herself had screwed things up big-time.

According to Buddhism, the good mother gives up her own ego and desires in order to be a mother. But until she knows what she needs, she can't become enlightened. Jules now felt desperate. Happy times with Mike and Zoë still were too far away. The sacrifices they both had made for her. And she had distanced herself from them.

Mike—what he had sacrificed for her, squelching his anger, swallowing his own needs. She would tell her parents they were on their own now. She had had enough. No more guilt and obligation.

She had disappointed Zoë. Again. Yesterday. And oh, how she had wanted to be there! Career Day at Carmel High School for graduating seniors. All the banners. Students so excited to meet "experts" in different fields: pilots, a screenwriter, an actress (former girlfriend of Clint Eastwood), doctors, research scientists, winemakers, to name only the most popular career presenters. And Zoë had asked her to talk about child psychology.

"Mom, you are amazing. You know that, don't you? All my friends think so. How you taught at Stanford. Are writing a book. Have your own part-time practice and still try to be there for your family. For Dad and me. We're all thinking about how to combine career and motherhood. Can you come? Can you? Please?"

Jules smiled, something deep inside her stable and relaxed. Breathing with more solid exhalations. Not jagged and tentative. How could she not make time for her Zoë? Her daughter was so forgiving, so generous of spirit. "I'll try, sweetheart," she said. "You know how I love your friends and don't want to disappoint you. I'll clear my schedule for you. When is it, exactly?"

Zoë came over to give her a big squeeze. She could feel her daughter's hands grip her around the ribs, fingers catching on her ribcage, just under the lowest rib. Love handles.

"Stephanie and Kristy both want to be psychologists, too. The three of us are going to apply to the same psychology programs. Stanford is our first choice. Actually my only choice. It's that or nothing. I know I'm obsessed, but they have the best psychology department ever. And it's not just about studying rats in cages and statistics either. People to people. That's what I want to learn about. How people think. What motivates them. How they feel. Why trying their best can still be so awful."

Jules looked at her daughter's face. Its certitude. The perfect radiance of youth. And its openness. Frightening at times. Envious at others. Jules looked into those green eyes, flecked with brown, so heavily lashed that her daughter's glasses had to be curved slightly outward so mascara didn't leave tracks on the lenses.

"You'll be the most popular speaker there. And I'll introduce you, Mom. Only Clint Eastwood's former lover will get more students." Zoë looked proud, glowing, savoring this precious thing between them.

The call came on the day of the event, just as school was getting out. Jules was dashing out of her office when the phone rang. She knew she shouldn't take the call, but she answered anyway.

"Mom, I've got to run. I'm late for Zoë's special day. Have to give a presentation." *Why did I pick up the phone? What's wrong with me?*

"Now, darling, that's just going to have to wait. It will only take a second, you hear me? It's an emergency. Our check for this month's fees at SafeHarbour bounced. The second time now. I told you at my birthday dinner that we'd be out on the street if you don't come through for us. By five o'clock today. You *did* get our message, didn't you?"

Jules had to think. Maybe Mike had erased it before she got home. Passive-aggressive.

"How much is it? I can go to the bank and wire more funds into your account."

"Well, hurry, won't you? Before the bank closes. Once they see the funds are being transferred, we can wait for the clearance." Pause. Her mother's silence was always hard for Jules to interpret. "Two months' rent is better than one. Eleven thousand should do it."

Jules called Wells Fargo as soon as she hung up. The bank was on the way to the high school. She still had time, she'd just be a few minutes late. She could do both. Her credit line would be exhausted now, and all of this would stop.

But the teller didn't have the wire ready when Jules got to the bank. It would have been faster, after all, if she had gone to her laptop and made the transaction online.

By the time Jules got to the high school parking lot, it was empty.

Stephanie's mother, Liz, called her minutes after she arrived home.

"Hope you're not worried. Zoë's with us. She's upset. I'm sure you understand."

"Let me talk to her. I want Zoë to know that I tried. I really did. An emergency came up." *Please, please, Zoë, I know you hate me now. I hate me, too.*

"I'll go get her. Just a second."

"Please, Zoë, come to the phone," Jules muttered to herself.

She could hear whispering, raised voices in the background. Her daughter's and Stephanie's. Then muffled sounds. Like whimpering. Tears, maybe. She swallowed hard. Then couldn't anymore.

Again, it was Stephanie's mom on the phone.

"Sorry, Jules, Zoë's just a bit under the weather. And tired. She wants to stay for supper and spend the night. Is that all right with you and Mike?" Jules could hear it in her tone: Stephanie's mother didn't want to go further. She was ready to be done with this conversation.

"Of course, that's fine. Zoë and I can always talk tomorrow." To her own ears, Jules's voice sounded saccharine. False. Clenched.

Embarrassed. She tried to ignore the sting of it, but couldn't. What a hopeless fool she was! She didn't even want to put up with herself. She felt wicked, diseased—something was not right with her. What kind of karma had she created for herself? How was it that she kept making those she loved suffer so!

Zoë stayed at Stephanie's for a week and didn't call Jules once.

Jules thought of the little boy she had tested the morning of Career Day at Zoë's high school. Max reminded her of her own little girl at that age. Same voice. Androgynous—before sexuality took over.

Max was a third grader at El Carmelo Elementary and couldn't read at grade level. Blond straight hair in a buzz cut, he could have played the starring role in *Dennis the Menace*. He grinned goofily at her, revealing a big gap between his two front teeth on top. "Mrs. Foster, do I have to take more tests? I just don't feel like it." He crossed his arms in defiance and grinned again, this time close lipped.

"We've been through this drill before, Max. Just thirty more minutes. Then you can pick out a book to read." It was ironic to Jules that some of the kids with the most difficulty reading loved books the most. They really wanted to read; they just couldn't fit the pieces of the puzzle together.

After the little boy had struggled with the test, twisting his head down to one shoulder then the other, mimicking the boxes drawn at weird angles to match up with other boxes drawn from a different angle, Jules took him to the shelf with age-appropriate books. She knew which two books he would choose.

Max reached for *Sylvester and the Magic Pebble*. And he slyly picked up *In the Night Kitchen*, too.

Jules raised an eyebrow. "I said one book, Max, not two!"

"Please, pretty please," he said. "That test made my head hurt."

Sitting next to her on the low squishy beanbag chair, wiggling and turning the pages at the right time, Max seemed to know how to read.

"Max, you know this story so well. Can you pick out words now?"

Max loved Mickey, the boy who lost his clothes in the batter and milk in the children's book *In the Night Kitchen*. Come to think of it, all the little kids loved seeing Maurice Sendak's drawing of Mickey's little penis. Always made her wonder why some adults had banned the book, protesting that young minds shouldn't see such explicitly drawn body parts.

"I just know how to follow along with my finger. My finger does the reading." Max looked delighted with himself. "That's why I fooled Miss McLaughlin. I just copy what everyone else is doing."

Jules laughed. Max had been diagnosed a little later than others. He was a great pretender. *But aren't we all at times?*

"Max, see the little boy sleeping here? See the letter *Z*? What sound does it make?"

"I don't know. I give up."

"Zzzzzz."

"You mean the letter moves?"

That was why she spent so much time with Max, more than with other kids. He was bright, original, and made her laugh. She needed more of that these days. It was good for her soul. She cared about these kids' future. Kids like Max. Zoë, though, was no longer a kid but a beautiful teenager, and time had run out. She would be going to college in a few months and Jules would become irrelevant. She had to choose now. The moment of everything.

Consequences, unforeseen consequences. But she should have seen that there would only be so much time to be a mother. Now there were just too many ghosts and too many birthdays, celebrating nothing.

GHOSTBUSTERS

They both took vacation time to be there. Uncle Wilson's memorial service. Mike had enjoyed the company of her favorite uncle, too. But only one week after her mother's birthday, Jules felt in no mood for more family affairs. Birthdays. Funerals. She was worried about their daughter. Zoë was still at her friend's house and refusing to take her calls.

The PowerPoint slides of family reunions and ordinary holidays were on a timer. One by one, at ten-second intervals, each photo—about four feet square—flashed on the screen. Some of the slides were very old ones—more than fifty years at least, Jules reckoned, converted from even older emulsion photos. Photographs had been expensive way back then, and her father's family had been so poor. There was one black-and-white of Uncle Wilson as a baby. There were lots of other photos, too: the wedding photo of Uncle Wilson and Auntie Alice, a black-and-white photo she would have had trouble identifying. The sporting goods store on opening day. Slides of good times with their large, boisterous family—two successful sons and six grandchildren. The other brothers included, her father excepted.

Then flashed the color ones. Some she remembered. The twenty-fifth-anniversary celebration of his store, for example. She heard the click-clicking of the space bar on the computer keyboard. More slides. The expected ones: the happy family gathered for first high school, then college graduations (for both sons—no playing favorites). The cap and gowns were the same throughout. Only the faces and the tassels were different. Then there was Charlie's medical school graduation. Lots of photos of that day. Repetitive, and a bit monotonous, perhaps, but a thoughtful and caring photographic tribute.

The Hyatt hotel in Los Angeles provided the easel for more old photos—hard copies, pinned haphazardly. There wasn't a single one of her dad. Nor any from her family, except one of her, standing on her uncle's commercial fishing boat, a bloody rag held over her left eyebrow.

Jules adored her uncle, and had hated returning to Ohio that summer after visiting him. She was almost sixteen years old. Grown up. California had seemed like another country to her back then. The water was still, the sun so hot on the Santa Monica pier that her flip-flops stuck to the planks, almost melting into the boardwalk. A Disneyland of rides—Ferris wheel, carousels, roller coasters, and the arcades, honky-tonk but thrilling. Andrew and Joanne, who was only eleven or twelve at the time, were going on Uncle Wilson's fishing boat, too. Jules absolutely loved riding in her uncle's old red pickup to the pier. Their dad had come along, but hadn't really wanted to. She had felt he knew he wasn't wanted. By anyone. Even then.

"Hey, little princess, ready to catch some albacore—the biggest and best there are?" Uncle Wilson gave Jules a long, delicious hug, his sun-leathered face all crinkly and grinning, part toothless and part gold toothed. She didn't even mind him calling her "little."

Jules always grinned like a freak around him. "Yeah!" she jumped up and down, feeling giddy. No one back home would know she had reverted back to being a little girl around him.

"Me, too," Andrew broke in. "Boys always get more fish. Dad knows I can get the biggest one. You just watch me. He's going to be so proud of my catch."

But Uncle Wilson ignored him. And Jules loved him for that, too. Andrew dragged his pole to the other side of the boat, but no one looked up.

Her uncle whispered conspiratorially, his Coppertone lotion smelling sweet and rich to her, a fragrance she thought for years afterwards was aftershave: "I told Andrew the other side of the boat's better. But the fish are biting here. He'll be out of our way. Guess he doesn't want to share the water . . . or the fish." He laughed.

Jules had felt honored that Uncle Wilson preferred her fishing skills. By then, all her friends called her "Jules." Not so girlie. But her uncle had called her that when she was in kindergarten, way before she had decided on what she wanted for her name. He had said she was like a chest of jewels, precious and beautiful. A family treasure. Jules loved the sound of it now. Her new name had sounded so grown-up and luxurious. Deirdre and her other friends thought so, too.

Joanne clutched Jules's hand as much as she'd let her. She was still the baby in the family, although she was past baby age, and almost as tall as Jules was. But Joanne had sponged up their mother's fear of boats and water.

As Jules was feeling the hot sun on her face, sticky with sweat and suntan lotion, her pole jerked in her hand. Squeezing her eyes tight and shaking off her sister's hand, which rested on her arm, she clutched the pole with all her strength. Nervous, twitching with excitement, almost dropping the pole, she screamed, "Uncle Wilson, help! Help me! I don't want to lose it."

"Don't you worry, pumpkin. We'll get this one good." He called out to her father, "Barbie, get the net . . . quick!"—all the while keeping a firm grip on the pole, his hand over Jules's.

Silence.

"Maybe he's taking a nap down below," Jules said, wishing her father had stayed back at her uncle's house with her mom and Aunt Alice. He just got in the way.

"You know, he's never there when you need him. Said he wanted to go fishing. But then all he does is sleep. Well, we'll have a good time anyway, Jules. Without him."

Uncle Wilson called to Andrew as they struggled with the line.

"Andrew, get the net. It's under the bench you're sitting on. Hurry!"

With one expert yank, Uncle Wilson had reeled in a stunning metallic, shimmering fish—somersaulting and panicking on the line the whole way in—and heaved it on deck. Andrew slowly waddled over with the net, probably hoping to sabotage Jules's catch. His face was subdued as he looked down at the squirming, lashing wild thing.

Jules yanked the net from her brother and scooped up her gyrating, flip-flopping trophy, but Andrew jerked back—so hard that the end flew up, just missing her left eye and cutting deeply into her eyebrow. A shocked look on his face, he dropped the net and ran.

Jules cried out in pain, dropping the fishing pole and holding the left side of her face. Then Jules bent down to retrieve the net, blood dripping into her eye. Uncle Wilson gently took it from her hand and scooped up the fish. The albacore was bleeding from its mouth as he unhooked it, her blood dripping, the two trickles of red mingling on its silver scales.

"Let's put it in the cooler on ice," Uncle Wilson chuckled, depositing the thrashing fish into the Coleman ice chest. "We'll have a feast tonight!"

Jules grinned, ignoring the blood—both hers and the tuna's.

"Now, let me see that eyebrow, princess," Uncle Wilson said as he matter-of-factly reached into his tackle box for bandage tape and gauze. "Looks deeper than it is," he said. He washed it in saltwater, so gently that it felt good. "We could go down and get your dad to double-check you don't need stitches."

"Nope." Jules smiled now, relieved. "I trust you. Let Daddy sleep. He likes to dream about marrying Donna Reed."

Uncle Wilson looked puzzled, but said nothing.

She beamed as Joanne opened the red-and-white Coleman cooler again and again to peek at the albacore. Andrew came back to take another look as well; he sulked as Uncle Wilson stretched his tape measure across the fish's glistening side. After that, Jules didn't see either Andrew or their father for the rest of the day. *So much for boys getting all of the fish,* Jules gleefully kept repeating to herself . . . silently, she hoped. It was the best day ever.

Jules liked *that* memory. A real family outing.

The banquet room at Uncle Wilson's memorial was full of tears. The first testimonial was from Charlie, Uncle Wilson's older son. The UCLA neurologist. He had pages of notes. The microphone at the podium was set too low for him to speak into it audibly at first. After fidgeting with the mike, he began:

"My dad was the best dad ever." Jules could hear that he was struggling to find his voice. "Never shirked his responsibilities to any of us:
my mother"—Jules listened to her Aunt Alice's muffled sobs—"my
brothers and me, our friends. We may not have had much in the early
days—when two boys and their parents live above a store in two tiny
bedrooms, and one was actually a closet, that's what they call 'cozy'—
but we never owed anyone anything."

Jules caught Charlie's smile as he looked down at her, picking at the
cheesecake, and it made her wince.

"What we didn't have in dollars we had in respect for each other.
And love. We had each other's backs, and we were and are stronger
for it. My parents have made lots of sacrifices for all of us, too many
to count. Our dreams became theirs. I can't say I even knew what my
father ever dreamt for himself. Everything was always for us. To you,
Dad; I'll miss you."

Slump shouldered, Charlie walked back to sit down across from
Mike, who patted him on the shoulder, man-style. "Hey, you did a good
job," was all he said as a gesture of comfort.

Jules wondered why she and Mike had been seated at the table for
guests of honor, as if they were the close inner circle. Family.

At first she thought there had been some mistake. Why was she invited
to the legal offices of Hawkins and Davis? Her cousins seemed to know.

The conference room was larger than the square footage of Jules and
Mike's entire home. Todd Hawkins's office was upmarket. The high-
est downtown rent. A commercial building in Los Angeles with views
of the mountains towards Pasadena . . . on a clear day, that is. Today
there was too much haze. By Thanksgiving, the smog would probably
be locked in for months.

Since Mike knew more about the law than she did, Jules figured
he would translate any legalese at the meeting. She felt uncomfortable being there. Her uncle's body was still warm, as far as she was
concerned.

Uncle Wilson's two sons and their wives were already seated on one side of the long table, facing the expansive views from the floor-to-ceiling windows. Alice, bent over, dabbing her eyes with a balled-up handkerchief, looked tiny and diminished. Hawkins sat directly across from Alice—he discreetly slid a boudoir-size Kleenex box closer to her as she cried.

When Jules and Mike walked in, Charlie rose from his chair and hugged Jules tightly, shook Mike's hand, and then motioned for them to sit at the end of their side, nearest the door. The family side.

"My dad wanted you to have this, Jules," Charlie said, handing her an envelope. "It was extremely important to him, and I promised I would give it to you. It was one of his last wishes."

Jules hesitated, mumbled "Thank you," then Charlie returned to his seat. She glanced at Mike, and he shrugged. She fumbled to open the envelope. With Mike looking over her shoulder, she read the note—written in an elderly hand, the letters almost quivering off the page: "To My Sweet Jewels, the only one in her family who knows and understands what obligation and duty truly mean. To protect and love you."

As Jules read the note, a beautiful secretary, dressed elegantly in a cobalt-blue suit that made her look very lawyerly, rolled in a cart with teapot, coffee urn, and cookies laid out on a silver tray, and exited without a word. Hawkins cleared his throat and handed out the documents.

"We want to make sure you understand the intent of Mr. Wilson Whitman's will."

Jules was a fast reader—one of those Evelyn Wood speed-readers, a remnant of her days at Northwestern, where she frantically revved up her reading speed for exams. But the legal jargon in these documents slowed her down, and she kept stumbling over the boilerplate in the paragraphs. So Mike, ordinarily a slow reader, was the first to catch the bottom line. Jules heard him make a little gulping noise.

Hawkins cleared his throat. "Mrs. Foster, I believe you are the named party and benefactor who is to receive a sum not figured into the annuity of the trustees."

"Huh?" That was all Jules could say. What was this all about? She was mystified.

"You have been bequeathed a gift today as instructed in this will. Hawkins and Davis have a fiduciary responsibility to carry out the instructions on behalf of the deceased. If you prefer, we can have the total inheritance deposited directly into your account, after you provide us with the necessary information for an electronic transfer. But we have written the check in the event that you would like to take it with you, since you are returning home to Carmel right after this meeting, I am told." The lawyer handed her an envelope.

Jules couldn't understand what Hawkins was saying. Was he speaking English? Mike elbowed her; he looked confused, too. She slowly slipped her index finger under the lip of the sealed envelope and pulled out a greenish-blue check—what she would call a "Ghostbusters" color, a Halloweeny, ghoulish hue—for $300,000. Almost exactly the amount her father had owed his brother for Charlie's medical tuition, taking inflation into account.

"Jules, your uncle just left you $300,000," Mike said, looking over her shoulder. He seemed elated. "It couldn't have arrived at a better moment for us! Your uncle always was a master of timing—not just in his ability to pull in a catch."

Jules felt in dreamland. A Disney kaleidoscope that had made her problems dissolve. How had she been so lucky! Now she could pay for both her parents and their daughter's needs.

Charlie walked over, inviting her with open arms. "My father loved you like a daughter. Like the daughter he never had. We always knew you were not like the others in your family. And we are so happy for you."

Jules cried.

That night they splurged for a room upgrade at the hotel. Jules felt flushed—with desire for Mike, joy for Zoë, and an exuberance and relief for all of them. No more mother-daughter fault line. No more decisions made against her better judgment. No more barely missing the rocks, avoiding a tempest. Jules exhaled upward, fluttering her bangs.

"See, darling? Everything turns out fine in the end. No need to be an Eeyore." She kissed Mike passionately, undressed slowly, playfully, throwing her underwear, humming to herself. She hadn't felt this light, almost giddy, for so long, and it felt so good.

Jules hated their lengthy volley of he said, she said, over all these years of dealing with her parents and their bailout. Now was their time. She savored the moment.

Afterwards, they FaceTimed their daughter.

"We have exciting news for you, Zoë," they said in unison, looking down at the minimized image of themselves, foolishly grinning up at Zoë on the monitor. Jules laughed as Zoë and her friend Deirdre jumped up and down in front of the computer screen.

Life would be good after all. Problems solved. She and Mike would deposit the inheritance into two banking accounts as soon as they returned home: half of the funds for Zoë and half for her parents' debts. End of story.

It was never too late. The three of them had a special kind of love. It might have been in remission for a while, but it had only been waiting to resurface, just as sweet and delicious as ever. They *could* have it all. Who said bitter disappointments always turned cancerous?

BATTING LIKE A GIRL

Joanne was convinced that Jules was the lucky one—and her brother said so, too. Andrew confided in her, "Did you know that Jules got an inheritance from Uncle Wilson? Who thought he would give her anything? Mother wheedled it out of Zoë."

She hadn't known about the inheritance. No one told her anything. But Joanne was happy for her older sister. She knew she took advantage of her sometimes, just like her parents did. But what else was she to do? Sometimes she had no one else to turn to.

Joanne didn't think she was the preferred daughter, though she knew Jules and Andrew thought so. Sure, she was the baby of the family. A good sport. Willing to do girlie things like makeup, shopping, and all that stupid stuff with their mother.

Sure, she still loved putting her mother's eye shadow on and comparing different shades. Going to monthly salon appointments with her. But sometimes she thought she would like to do something else—maybe read a book, or paint. Jules didn't care about all that copying mother stuff, and that made her different. Or it seemed that way anyway. Jules studied even though their mother made fun of her and called her a wallflower and an egghead. She envied that. But on the other hand, her mother was right, too: Jules needed to do something so she wouldn't look so plain. Why didn't her sister seem to care about those things, important things?

Joanne had lived alone with her parents after Jules had left for Northwestern and her brother had left for George Washington Military Academy. And she had missed Jules and Andrew. Having her brother and sister there to share in the parental attention. Once they'd left, it had been all on her. For ten long years—a decade that felt like two. Perhaps that was why she married him. Al.

The year Jules left, 1968, there was political turmoil throughout the country. Civil rights. The Vietnam War. A nascent feminist uprising. Joanne was only thirteen, almost fourteen—a vulnerable age. And she had her own turmoil. All her friends had always been so jealous that she had a big sister to look after her. She'd felt special. And all of Jules's friends had always fussed over her, saying she was so cute. But she knew she would never be as eye-catching as her mother still was. Even now, as a mother of two teenage girls, she yearned for her mother's beauty. She couldn't reach her level. No matter how hard she tried.

"Joanne, you're the pretty one, the one who will take after me in my old age," her mother often said as they sat in salon chairs, hoisted up so they could admire themselves in the mirror. Their stylist, cutting first her mom's hair and then hers, moved easily from one bob to the other. Identical haircuts. When she was done, she passed them each a mirror, and Joanne and her mother would smile first at each other, then at the mirrors in their hands. The same thing every time, ever since she was a teenager. Now middle-aged, she was still gazing at mirrors with her mom.

It was really all about Mom. She had never worn shorts or an old skirt to pick Joanne up from school. No way! Instead, she looked as if she had just walked off a television set—maybe *The Donna Reed Show,* her father's favorite. The other mothers looked normal. Funny looking, though.

Girls smuggled *Seventeen* magazines into the bathroom at Our Lady of Sorrows under their blazers. The nuns told them the magazine was indecent and they would go to hell, but that made it even more exciting. They would pore over the photos to find out what "normal" girls wore—that is, girls who didn't have to wear uniforms with plaid skirts hanging down almost to the ankles and navy-blue blazers with suede elbow patches every day. Some of the nuns thought Jules was going to be a novice once she graduated. They were sure wrong about her.

Joanne never wanted to dress up as a nun, not even for Halloween, the way Jules sometimes did. For laughs, but still. Jules sprayed different color paints in her hair as soon as school was over, the wash-off spray-paint kind. Said she liked doing it because it reminded her of fun times with their mother when she was a Brownie. Joanne always thought it was a bit theatrical.

Everyone believed the Whitman girls had the mother they all wished for back then. "Oh, your mom's so much fun. My mom's not cool and my dad thinks your mom looks like some movie star," Ann had said on more than one occasion. But what did her high school friends know?

Deirdre, Ann's older sister, was Jules's best friend, and Ann was Joanne's. And Pat, Ann and Deirdre's mother, was their mom's best friend. They liked keeping friendships in the family. Easier that way—if the mothers wanted to see each other, the daughters could be together, too.

Ann came over almost every day in the summer during those high school days. Too hot to do anything but go to the pool or experiment with art or makeup, sometimes both. Ann had trouble telling the difference between the two: makeup and paint. Both had to do with the imagination—Joanne had plenty of that. Ann didn't. But Joanne liked drawing: snakes, tarantulas, and Nazi swastikas, preferably all in the same picture. No color. Just ink and charcoal, so she could get all the details just right. Her friend liked conventional, colorful, pretty things: flowers, leaves, nothing scary.

Their house had a pseudo-Victorian/French sensibility. There was a "solarium," not a TV room; a "foyer," not a hallway; a "salon," not a living room; four "boudoirs," not bedrooms; and a *salle de bains*, not a bathroom like other families had. Dark-green wallpaper with white dogwood flowers lined the walls. Her parents' boudoir had a Duncan Phyfe mahogany dressing table banded in brass, with a seat in striped beige-and-gold satin. Joanne would sit down carefully on the seat, as if she were sitting on a throne, and she and Ann would spritz each other with perfume from beautiful purple and gold atomizers and translucent glass, spraying and spraying until they sneezed. Joanne once powdered Ann's cheeks and nose—gently dusting the makeup on her friend's upturned face—before remembering that her mother dusted her panties with that puff. She didn't tell Ann.

They always ended their makeovers by staring at the photo on the dressing table—her mother in almost the exact same pose and color blouse as Elizabeth Taylor in the cutout magazine photo taped to the side of the frame. Joanne could admit that there was some similarity, if she stretched her imagination a bit. But she never said that to her mom.

Her mother's special ring—a sky-blue topaz ring, the size of a beetle, surrounded by diamonds—sat on top of a special stand, a tiny altar. The two of them would fight over who got to wear it first, and longest. But Joanne always gave in to Ann. After all, her mother had promised her that ring someday. "You know, sweetheart," she'd said, "you are so much more like me than your older sister. This ring is for you. I'm saving it for my special girl. I promise." That ring had her name on it.

When her brother and sister went away to college, Joanne's parents let her have Ann sleep over even on school nights. Less trouble, her mother said, than putting up with her neediness. How was she needy, she wanted to know? But she never asked.

They'd watch TV, make pizza, and talk of becoming movie stars as they sought refuge from her parents in the solarium. Joanne never got to make pizza, but her mother wanted to be nice in front of her friend.

"'Pizza face,' that's what you'll turn into if you eat all that grease," she said when Ann wasn't around. "Nothing but zits. You'll thank me some day. For saving your skin from disaster." She told Joanne that over and over again, too many times to count, but never in front of anyone who was not family. "Look at my skin. Flawless. And I'm forty now."

Joanne knew she lied about her age.

"Everyone has such ugly faces now—and teenagers should be at their peak. Not eating hamburgers or pizza."

On those nights with Ann, Joanne would plop down on the faded, overstuffed sofa and sink into the cushions, feeling the pinpricks from the feathers that stuck out. Ann would curl up next to her, a few lumps in the cushions separating them. Usually her dad sat in the wing chair, fidgeting in the corner with one of their mother's favorite pillows—puke green, embroidered with dogwood blossoms.

Her dad crept up silently, lurking from behind the curtains or near the solarium door, like a shadow. They hardly saw him. He usually napped on the living room sofa after dinner—if he got home in time for dinner, that is. She and her mother were often asleep by the time he had finished examining factory workers after their night shifts. The three of them hardly ever ate together on weekdays.

One evening, watching TV with Ann, Joanne heard the weighted thud of footsteps overhead, footsteps of different weights. Ann gently reached for her hand and squeezed it.

"Come on, Daddy. *The Donna Reed Show* is on—your favorite!" Joanne shouted, singsong style, towards the upstairs, hoping that would make the footsteps and voices stop. On TV, Shelley Fabares was singing "Johnny Angel" while her sitcom mother, played by Donna Reed, grinned at her adoringly.

They both loved that song. Joanne liked that it was about dreaming. Dreaming about a true love who didn't know she existed. So romantic.

Her mother entered the room and joined in, singing in her clear alto, a glass in her hand.

Ann giggled. "You sing better than Shelley Fabares, Mrs. Whitman. You really have a wonderful voice." Joanne knew that her friend complimented all the other moms, but her mother was the only one Ann really thought was beautiful.

"I want to be a mom like Donna Reed when I grow up," Joanne said to her friend, ignoring her mother. "The mother of my dreams."

Her mom walked over, sat down on the couch next to her, and put her arm around her as she swept the hair out of her eyes with her free hand. "Do you think I'm a perfect mom? Like Donna Reed?" she asked.

"Sure, Mom. But your voice's not as soft. You don't smile and laugh as much," Joanne said. "But we have a real family, not a fake family," she said too late when she noticed that her mother's smile had disappeared. *Oh no.* Her mother quickly left the solarium before either girl could add sweeter-smelling words, a sachet packet to improve her mood.

Next, the shadow moved into the room. "I always liked Donna Reed," her father said as he nudged her over on the small couch. The program was half over. "You know I met her once. Might have even married her." He stared at the television screen. "I might have been a different type of father," he said quietly, to no one in particular.

Joanne didn't ask why.

"Your mother was a looker. Always was a sucker for good-looking women." Her father's voice sounded worn out, distant—he was almost panting. "You know, one of my classmates became Donna Reed's first husband. It could have been me." He waved his hand dismissively. "What the hell do you kids know about life? Wait till you see what it does to you. Life never turns out like you think it will." He seemed wound up, perhaps from being upstairs with her mother. He had a glass in his hand, but it was almost empty. Plainer than the one her mother had been holding, not as pretty. Most of the other moms and dads drank from glasses like her parents', too.

He went back upstairs before the program ended, without so much as a good night. Ann didn't seem to notice. Joanne turned off the sound and they just watched the picture, making up their own script to *Father Knows Best,* their second-favorite show.

The house always seemed too quiet, even in those days, before her parents became seriously old. Just the softest tap of feet upstairs. It was sometimes scary, she recalled. Joanne remembered the sound of her father's belt slapping Andrew's body, a thud so heavy and sad, unrelenting. She had pretended to be busy watching TV. She was only a little girl then. Couldn't say anything. Didn't want to say anything either. But if her parents moved in now with her, instead of continuing to live at SafeHarbour, would it be even scarier?

One bright Saturday afternoon, Andrew dragged out the baseball bat and softball from the hall closet. He had just come back from lifeguarding at Lake Tamsin.

"Come on, Jo, I'll teach you how not to hit like a girl."

"Maybe some other time. Going to go shopping with Ann."

"It's either now or never. See if I care that you don't make the team."

Andrew had loved to teach her "boy" sports: wrestling, soccer, karate, and baseball. He liked to tell her he was more of a coach than a brother. That was before he left for George Washington Military Academy and forgot about his family. But the wrestling and karate moves he taught her did turn out to be useful later on.

The first time she brought Tim home—that summer, when Ann

was away on vacation—he had just gotten his license. He was a year older. Even after three years, she still wasn't sure why he was her boyfriend. He seemed conventional and pretty. All the other boys seemed to stare at her breasts under all that wool: the scratchy blazer and starched white blouse, undershirt over the bra so no shadows peeked through, tucked into a plaid, pleated skirt, and thick argyle knee socks that itched. Sweat left a dark streak, soaking through her blazer, down the middle of her back, once the temperature hit seventy-five degrees. Maybe that was why she liked Tim. He didn't pay attention to her, never stared at her breasts, and all the girls adored him.

"Hi, Mom. I'm home. I have a new friend I want you to meet," Joanne shouted towards the living room.

Her mom came down the stairs, overhead chandelier brightly lit, even though it was daylight saving time and the sun wouldn't set for another three hours. Backlit, in a pink see-through nightie—Valentine's Day pink, her mother called it—she glided down to greet them. Joanne remembered how impossibly thin the material had been, and sleeveless, and far more low-cut than anything she ever saw the other moms wear.

"And who is this handsome young man?" her mother asked as she landed in front of them, turning her cheek for a kiss, a bit unsteady in her slippered feet. Those glamorous, pink-feathered pompom slippers. The kind Joanne's Barbie doll had.

Tim looked startled. "Uh, uh, I . . . I'm Tim," he stuttered. Joanne had never heard him stutter before.

Her mother kissed him—a firm, aggressive kiss. "It's about time I got to meet one of my daughter's boyfriends." She looked more closely at Tim's face, and Tim started picking at one of his zits, the big one in the center of his chin, and shuffled his feet, putting one shoe on top of the other.

It must hurt to do that, Joanne thought, *with cleats and all.* He was still wearing his baseball shoes, having come straight from practice.

"Has anyone told you that you look like a blond Paul McCartney, my favorite Beatle?" her mother asked, reaching up on tiptoe to rake her fingers through his long, shaggy blond hair.

Tim mumbled something, but Joanne couldn't tell what he was trying to say, if anything.

"You know what I think?" he said when her mother was done fawning over him, and he and Joanne walked out on the porch that edged the solarium. "You don't think I'm good enough for you. That's what I think. I'm just convenient, while you wait, biding your time until college starts. I may go on to college, too, you know. I'm just working at McDonald's until I can save up enough. Not everyone has rich folks like you. You're just a spoiled brat, if you ask me."

Joanne looked up as she slipped her arms under his armpits, bringing her face close to his. "I would never dream of dating anyone but you. We've been together for three years now. Nothing's changed. You're my angel. You know that."

"You're lying, you little bitch. I see how the guys stare at you and your friend when you think I'm not looking." He raised a hand, and before Joanne could pull away, he struck her across the cheek.

The slap was loud. She hoped her parents couldn't hear from inside the solarium. The TV was blaring. Seeing neither one of them had looked up, she rubbed her cheek and looked back up at Tim. He hung his head, just for a second or two, but then he stormed off into the dark. She watched him start the car; then, when he turned out of the driveway, she ran upstairs to see what damage had been done to her face.

Ann stopped by twenty minutes later without calling first. She never called first. This time Joanne wished she had.

"Let's see what the choices of dorms are," she said. "Let's pretend we have to make the selection for first choice and second choice right away. Before others take your spot."

"I'll want a dorm next to the boys' dorms. That's my first priority," Joanne said, rubbing her cheek.

"This is so much fun. I'm going to be living at home—God, how awful. But you have the chance to get away from this place and meet all kinds of new people. You're so lucky. I wish I could trade places," Ann said, flipping through the flyers scattered all over her bed. She glanced up at Joanne and, finally noticing her cheek, gave her a worried look.

Just then, there was a tap at the window. A whisper. Tim. "Hey, beautiful! I'm so sorry, you know I am. I love you so much. I'd never want to hurt you."

"Yeah, right, asshole," Ann said. "Don't say a word, Jo."

Joanne flinched. Now her friend knew what had happened.

"But my Mom—she likes him so much," she said, turning her back to the window and speaking low so Tim couldn't hear. "Maybe it's my fault. I'm to blame for putting him in a bad mood."

"Does your Mom know how he treats you?" Ann seemed incredulous.

"I can't bring myself to tell her. Mom always says it's a woman's charm and beauty that keep her man happy. I guess I'm not beautiful enough."

Ann yanked her away from the window, and slammed it hard in Tim's face.

Joanne finally did decide to break it off with Tim before college started—or maybe it would be more appropriate to say that Tim self-destructed. It happened when her parents took them both on an Alaskan cruise as a graduation present for Joanne. *The Seven Seas*, a luxury liner, had suites with adjoining rooms, each with its own little balcony and view. Her mother was slightly claustrophobic, so they had the spacious Silver Class suites. Not spacious enough to keep her mom from hearing what happened in Joanne and Tim's room on the second day of the cruise, however.

"What's all that racket? I hear knocking and pounding through the wall. What's going on in there?" her mother shouted, pounding on the locked door that separated their suites.

Joanne could hear her tears catch in her throat. "I'm all right, Mom. Just fell. No need to worry. I'm just practicing my karate moves Andrew taught me with Tim. Go back to sleep. I'm fine."

"No, you're not. I can tell. Open this door!"

Joanne folded up inside, and let her mom in. Tim slept and ate by himself for the rest of the cruise—in her parents' walk-in closet.

Her mother was her hero. Forever and always.

Her sister was, too. Especially now that she could pay for more of their parents' debts with the windfall inheritance she had received from their uncle. Thank goodness for Jules.

HAMBURGER FACE
ON SARAN WRAP

"Your luck will improve now, darling," Joanne's mother said after meeting Al, a fellow student majoring in art.

Santa Monica City College was all Joanne had expected it to be and then some. Jules had reviewed the flyers with her and they had both agreed on two things: that she had artistic abilities, and that putting some distance between her and her parents would be a smart move for her. The Gemological Institute of America had a joint program with SMCC so she could pursue a dual career as an artist and a jewelry appraiser.

"He may not be as handsome as Tim was, but he looks more agreeable," her mother said. "Someone who can listen. Who appreciates your beauty, your artistic nature. I think he'll make good money someday, too. Being with someone ten years older can be a plus, you know. He's probably more mature, too."

Her parents were more delighted than she had thought they would be. "I just don't know if I want to get involved with anyone else right now, Mom," Joanne said. "Tim made me such a mess. I just want to hang out with my new girlfriends. And draw."

"You're not getting any younger, you know," her father said—during this conversation, and on more than one occasion throughout that first year of college. "The best age for having kids is in your late teens or early twenties. Before you know it, you will be perimenopausal. It's a woman's duty to be a mother, you know. It defines her essence." Joanne ignored her father's medical opinion. She was eighteen, not eighty. But she couldn't help but be influenced by her parents' enthusiasm for the match.

It seemed somehow inevitable that she would eventually hook up with Al. His parents were Southern Baptists from Texas and wanted him to be an engineer, like his father and brother. One problem, however: Al had no aptitude for math. He started flunking all of his engineering courses, and finally his parents stopped paying the bills at UCLA. That was when he decided to transfer to Santa Monica City College to study art. He shared a grimy apartment with four other guys on the outskirts of Santa Monica, an easy commute from campus. He fell for Joanne the first time he met her. When he saw her high-rent apartment, he loved her even more.

Joanne's parents paid the rent without being asked and made frequent visits to California to see their baby girl. They were happy to take care of her, her mom said. Someday Joanne could support herself and them. But that never came to pass. Sometimes Joanne wondered what would happen if they ever ran out of money. Daddy had reassured her that would never happen. But Joanne didn't want to depend on her parents forever. She wanted her own dream: to become the owner of a jewelry store.

Joanne had decided Al was not so bad the first time he invited her to his student apartment. "Love the smell," she said.

"I'm making spaghetti for dinner. That's what you smell," he told her with a grin on his face. But the smell she was referring to was patchouli, not *pasta e fagioli*. And really, what was irresistible about Al was his choice of art: nightmare-inducing Nazi images, disembodied mutations, and predatory insects and animals. Just her style.

Al was a closet geek, and older than Jules. Like a docile Labrador, Joanne's favorite breed, he hovered around her. By the time they celebrated their first Valentine's Day together, Joanne knew her future.

"Oh Al, you know, you could do much better and save money to boot," Joanne's mother had said to him after hearing about his living situation when they came for a visit in early February. "Why don't you move in with Joanne as her Valentine's Day present? Don't you think she's beautiful? Takes after me. Everyone says so."

Joanne had felt herself blush. She had only known Al a few months. The next day Al had sent a dozen roses. Then another dozen the following day. For a whole week, seven dozen in total, a different color each day, until Valentine's Day. He made reservations for them at a famous restaurant, requesting the most coveted table in Beverly Hills. He also started to cook for her after classes.

"Al may not be exactly your type, but his devotion is impressive," her mother said. "And you know, none of us gets what she wants all wrapped up in one package with a pink bow on top. He may be as good as it gets. I should know—I married your father, didn't I?" she laughed.

So she married Al. And just as she was concentrating on getting pregnant, Al lost his job.

"No one should love work. That's why they call it work," Al grumbled.

Joanne remembered saying that she felt fortunate snagging an instructorship at the Gemological Institute in Santa Monica right after graduation, and regretting it as soon as the words flew out of her mouth. Al never liked anything. He didn't trust the concept—let alone the prospect—of happiness, either his or hers. That Southern Methodist upbringing. He didn't even like sex—or at least, he only liked sex before they were married. When it was forbidden by his church.

When Al picked up her class list, Joanne knew her life would change before he even spoke.

"Hmm, mostly guys, judging from this list. Are they interested in the subject matter or just you?"

"You're not jealous, are you? There's no need to be, you know." She laughed.

Al wasn't smiling. "Tomorrow you hand in your resignation."

"But you just lost your job. We could use the money." She could hear the pleading in her voice as she slipped her arms under his armpits. The way she had with Tim when he used to get angry. Her own voice was scaring her.

"No way you're going back there. Pretty soon you'll be huge, anyway. Like a fat cockroach. You won't even be able to fit behind the steering wheel. Quit your job. You can sew baby stuff to get ready for the big day. We'll live off my severance and then my unemployment, if we have to. Until I find another job."

And that was how Joanne kept out of harm's way: by sitting in front of her new Singer sewing machine all evening, waiting for Al to come home—where did he go all day?—and creating baby clothes, unisex ones. When her hands were tired of sewing, she created serigraphs, her most accomplished form of printmaking—shifting and morphing shapes of uncommon virospheres and body parts. Her favorite subject was the spleen.

Six weeks later, she became pregnant with Megan. Her first baby was born bright and healthy. Al adopted Koko, a chocolate Labrador, from the SPCA, to be Megan's playmate, but the dog turned out to be vicious, except towards their family.

Soon after Megan's birth, Sarah was on the way.

"You know, darling," both her parents observed, "you make such beautiful babies. Thank God they take after you in the looks department." Joanne could never figure out how they could both say that in front of Al, as if he weren't there.

"And why on earth did Al buy that filthy dog . . . and around small children, no less?" her mother asked once, when Al was out at the store. "Don't you have any sense of hygiene?"

Joanne laughed it off, recalling her mom's disgust when she first saw Megan crawling to catch Koko and suck on one of his paws. "I think Koko is more lovable than Al," is all she said.

Al was gone now, but Joanne still had Koko.

Al's search had paid off, landing an engineering job at less pay at Boeing in Seattle. Well, it wasn't actually an engineering job. He drew the schematics for aeronautical parts before they were adapted for CAD-CAM input.

"God, I hated looking for a job, day after day, month after month," Al complained to Joanne after getting the news. "It's not easy, you know, having to provide for the family. I hate having to be approved by some asshole. And goddamn those LA riots. Those riots caused our bankruptcy. The looting scared off any buyers." Echoes of her father's ranting long ago at Lake Tamsin during the civil rights movement. The violence.

Her parents had put a generous down payment on a large house in a good neighborhood overlooking the Cascades, big enough for all of them to move in together, if that day ever came. Her father's investments would bring in more profits when they needed them down the road. No worries. Just like the good old days on Crestview Avenue in Akron, her father said.

They would move to Seattle to start a new life. A better life. For all of them.

"I think you have some crumbs on your cheek. Maybe from a bran muffin or something," a neighbor had told her when they had a welcome-to-the-neighborhood lunch at a local restaurant in Edmonds, the Seattle suburb where she and Al had just moved .

Joanne had casually brushed her cheek, where her neighbor had been staring, and felt nothing. She ran to the bathroom to have a closer look, pulling down on the skin on her face. Those garish overhead neon lights magnified everything, including the tiny scars on her left cheek—leftovers from some pustules a distant memory away. What her mother had called a "pizza face" or "hamburger face" from acne she'd had as a teenager. *How embarrassing.*

Joanne had carried those comments with her all these years, and now it was time to do something—to enhance her beauty so her skin would be more like her mother's. Hollywood had always been plastic in so many ways, and Joanne never had forgotten her own aspirations to be an artist to the stars. But you couldn't be a famous artist without looking like one. Her only job now was working on her own body. She was a work of art, after all.

It was the weirdest feeling. He reminded her of a large black spider on a white wall when you least expect it. Scary. No one else was in the waiting room. With its overstuffed white sofas, white marble counters, and bleached oak floors, the doctor's office was a blinding, spotless whiteout. It was hard to see Dr. Payne in all that white. His dark hair and eyes. His voice sounding raspy and irritable to her, as if he had swallowed something too peppery.

Dr. Payne, plastic surgeon to the stars, came highly recommended by customers who had frequented the Gemological Institute to have their diamonds appraised. Dr. Payne's office had formerly been next to Grauman's Chinese Theatre, then a more expensive high-rent district in Beverly Hills. Now he was practicing near Pike Place in Seattle.

Joanne felt like she was neon glow . . . a diner's street sign. Dr. Payne's magnifying goggles underscored his buglike appearance, bulging eyes like opaque marbles. "So you're here for your droopy eyelids, huh? Just a tweak here and there. Eyelifts are very routine, you know. Not a complicated procedure at all. But expensive, because eyes are considered nature's treasure. We can do the tummy tuck at the same time. Different body part."

The plastic surgeon's comments made her wither. She felt foolish, a frog-beetle under a microscope. And what about the cost? Maybe Jules's windfall could be shared. After all, Uncle Wilson had been her uncle, too . . . and she shouldn't have to find out about her sister's inheritance from her brother. *Why would Jules keep that from me, anyway?*

"I guess, whatever you suggest, Doctor. Just as long as I come out more beautiful than when I went under." She really wasn't getting any younger.

"Well, I'll tell you a little secret, just between the two of us," Dr. Payne said, touching her arm. She pulled it away, but he reached for it again and held her in an armlock. "Most of my patients come back again and again for other enhancements. Once you know what true beauty is, there is always room for improvement. We're all a work in progress, as the cliché goes."

His breath smelled like garlic; Joanne drew her head back.

When the day came for the procedure, her mother came with her.

"I'll be right there when you come out of anesthesia," she said, patting Joanne's hand as she rode the gurney into the operating room. "It'll be worth it, you'll see. Beauty is priceless. And you have to start maintenance while your underlying muscles are still strong, not flabby.

It's too late for me now. Way too late. Just can't believe I've already turned eighty."

These were her mother's last words to her before she went under.

Oh, the incredible pain. Joanne gulped hard, slowly awaking in her bed after being wheeled out of surgery. Her face had been resurfaced like the blacktop on a road—abraded with an electric sander with a special type of gritty sandpaper, then peeled with acid. She felt like her face was raw hamburger. Where was her mother, anyway?

The nurse said she was outside taking a smoke. Joanne fell back to sleep, waiting.

The night she came home she slept on a special pillow covered with Vaseline-smothered Saran wrap. Her eyelids were lightly bandaged so she could partly see through the gauze. Her mother had prepared the pillow ahead of time, according to Dr. Payne's instructions. Special satin pillowcases, two to a package, in petal pink. Her mother had ordered them from Victoria Secret's boudoir collection. It took three more days for scabs to form on Joanne's face, and in the meantime her hamburger face almost peeled off onto her pillow, slipping and sliding like her two young daughters on their Slip'N Slide.

On the fourth day, Joanne steeled herself to look in the mirror. She loved mirrors, but not as much as her mother. And not now. Her face looked shattered.

"Mom . . . Mom!" she cried out. Her mother had been sleeping on the couch. No one else was home. Al had taken the girls on a camping trip.

"I can't have Megan and Sarah see me like this. It's still too soon. Call Al and let him know not to bring them home for ten more days. The campground number is on the coffee table next to the sofa." A tear slowly slid down her face, making her wince, feeling like it was traversing bumpy terrain, a switchback. *Beauty is its own reward,* she told herself.

Her mother dug her nail into her hand. "Don't you cry, you hear me?" she demanded. "The tears are salty and will burn. Besides, your skin is raw, and it won't heal if it's moist."

Looking in the mirror after surgery, Joanne was not completely satisfied. Some of the spots on her cheeks were still visible. And the little stitches behind her ears and in her hairline were neat, like stitch number 23 on her Singer, but would they show if the wind blew her hair up? Dr. Payne had been right—about coming back for more enhancements, that is. After she healed from these procedures, she was going to schedule a second dermabrasion for wrinkles, and a tummy tuck. Everyone—that is, Al and her mom—had long said that her stomach was too flabby ever since she'd had Sarah.

"God, Jo, you're letting yourself go," Al had said to her when the girls were still little. Joanne had gained about fifteen pounds that she just could not lose. "I thought I had married a red-hot mama, not some dumpy housewife with a gut."

"You could use a tummy tuck," her mother advised. "Nothing too extreme or dramatic. Just a little one."

She had waited a long time, but she was finally going to do it. As soon as her face stopped looking like hamburger meat.

The tummy tuck was awful. She had to wear a girdle so her stomach muscles wouldn't pouf out into a big, ugly bulge. The worst of all, though, was the boob job. She'd just wanted to make them more perky—not too much larger. They had been hanging around her navel ever since she nursed her daughters—each of them for over a year—to the point that, to her, they'd looked like baby-foot-shaped raw pizza dough.

After the procedure, dragging a morphine drip—prescribed to help cut off the relentless, excruciating pain of recovery—as she limped from room to room, Joanne had stumbled sometimes. Experienced blistering headaches. Vertigo. She'd really thought she was going to die. Breasts were unbelievably sensitive tissue.

But now she truly was a work of art, and she could take great satisfaction in that. A serial artist. The human mind isn't Pyrex—it can shatter. So can the face. And she had to think of her future. Getting a man in her life. The way to true happiness. Her mother had told her so. Her face was her birthday present to her mom—a belated eightieth birthday present. After all her mother had done. Jules would take care of all of them, as she always had. All she had to do was ask.

There were stunning views of the Cascades from Joanne's tiny living room in her new apartment, after leaving Al. She could see all the beautiful, perfectly honed bodies on bikes or just jogging in expensive tracksuits down on the trails below every day. Her mother loved the human scenery.

What was the problem? Why couldn't Mom and Daddy move in? Her mother had pushed for Al to move in with her back in her student days. *But look how that turned out,* she thought grimly. Maybe that's why her parents didn't want to move in with her—too much togetherness. Her place was small, she had to admit, but Megan and Sarah could sleep on the futon couch if they needed to.

The SafeHarbour director had discouraged the proposal to have her mother and father move in with her. "There's no support there," she said. Maybe she just didn't want to lose the rental income. But she had offered other reasons for suggesting that her parents' living situation should stay the same, if at all possible. According to experts in cognitive deficiency, the director said, changing an elderly person's environment could be deeply disorienting and worsen their condition. Both her parents were showing signs of dementia and perhaps Alzheimer's.

Maybe they had to think of another plan.

"We have to talk. I just got off the phone with the SafeHarbour director, Ann Pike," Jules said.

"What's going on?" Joanne asked.

"Their housekeeper just informed her that an unauthorized surveillance system has been installed in Mom and Dad's apartment."

"She should have talked to me first. I'm the point of contact—I'm the one who lives nearby, Jules. Why would she go behind my back like that?"

Joanne hadn't expected the subject of surveillance equipment to reach Jules. She was a little embarrassed. But then again, hadn't Jules gone behind her back and told everyone else in their family besides her about Uncle Wilson's bequest? Why couldn't everyone in her family just be direct with each other? Her face and body ached from the surgery.

"That's not the point, Joanne," Jules said. "Where did this surveillance stuff even come from?"

"I was worried," Joanne said. "What if something happened and they couldn't reach the emergency pull in their room? That's why Al installed the surveillance system. For their safety. That's all." She hated how defensive her voice sounded, strong and clear. She knew her sister, with her psychology training, would understand.

She hadn't planned to tell Jules about the surveillance stuff. That cat was out of the bag now—but she still wasn't going to say anything about the content of the recording she had heard between their mother and Andrew. That she would keep to herself.

SAFEHARBOUR

Aida had had to find out from her granddaughter—Zoë, no less. Three hundred thousand dollars! Who would have imagined that? And nothing for her husband, after all he had done for his brother? They had always seemed so close.

She was sure that Zoë hadn't known she was revealing her family's secret when she mentioned the money to her grandmother. But you never knew with families. Secrets. Lies. The unforgivable. How long would Julia have kept it a secret from her?

Aida knew SafeHarbour was the last "harbor" for the wealthy and elderly. There, the frail and disabled were pampered amidst green woods and tennis courts, gym, and swimming pool. Having lost spouses, friends, and even adult children, SafeHarbour's elderly were tiptoeing around their final loss: their own death. Social calendars were filled with bridge clubs, shopping, exercise classes, stage performances, and field trips. The residents themselves were reduced to a useless minority.

They had moved to Washington from Ohio for their sunset years. Aida had become tired of the harsh winters and had waited for a long, long time to move into a place like SafeHarbour. Her husband had denied that he was at retirement age for longer than he should have. It wasn't until his patients started voting with their feet in the late nineties and moving on to younger physicians that he finally gave in. And by then, Aida had felt that her husband "owed" her—owed her a life focused on *her,* a life where her identity was not exclusively being a doctor's wife. Finally, it wasn't all about him anymore.

When one of the "penthouse" apartments had become available,

Aida had pounced. Overlooking the woods, the penthouse had a kitchen/living room facing the front door, with two bedrooms, two bathrooms, and a study with a small balcony. Spacious for senior citizen communities, though it was still several magnitudes smaller than their home in Ohio. But now they were being squeezed into smaller and smaller spaces, until finally their remains would be in a tiny, decorative urn. Her children may consider this new efficiency apartment safe and economical, but she was confused—couldn't find things sometimes. And people seemed strange, the way they talked. "Mom, we'd love to have you move in with us," Joanne had said. "Jules thinks it would be a great idea, too."

Why would that be a good idea? Burdening her favorite child? She'd refused. "Sweetheart, you're way too busy to put up with your father and me. Why would you even think of such a thing?"

"Just because we want you closer to us."

"Your sister put you up to this, didn't she? No way. We'll just continue to live here, thank you very much."

Aida didn't like change—especially not at her age. She liked routine and her familiar furnishings. But now their Duncan Phyfe furniture looked tired and dislocated in their one-room efficiency, like play structures in a day-care center for the elderly. So did the pale-green jacquard sofa and the glass étagère with its collection of fake food— jade fruits, papier-mâché peppers and broccoli—and lifelike dolls on the upper shelves. The dogwood curtains had disintegrated; they let in too much light now. The small kitchenette was bursting with pots and pans, the result of sixty years of accumulating kitchen stuff in Akron.

Except for her husband's blood pressure monitor, the mahogany coffee table, with those weird animal-feet legs, was bare. The PC—a Christmas gift from Mike and Jules—sat on top of her husband's old physician's desk, which was crammed in one corner. Bob spent all day looking at the ticker tape moving along the bottom of the screen.

But Aida had never asked to be happy. Just content. And for her, SafeHarbour was a seniors' sorority, "love boat" for the old. And it also provided her with an audience. She always volunteered, along with less talented old broads, to sing at the annual talent show, and always won first prize for her signature song, "Doin' What Comes Natur'lly."

Encores, too, for "Someone to Watch Over Me." That always brought the house down.

There also were musicals, mostly Rodgers and Hammerstein. She guessed there were comforts at SafeHarbour after all . . . small details that made living there more bearable, if you had the requisite amount of "perkiness" and positive energy like she had. It was certainly a better place than Akron. And she felt protected from the outside world there. Aida liked being the energetic one in the room, and around all these decrepit old residents, she felt decades younger, even though she wasn't.

As she walked across the dead-end street to the short block of quaint stores opposite SafeHarbour's gates, she reminded herself that seniors were not a pretty sight. Despite that fact, she liked spending her time—lots of it—volunteering in the women's clothing section of the second-hand shop, Yellow Brick Road. Proceeds went to the local SPCA next door. A convenient arrangement—old biddies replaced their dead spouses with a neglected animal from the SPCA and donated their dearly departed husbands' old clothes and golf clubs to the consignment store next door.

As she approached the door to Yellow Brick Road, Aida spotted a SafeHarbour resident walking her small, silver-haired Lhasa apso out of the SPCA. They were both modeling the same haircut. Aida couldn't remember the woman's name but a residue of dislike registered. She pretended not to see her. "A move up in the world," she snickered to herself as she stepped into the thrift store: from dead husband to cute little dog, from silver hair to silver fur. She had such a great sense of humor, but not everyone appreciated it. That was their problem.

Residents of SafeHarbour took great comfort, she felt, in fondling a furry little pet when widowhood hit. She didn't care for pets; she liked people. Those who were worthy of her, that is. She needed an appreciative audience. She was through being ignored. Even more so with cleaning up others' shit.

"How's our favorite volunteer?" Francine cheerfully greeted Aida as she entered Yellow Brick Road, the buzzer sounding off.

Aida smiled. She derived energy from the other "senior" women at Yellow Brick Road. By comparison, she was a showstopper. Francine had come out of the back room to say hello—Aida guessed her covolunteer must have been back there tagging new donations and entering them into a ledger before hanging them on racks. None of that for her—what a snooze. She had to be in the front, where the action was. Where people could see her. Not in the back room, far away from admiring eyes. She was good for business.

"My, oh my, Aida, you certainly dress up," Francine said, looking her up and down. All the women did that, and Aida loved it. She knew she was still attractive, even at her age. *You're only as young as you feel,* she thought. That's what she tried to impress upon her two daughters, but only Joanne listened. She often felt she had spent most of her life as an old woman, not a young one. Seemed unfair somehow. But her greatest asset was still there to pull men in. She just had to accept that her admirers had been age-appropriately adjusted. The looks she got now were from old men, not the young Turks of her diva days.

"Oh, this old thing? I just rushed to put it together." *Lie.* It took Aida at least an hour every morning to decide what to wear. And this particular outfit had maxed out her major credit card, the one she used exclusively for replenishing her wardrobe. But no matter. Aida was proud that she dressed as if she still attended Junior League luncheons. And customers seemed to appreciate her air of entitlement, as well as her fashion sense. She was highly valued. She just knew it. So obvious. She was different and always had been. Went after whatever she wanted.

"I can't stay long. My older daughter, Julia, was just here from California to celebrate my birthday. It was okay—too much fuss, if you ask me. But you know how it is with guests. I had to put everything on hold when she was here. Lots to catch up with. And Sarah's coming over after school for her scheduled playtime with her grandma." She liked using the word "grandma" as if it belonged to someone else. She had never imagined herself being called that by anyone. Ever.

"You never told me you had another daughter, Aida!" Francine said, interrupting her thoughts. "And we've been working together for three years now, haven't we? Isn't it wonderful to have daughters? Must have been special with all your kids here to celebrate."

"Oh, I'm absolutely positive I've mentioned my older daughter to you before." *Francine can be so irritating,* she thought, looking over at her.

Chunky reading glasses, nose pointed down. Dressing as she does, as if she were going to weed her garden. Probably a hand-me-down from one of her teenage kids, or maybe something that couldn't be sold even here. Like my son's wife, Abigail—looking like a hayseed. No self-respect.

"Nope, I'm certain," Francine insisted. "You only talk about Joanne and Andrew. This is the first I have heard about another daughter."

Aida sniffed. No reason to mention that Andrew hadn't come out for her birthday. Francine was so forgetful and nosy. How could she not have mentioned Julia at least once in the three years she had volunteered there? It just wasn't possible. *Well, Francine's got to be at least fifty—almost the same age as Julia,* she thought. She wondered why her coworker was aging so rapidly. You just had to fight the inevitable and maybe it would go away. *I'm not going down that path—not just yet, anyway.*

She felt her irritability was showing on her face. Why hadn't Francine learned how to filter her words, to know the margins of accepted behavior? She had no social skills. At least Aida had taught Julia and Joanne that much.

"I'm certain I've mentioned Julia before," Aida said, digging in. "But you know, I've noticed you've been repeating the same old stories and instructions over and over again. Starts to set in around menopause, you know—along with the middle-aged spread." She smiled to herself, knowing Francine was sensitive about her weight.

Francine said nothing.

Aida wasn't done yet. She went over to give her a squeeze around her waist, making sure to feel her rolls around the middle. Kind of disgusting. *She should do something about that.* But Francine was too out of shape for a tummy tuck.

"You just get used to not being noticed anymore. A kind of encroaching invisibility," Aida continued, gaining momentum. "There are benefits to a place like SafeHarbour, you know. You should apply for an apartment. You might find some old geezer—I could make some introductions for you. The rich old farts are unaware they're surrounded by old hags." She chuckled softly, knowing Francine had financial worries about paying for two kids' college tuition. She was recently divorced, with a deadbeat ex. Good riddance, if you asked her.

"Why don't you tell me a little bit about Julia," Francine said with a forced smile. "Is she married? Any kids?"

Aida's cheeks puffed out. She could feel them heat up. "Since you can't remember anything, sweetie"—she paused and reached for Francine's hand, but was startled to see Francine recoil from her touch—"I'll tell you again, hon, but you'll probably forget by the time tomorrow comes around." She laughed. Sweetly, she thought. "I gave her the beautiful name 'Julia' and refuse to call her anything but that. She's an academic—or should I say, a failed academic. I think she is having problems with her husband and daughter but she doesn't tell me anything. What more can I say? Hmm. She's a royal pain in the ass sometimes. How about that for an answer? But the birthday celebration was good enough, I guess."

"Oh my, you're always a surprise, Aida," Francine sighed, looking nervous, avoiding her eyes.

Aida sighed. All that phony nicey-nice crap. "Julia lives in Carmel now, and got a PhD so she could become a psychologist. She's one of those psychologist types who have the biggest neuroses of all. That's why they go into that field—to try to figure themselves out."

"So, what kind of psychologist is she?" Francine asked.

"Oh, not the inkblot type, thank God, or those who study rats in cages all day. Nah, she tests kids in school who can't read. They call it 'learning differences' now, instead of just 'slow learners,' like it was in my kids' day. Back then, 'slow learners' was the nice way of saying 'dumb as a doornail.' "

"Well, that sounds like a real contribution to improving kids' lives, their self-esteem and all, don't you think?"

"I guess . . . but I don't believe in all this 'self-esteem' shit. Some kids have confidence because they're natural-born winners. Others are losers, just plain-vanilla losers. If you ask me, they're going to have low self-esteem no matter what. Not everyone can be a winner, you know."

Aida fingered the new merchandise that had just come in. "New" used-clothing donations, that is. She usually stroked the donated clothing as if it were from Saks, but now she twisted and yanked at the blouse neckline on a shirt she was hanging, wrinkling the thin cotton, which had clearly been meticulously ironed by another volunteer. She let go of the cotton blouse, straightening the hanger. The wrinkles looked embossed, like one of those crinkly Indian patterns. She tried to smooth them out. Hated wrinkles, even on fabric.

Francine laughed, interrupting her train of thought again. "Well, it's probably a blessing you didn't go into counseling and have to listen to other people's problems, Aida."

"Yeah, I've had enough of my own. At one point, my kids were the source of a lot of problems in our household. Always had five cars for the five of us. No one learned to share. We all felt like we had to have our own. Go our separate ways. They were so goddamn spoiled— always getting what they wanted. Bob got so upset when our son had a car accident, crashing into a steep snow bank. The bills were so high, he started playing the stock market. That's probably what he's doing right now, as we speak."

"Well, kids can be expensive, but you can't worry about the money you spend on them too much. It's the love that counts in the end, now isn't it? And how are Julia's own kids, her being a child psychologist and all?" Francine asked.

"She only has one: a college-age daughter. Zoë. She's fine, in spite of her mother." Aida laughed at her own joke. "She's a very good student, thanks to lots of nagging from her helicopter parents. But we don't see Zoë much. They say they're too busy . . . just an excuse, though, if you ask me." Whenever she thought of Julia, she envied women who were close to their adult daughters. Must have just been her fate. She'd had no choice—in who her daughters would become, what personalities they would have. She and Julia were just mismatched. That happened sometimes. Like her and her own mother. At least she could depend on Joanne and her two girls. She could still influence them.

Francine had put her in a bad mood.

"Got to go," Aida spit out, shooting a stink eye at her. She hustled through the door before Francine could respond.

Yep, she thought, *Francine doesn't get any action.* That explained it. Probably hot flashes were making her bitchy today. *She'll love me again when she gets back to her old sweet self.* She wished she would just do her makeup once in a while, though, and make herself look more presentable. But Francine probably didn't give a damn. Didn't care about what was really important for a woman's well-being.

While she waited in the parking lot for her youngest granddaughter to arrive, Aida thought about the differences between her two daughters and their daughters. Three generations, yet so different. Julia had been difficult from the get-go, no common ground with her. Julia's daughter, Zoë, was a compromise, an in-between granddaughter: beautiful, sweet, good natured, but so serious and studious—a real drawback, in Aida's humble opinion. She saw Zoë annually at best, more like once every two or three years. She would have liked to have been closer to her. Like she was with Joanne's two cutie-pies; they visited her at least once a week.

No matter how Aida had tried, her older daughter just never cared. Julia could have been pretty if she had only shown any interest. Aida remembered their last heated argument, over the telephone, during the obligatory Sunday-afternoon phone call to the old folks.

"Mom, stop fussing over Sarah and Megan's appearance, their weight, their clothes. Will you, please? You're going to make them obsessed like you did with Joanne: eating disorders, body image problems, that kind of thing."

Aida could hear the edge in Julia's voice. It never seemed to go away, no matter what they talked about. "All that psycho mumbo-jumbo, darling. You know, a girl's best asset is not her brain. It threatens men, and you should know that more than anyone. You needed to play the game more—tell them how they are all God's gift to women. That's why you didn't get tenure. I bet that chairman could have been charmed into submission. Into giving you that tenure you wanted so badly. And Mike . . . well, you just think you know your husband. Men hide their true feelings, you know. Like your father. Mike does it, too."

"Mom—" Jules began.

"And *are* the boys after Sarah already!" Aida continued, ignoring her daughter. "One reminds me of your sister's first real boyfriend, Tim. Only in the looks department, though. Not all that other stuff—such bad news. What a nightmare he turned out to be. Having to sleep in our closet on that cruise ship. Who would have guessed? And you just leave that little girl alone, you hear me? Sarah's the little girl of my dreams. Looks just like me when I was her age."

Why did they always end a conversation so tense and disagreeable? Even when they talked about Sarah, who was none of Julia's business. With her, Aida had truly fallen deeply in love, perhaps for the first time. And this time she would get the relationship right. Many of the aunts and uncles on both sides of their family thought that Sarah looked like Julia. Even Joanne did. How could they think such a thing! How could a mother not know what her own daughter looked like, what she was interested in, or what she dreamt of becoming?

"She does look like Jules, Mom," Joanne said. "The same black eyes and gorgeous, wavy, jet-black hair. And she has those same skinny stick legs Jules had when she was ten years old, too. I've seen the photos!"

Well, not even Joanne knew her own daughter as well as she thought she did. Not as well as Aida knew her. Well, it is what it is. It is what it is.

While she was on the phone with Julia, Aida had seen Megan sit at Bob's desk in the corner of the room to do her homework. After that she would sketch for hours, lost in her own little world. Sweet. Megan should watch her weight, though. You could never be too skinny, as Gloria Vanderbilt used to say. Or too rich. Aida preferred Sarah: her second chance. With her she felt reborn—she felt like a mother. Sarah *was* a bit too organized sometimes, a wee bit too fond of structure, even at the age of ten. She aspired to be an orthodontist and straighten other people's crooked teeth. Aida promised herself she would work on that, and on Megan's seriousness—promised herself that she would cultivate in both her granddaughters a preference for enhancing physical appearance and a sense of fashion instead of a focus on school and studying. It was probably just a phase they were going through. Academics were not the key to a woman's success.

Aida thought of Nancy, way back then. Star student. Why had Aida hoodwinked Bob into marrying her instead? *That was one helluva misstep. One bookworm should have married another.*

Aida had to remind herself that Sarah was not a plaything, a "reborn doll" like one of those displayed in her étagère. She had a case full of the humanlike dolls, each one in hand-sewn attire from different periods in American history. She had a Betsy Ross doll, a Pocahontas doll, a Southern belle antebellum doll, First and Second World War dolls,

Great Gatsby period dolls, and frontier dolls, too. An expensive—but not a frivolous—hobby.

Sarah seemed to love those reborn dolls as much as she did. They shared a ritual. Now that Sarah was entering her teens, Aida hoped that her granddaughter wouldn't outgrow her fondness for the Sarah doll. Or become like Megan, who studied the historical background for each doll, ominously like what Julia would have done. Megan was never going to be anyone's plaything.

When Sarah was little, Aida had described to her the time-consuming process of creating the Sarah doll. Every apartment at SafeHarbour had a decorative tchotchke displayed in the alcove by the front door where a plaque hung with each resident's name. The O'Reillys had a photo of Stonehenge. The Ludwigs had a family photo of three generations. The Whitmans had a photo of Aida's Sarah doll.

Her granddaughter had peeked up at the shelf. Aida, only slightly taller than Sarah, had unfolded the stepladder because she herself couldn't quite see the top shelf either. She explained how she had looked at boxes of Sarah's baby photos, compared them, and decided which one captured the essence of perfect babyhood.

"Sarah, you just knew when a camera was pointed at you. Always so cooperative. Doing what you were expected. Not like other babies. You knew how to pose."

"Well, I hate having my picture taken now," Sarah said. "They all make me ugly as sin." She had taught her granddaughter that expression. "I look fat in most of the photos anyway."

"How can you say that, darling? You're beautiful. You could be a model. I pored through boxes and boxes of scrapbooks. And then I found the one. Finally sent the doll manufacturer this photo of you at about eight months old. See?" she said, passing the baby picture to her granddaughter, excited about its pristine condition. "Here's a lock of your baby hair I sent FedEx insured. The 'Sarah doll,' custom ordered, came by express mail about a week later, a month before you entered kindergarten."

Today, on their special afternoons together—even as a teenager, way past the age for dolls—Sarah asked about her reborn doll. With an exaggerated dramatic gesture, like the ones she practiced for the musical *Oklahoma!*, Aida reached for the doll, loving the buildup of suspense both for her and for her granddaughter. She had gotten all dressed up for Sarah—was wearing a pale Valentine's Day–pink blouse, the sheer, low-cut type she preferred when singing in Rodgers and Hammerstein productions.

"Well, you know, Sarah, this *is* my favorite," Aida singsonged, absolutely delighted. Gently lowering the baby doll from its stand, she kissed it and stroked its skin and wisps of hair. Stepping down, trying to conceal her arthritic hands, she handed her prized doll to Sarah, presenting it as a gift.

Sarah's face glowed with the honor of holding her namesake; she hugged it awkwardly, perhaps afraid she would drop it.

Aida was pleased to see that Sarah was not too old to play with dolls. "This baby photo was the right one for your doll. I keep it in an envelope in the display case, too. Right here," she said as she patted the envelope where it sat in the étagère.

The Sarah doll, which had cost more than one thousand dollars, looked as human as possible without being quite a corpse. That was part of its ethereal beauty for Aida: a statement of beauty from cradle to grave.

When Sarah was little she had stroked the doll's skin and looked under the white "christening" dress at its diaper, and her eyes had grown large. "Sarah's skin looks just like mine," she had muttered, touching her chin with her index finger and then the doll's.

"My doll even has the same birthday as yours, hon. Do you want to see her birth announcement?" Aida had asked. "My Sarah is made from some pricey silicon-vinyl mix. Doesn't it look like real skin though? You can touch it again if you want."

"I want to look at my doll, Grandma—the Sarah doll—in my own way," Sarah had said, putting the announcement Aida handed her on the coffee table with barely a glance at it. She looked closely at the doll, then at her baby photo, and back at the doll. She didn't say a word.

After a long inspection, she finally spoke: "The eyes are too real." That was all she volunteered. She seemed spellbound, unblinking, staring at the doll's eyes. They looked like glass to Aida.

There were two birthday cakes, always, for Sarah's birthday every year: one for Sarah, and one for the doll sitting next to her.

"I can't remember, Grandma," Sarah said, interrupting Aida's thoughts. "I know you told me before, but is the hair real?"

"Sure is. I've told you before, many times. The hair is yours. And the eyes look so lifelike because they are made from an advanced material, a sort of synthesized form of Pyrex."

"The skin's kind of reddish and veiny, though. I'm not sure I like it. Was I that way as a baby?"

Pausing, Aida thought of Sarah as an infant. The sight of her had taken her breath away. As if she would have shattered if she had stared at her too long. Delicate—a fragile, almost supernatural beauty. "My Sarah weighs exactly the same as you did at three months of age," she answered. "That's the age when you could focus on your mother's face. And mine, too, of course." Stretching the voile fabric between her fingers, she admired the delicate French ivory silk. "This was actually *your* christening outfit. I've saved it all these years. And I get it dry-cleaned and heirloomed on your birthday each year." She sighed, and drifted in her own thoughts for a moment. "We can dress her up in your old baby clothes, too, if you want. I've saved the prettiest ones in special zipped organizers so they won't get dirty or musty. Nothing old and ugly for my Sarah."

Sarah nodded, smiling and obedient, looking past the doll, staring off. Was her favorite granddaughter bored of her?

"Hey, Sarah, before we have a snack, let's look at baby Sarah a little more closely. All of the other babies in my little nursery can be ignored. Their skin and their bodies aren't as perfect as yours, baby Sarah."

"I'm not a baby anymore, Grandma," Sarah said, hesitating. "And I don't want to touch the skin. I don't like how I can't tell the difference between what's real—natural—and what's not with her." Sarah smiled sweetly, her face relaxed. Aida liked to think it was a special smile reserved only for her, and she focused on that—rather than on her annoyance at the girl's constant use of the word "Grandma." Made her seem so old.

"You won't have a pizza face, darling. A face of zits like so many of those homely teenage girls. Your skin will be without blemish, like mine. Even at my age, I like to pamper my skin."

"Oh, Grandma, you're the most beautiful one in here. Everyone else is so old and funny looking," Sarah said.

Aida drew closer to her granddaughter and gave her a kiss on the forehead. How good her Sarah's soft velvety, perfect skin felt against her lips.

"Grandma, you're getting extra skin around your face and neck," Sarah said. "I think that's cool. Didn't know you could keep adding skin."

Why did she have to ruin the moment? Aida thought, her temper flaring. *Then again, what do kids know?* She fluffed the pink ruffles around her neck, the way she'd done when she had a date back in the day.

"But I want to be more than just pretty," Sarah went on. "I want to be an orthodontist. Have a career using my mind—like Aunt Jules."

Aida no longer heard Sarah's voice; she was drifting to a time, far away, when she was young, beautiful, and a singer. Her Yellow Brick Road to a Land of Oz where dreams could come true. She caressed the skin of the Sarah doll as if it were her dearly beloved in an open casket. Humming "Doin' What Comes Natur'lly." Time stood still.

THINGS UNSAID

She tried to breathe, but the air came in jagged. She inhaled and held for far too long. She choked, and then she read the note again, panting and trembling. Jules could smell her own sweat. She vomited until nothing but yellow, piss-colored liquid rained down on the welcome mat.

> *Jules,*
> I can't stand by and watch what you are doing to all of us in the name of duty and family obligation. We're family, too. Your real family. Not the fake one you insist on choosing over us. Until you know what we mean to you, I am taking Zoë on a camping trip across the country . . . for two weeks, maybe more. When we get back, I hope you will have made the right decision. You have no idea what sacrifices I have made for you.
>
> I still love you, no matter what.
> *Mike*

Mike was planning his way out. He'd found an escape hatch. And she wanted to escape *with* him and Zoë—otherwise, there would be nothing left. Everything was the opposite of what it was supposed to be right now.

She carefully folded the note into even rectangles, origami-style, and slipped it in her purse. Why hadn't she seen this coming? What a fool she had been—so blind, so driven to be a good daughter and get her parents' approval, to prove she was a better person than either one of them. Children took care of their aging parents, didn't they? Mustn't they?

∾

Jules hadn't slept in days. She looked at the answering machine. Not a single message. Over one week had gone by since she'd found Mike's note. That wasn't like him— not to text or even send an e-mail, however curt. Just silence. No Mike and no Zoë.

She texted them both, hoping that Zoë, too, would text her back, just this once. *"Please, please come home. I can't live without you. You know how much I love you, don't you? I have been so stupid! Can you forgive me?"*

∾

Then, only three- or four-word text messages—and from Mike, never Zoë. *"We're fine." "Don't worry."*

Yeah, right.

Mike was still refusing to talk to her, camping only-God-knew-where with Zoë. Or was Zoë hanging out at Stanford already? She had called Zoë's friends but they'd all acted as if Jules were diseased. She let it all sink in, taking her down. A rabbit hole. No worse, an abyss. An awful, frightening lethal silence. She wondered what Mike had said to their daughter about their problems. How could she redeem herself in their eyes? How could she have lost all sense of consequences? They no longer assumed she loved them; and why should they?

The phone rang. Jules picked up.

"Mom?" It was Zoë! But the connection was unclear, full of static.

"Zoë? It's so good to hear your voice."

"I miss you, Mom. What's going on? Dad doesn't say much, and I'm tired of camping now. With just him. I want to come home. Besides, I'll miss Stanford classes if we're not back in a few days. Dad said I could go to summer school there. He's going to sell his car and start biking to work."

Jules's sucked in her breath. Maybe they would be back soon. Zoë's voice was like a symphonic chorus in her ears.

"I miss you, too, sweetheart. Where are you?"

Zoë explained they had gone up the coast to Oregon. To look for rocks at a jade beach. And would be at Stanford in two days.

"You can come home whenever you want to. What does your dad say? Can you put him on the phone?" Jules waited expectantly.

"Dad's being vague. Says it's up to you. That you need to have a break from us. Is that true, Mom? Do you need a break from us?"

"No, honey—well, it's complicated," she answered. She was trying to be honest, but she didn't want to blame Mike. This was happening because of her mistakes, not because of him. "I love you. And miss you. You know that, don't you?" Mike had not picked up the phone since they left. Two weeks since her mother's birthday, and in that short time, everything had unraveled.

"I can still find a way to go to Stanford, can't I?" Zoe said, more hoping than asking as far as Jules could tell.

Jules remembered how the multicolored, glossy college brochures and admission forms had looked like some kind of messy buffet on their dining room table when Zoë had spread them out. Always a hard worker, she had spent four summers at Double Rainbow, scooping ice cream for young families with kids and swarms of teenagers in order to help with college expenses. Jules had waited every day for her daughter to return from work. Waited for that sweet, sticky kiss to be planted on her cheek.

"I got into Stanford, Mom. I know it'll be tough there. But I just have a feeling I can do it. I'm not too worried," Zoë said.

"That's not it, cutie-pie," Jules said. "I know you're smart enough. I just don't think it's going to be possible now. Financially. But I'm working on it for later."

"What? I just don't understand! Is it that you just don't want me to go there because they screwed you over? That's it, isn't it?"

Jules sucked in oxygen, preparing to inform Zoë about their financial situation, about putting her dreams on hold.

"No, sweetie, that's just not true. Your life—present and future—is your own. Whatever you want it to be. We want you to go wherever you want to go. And we know you have your heart set on Stanford. We'll try to make it happen down the line. Perhaps with some student loans and your earnings from your summer jobs, we can eventually swing it. But we can't make it happen yet—not now. I have an obligation to help your grandparents, and—"

"I'm so sick of hearing about duty, duty, duty," Zoë cut in. "Obligation this. Obligation that. It's just insane. You're ridiculous."

Her daughter was right. What had she done? All this time she had wanted to help her parents and sister, but she hadn't realized it came at such a great cost. Now she wanted to take away all the wrong choices she'd made so her family could start living again.

Still . . . there were so many excellent universities in the state. Why was Zoë being so single minded? So one sided? All these months they had talked about other potential colleges—Berkeley, other UCs, places where Zoë could get in-state tuition. And she had such good grades. Her daughter certainly knew she had other options and could go somewhere else. Just until they were back on their feet. Then she could transfer to Stanford.

"Don't you see, Zoë?" she tried. "You're so smart—you could even take a break for a year or two and earn some money before going to college. Get some work experience. Maybe take a few classes at a community college, if you want to. Then we can figure out financial aid and you can reapply."

God, she hoped Zoë would understand. In the Whitman family, Uncle Wilson had always bailed out everyone—even his parents' friends. It was a question of honor and of pride. And he'd been able to do it because there was never any doubt—ever—that those friends and family would pay him back. All except her father. But his debts, like all the others, would be repaid. Maybe not right away, but eventually. Even if it took generations.

Jules could hear the tears in her daughter's breathing.

"This is the worst day of my life. I can't believe you're my mother! You've screwed me over," Zoë sobbed.

The phone went dead.

Tears rolled down Jules's cheeks. The tears came and came, and wouldn't stop, like nothing she had experienced ever before. She never cried. How could she have thought she was doing the right thing?

For the next week, Jules tried almost every day to reach her daughter—calling, texting, and then, when that failed, calling Zoë's friends. They told her not to worry—if they said anything at all to her—but all they would say was that Zoë was in Palo Alto, taking classes. Mike seemed to know where their daughter was, but his texts were vague. He was staying with a friend in Palo Alto, and said they spoke by phone occasionally. That he'd seen her once in the past couple of weeks.

Jules was beside herself. What if something awful were to happen to their daughter? What if something awful had already happened?

MENDEL'S THEORY

"Jules is the one who has to support us. That's all there is to it. They have Uncle Wilson's inheritance—and you have to provide for your own sons, don't you, honey? You have professional goals of your own. Dreams, too."

Andrew knew his mother was livid over Uncle Wilson's snub to their father. Who cared? He didn't. You should be able to do what you want with your money. But he bet Jules was beside herself that Zoë had let word out about the inheritance. Now all of it spent to recover from their father's stock speculation. How could they have such enormous debts, anyway?

"You have so much on your mind," his mother went on. "We understand the pressures you must be facing."

Andrew loved having an older sister at times like these. Still, even if she was mommy's little helper with a neurotic sense of obligation, she should cut her losses. He certainly wasn't going to get sucked in. Jules kept calling him, leaving messages, and he knew why. He wasn't going to call her back. Pressures were there only if you felt them. And his sister felt both Catholic guilt and Buddhist karma. A double whammy.

The moment passed in silence. Andrew exhaled. His mother didn't understand any of them. Only her own needs. It had always been like that.

"Well, this phone call does have an ulterior motive," his mother said. "Not like our other weekly calls. Which're all just pure fun for all of us, aren't they? About good times. Family memories. Togetherness." She paused. "Go on, Bob. Have the guts, for once in your life, to tell our son what's going on." Her voice sounded stone cold now.

His father's voice had trailed off, sounding like a whimper. "Dad, I can't hear what you're trying to say."

"I said our portfolio has tanked," his father said, sounding angry. "Credit cards, line of credit, Social Security checks. All gone. Things got so much worse, instead of better."

Andrew felt endangered. How high was their debt now, anyway? Their expenses should have been cut by more than half with their move to the one-room efficiency. And between Jules's second mortgage, Joanne's loan, and his own admittedly token check for them, they should be doing fine.

"It's just not what I expected when . . ." His father's voice trailed off again. Was he just distracted? Or was he disconnected? Was this dementia?

"Dad, I do have to think of my own kids, you know that. I suppose Jules and Joanne do, too. I wish I could be of more help." Andrew tried to think of something else to say but nothing came. His own family had to come first.

"Well, you're the biggest help of all. Being the best son a mother could ever have," his mother said, getting back the receiver. "Tell him, for God's sake, Bob. We can't move out of SafeHarbour. I just won't stand for it. No trailer park for me. I'm not moving in with Joanne either. After what I've put up with all these years. Not on your last dying breath am I settling for anything less in my goddamn golden years."

"Mom," Andrew said, "Mom, please. We'll figure something out. We can and *will* take care of you. What are we talking about, anyway? A few thousand dollars more, right?"

"We use our credit cards for everything now." His mother sighed. "Never thought we would be reduced to this. Not in my wildest imagination. We barely can make the interest payments—minimum ones. Collectors are hounding us. The only bills we can pay are the small ones."

Andrew heard her take a deep breath. Holding the handset farther from his ear so her voice didn't seem so loud, he inhaled deeply, too. *Jesus, how did they lose so much money?*

"Oh, by the way, I am mailing—insured, of course—my topaz ring to Ashley. You know, the one with all the diamonds? She loves that one so much—I see her looking at it on my finger. You need to get off on the right foot with her. It's time you settled down. Besides, I don't need it."

"Didn't you promise that ring to Joanne?" He felt uncomfortable. After all these years, Joanne must have thought she would get that topaz. *Not my problem,* he reminded himself. He needed to focus on his kids' future, and his. Just like his dad, he had learned to save. He had to maintain his family values now—that's why he was keeping his sons in a private Christian school. Tuition was high, but necessary.

"What Joanne doesn't know won't hurt her, now will it?" was all his mother said.

Ashley would love the ring, a blatant bribe from his mother. But it was Abigail he was thinking of. His first wife, the mother of his twin sons. Abigail—named after the Foursquare religion's founder, Aimee Abigail Simple McPherson—had read her Bible between cleaning patients' teeth. He had fallen in love with her at first sight.

Andrew had never been a religious type of guy, especially after George Washington Military Academy. But at Abigail's insistence, he'd converted to Foursquare—a form of Christianity that believed in a strict sense of healing sins by prayer and strict abstinence from alcohol and premarital sex—before they had sex. Andrew didn't buy into all of it, but it seemed to make Abigail happy. His quirky sister a practicing Buddhist and Abigail with her peculiar religion. Go figure.

Andrew had been a newly minted dentist at the time, the only one serving an Indian reservation in the hinterlands of Colorado, almost 1,400 miles from Akron, in what was known as the Four Corners area of the United States. Somehow it all seemed auspicious—Four Corners, Foursquare, that sort of thing. A box—but a box for containing an orderly life, a life that he could control.

The Navajo on the reservation lived in a range of dwellings: poor pit houses, pueblos, some with wooden ladders strapped with rope so the visitor's feet would be stabilized while moving into the common room. Originally, the ladders purportedly provided security, an escape route in case of an emergency. Now, only the kids played with them, as if their families lived in playhouses. Because of government financing, most of the dwellings now had steps. And there was funding for health expenses, too, which Andrew loved. No arguments about fees, no competition from other dentists. He could live near that reservation forever. Lead a simple, Christian life.

Life on the reservation had not continued for long, however. Abigail had wanted a family and a reliable, much larger stream of income. After she had accepted Andrew's proposal for marriage, he noticed a change.

"Hey, what's up with your reading plan?" he asked her while she sat with a patient's head in her lap. His favorite position.

"What are you talking about?" Abigail said, the patient jerking his head around while her hand was moving inside his mouth. "What plan?"

"You know, reading the Gospel. You always do that after you've stuffed cotton inside the patient's mouth. Haven't seen you do that once this week."

"I'm distracted, that's why. We've got to think of our future. After marriage. Do we want to be in the middle of nowhere for our family? Do you want our kids to be schooled with Navajo kids? To drop out after completing one year of high school—if we're lucky? Is that what you want?"

So Andrew had started looking for a private practice. Shrewsbury, Vermont—a small nowhere town—had offered him an office and moving expenses. Just like the offer Akron had made to his father. He would be the only dentist in over 150 miles, not much different from the Navajo reservation. At least he would be able to use Novocain— although if he were being honest, he didn't really care. He had become used to strapping kids down, like the cat corpses he had practiced on in high school biology class.

The addictive beauty of the changing of the leaves hardly compensated for the frigid winters in Vermont. Still, there were financial incentives for raising a family there. That would satisfy Abigail.

After two years of marriage and twin sons, Adam and Jake, Abigail's devotion to the Foursquare religion had grown stronger. Their twins were raised in a strict no-alcohol, no-smoking, no-swearing, no-sex, no-drugs environment. By the time they were thirteen, paintball, motorbikes, and hunting had become the boys' guilty pleasures. Ribbons from competitions and tournaments wallpapered the TV room.

Andrew's parents had moved to SafeHarbour when his twins were thirteen, just beginning high school, and their new little baby, Ethan, was starting to hold his head up. His dad had finally retired from medical practice, and Andrew was beginning to wonder about his mental health. His mother's, too, for that matter. Soon after moving, they had come for a visit—they arrived two days before Christmas Eve, in midst of a mild snowstorm (by Vermont standards, at least). Andrew had driven into Manchester to pick them up. They were both too old to drive by then and he felt too guilty to let them take a taxi, a very expensive fare. He also suspected their dementia was worsening and he was afraid they might have trouble even hailing a cab.

"Oh Andrew, honey, why can't you visit us instead sometimes?" his mother said when he picked them up. "We're getting older now, you know, and we just can't handle long flights anymore."

"My practice just can't be put on hold," Andrew said, defensive. "I can only take vacation time on Christmas Day and New Year's. Why do you have to nag me about this, Mother? How many times do I have to repeat myself? You know kids visit the dentist during school breaks and summertime."

His mother sighed and looked out the window.

Andrew steeled himself as they pulled into the driveway at his house. *Here we go,* he thought.

"Oh, hello darlings," his mother greeted the twins, some little gift in her hands for the two of them. Then she turned to Abigail—Andrew saw his wife wince. She wasn't a fan of his mother.

"Here is some smoked salmon—your favorite. I even buy the wooden box kind. Much more expensive, you know. It has some kind of Indian—Inuit, perhaps—fish design on the box. Thought you'd like it. Reminds me of that godforsaken outpost you were stuck in, treating all those Indian brats."

Andrew would save the box for Jules; he knew she loved them. That was the least he could do.

"Oh, Aida, how thoughtful of you," Abigail said. "You shouldn't have." It looked to Andrew like her face hurt. Probably from all the forced smiling.

"And I know you can't get the right kind of beauty supplies out here in this hick town—or should I call Shrewsbury by a nicer name? 'Hamlet,' perhaps? Anyway, I brought you a few cosmetics. Can't have too many, I always say. Although I don't expect you have much, if any at all." She offered up a bag of her latest free samples from Clinique or Estee Lauder, some slightly used. "See, Abigail, these colors would look good on you. With your coloring, your blue eyes. Brighten up your skin. I just tried the red lipstick once. Just to see if it would be a good color for you."

Andrew watched as his wife carefully accepted the gift, then exited the room. He knew she was depositing it under their bathroom sink, adding it to the stockpile of other free samples his mother had given her over the years.

They all plopped themselves down on the huge sectional couch in the living room. Andrew had bought it because it was large enough to accommodate their sons and their friends.

"Now, how long are you planning to stay this time?" Andrew asked.

His mother calmly stroked his face with her perfectly manicured red nails. "What kind of question is that? There isn't some sort of deadline I don't know about, is there? I don't need an invitation, do I, to come for a visit?"

Andrew took a photo of all of them around the coffee table. To go along with all the other photos shoved in the attic. All those pictures of her standing next to him, beaming—the skin on her face so tight that her smile looked like the Joker's.

Abigail always wanted the house to be spotless for guests, and the Christmas decorations she'd put up looked like they'd come straight from the cover of *Martha Stewart Living*. (They had, actually, Andrew realized as he thought about it. Abigail loved to order from the Martha Stewart website. Each year it became more excessive.)

His mother moved to hug Abigail and kiss her good night—then blushed as Abigail turned her back in a defensive block. Andrew couldn't remember the last time his mother's face had turned red like that. Abigail hurried out of the room and came back with fresh towels—the kind reserved only for very special guests—while Andrew struggled with his parents' two heavy suitcases, which he deposited in the hallway, to the side of the guest bathroom. Why did his mother have to pack so much for a few days' stay? Their guest room was too small for anything but one queen-size bed and a small nightstand. Even the closet wouldn't hold a standard drag-bag suitcase on the floor.

"My, the weather is frigid this time of year. And oh, my arthritis," his mother said, rubbing the gnarls on her knuckles. "But nothing would keep me from seeing my 'sun,' my one and only son, the sunshine of my life. A mother's love is always constant, you know. And soon my two grandsons will be off and about, not remembering me. How very sad. That's why we must make our visits longer," his mother said.

His father was quiet. Andrew was worried. He had followed his investment advice in the beginning and had lost everything. Now he left it to others—mutual fund companies. Once, he remembered, Jules—or was it Joanne?—had asked if their mom had her jewelry in a special place, just in case they had to find it. In an emergency, is the way whoever said it had put it. Well, their mother had just started yelling: "You can tear the house apart. Look in all the closets. Inside pots and pans, for all I care. When I'm *gone*!" That had been the end of broaching the subject of their parents' assets.

It's none of my business anyway, Andrew thought. He had his own problems.

Sitting down next to the Christmas tree—that year the Martha Stewart colors were white and gold—Aida seemed to Andrew to be displaying a general sort of weakness, the kind he remembered his grandmother sometimes experiencing under stress. She reached out for her son's arm, to steady herself, to avoid tumbling over. Abigail offered her hand instead, but she pushed it aside and fell back into the overstuffed wing chair.

"My mother said my life would be easy if I married a good provider. 'Become a doctor's wife,' she said. Well, if she had lived to see me now.

My troubles *began* when I got married." She paused and looked at Andrew. "I didn't mean for your father and me to be such party poopers. We can talk about this later. No need to ruin our visit. And Abigail, you needn't get involved with our petty personal problems. That's just for family to deal with, you know." She smiled at her daughter-in-law— a fake smile, Andrew thought. He knew Abigail would never be family to his mother. "Have you been busy with that Spiegel seed catalogue again, honey? That's where you do most of your shopping, isn't it? A regular farm girl."

Abigail fingered the buckle on the strap of her overalls. "No, these are from Sears, down in Manchester," she said. Her tone didn't hold the slightest trace of offense, but Andrew knew better. "Andrew likes me in overalls. Says there's no place for fancy clothes and makeup in Vermont."

"Andrew's so handsome, you know," his mother went on as if Abigail hadn't even spoken. "I would be worried, if I were you."

Ouch, Andrew thought, belching a baby-burp-up taste.

"He's such a looker. We had to fight the girls off, throwing themselves at him in high school. He favors me, you know. Same dark chestnut hair, Italian lover eyes." His mother laughed and girlishly tossed her dyed locks.

His first serious girlfriend, Carrie, had been his college sweetheart at Wooster College. How his mother had loathed her. Nearly fifteen years earlier, before he had met Abigail, he had taken Carrie to Wong's Chinese restaurant, the only decent restaurant in Akron, to meet his parents, announce their intended engagement, and celebrate his father's birthday. Wong's was considered very exotic for northern Ohio, a region of the state not known for "ethnic" anything—clothing, food, residents—outside of Cleveland, that is, which was an ethnic mishmash that the Whitmans found unnerving at that time. They felt safer back in their own white enclave.

At Wong's, white waitresses dressed in tight, gold-and-red-embroidered, Suzy Wong–style dresses. The bar was very popular; Andrew always felt he was in some exciting country in Asia—or at least on a Hollywood set—when he was there. Definitely not in Akron, anyway.

Andrew had insisted that Carrie, his soon-to-be fiancée, be invited to celebrate his father's birthday. Halfway through the evening, his mother stood up in a silvery satin cocktail dress and toasted her husband with her Tsingtao beer. His sisters, Jules's husband, Mike, and Carrie—all dressed in jeans—raised their beer mugs, too.

"To my dear husband, whom I saved myself for, not giving away the ranch before we got married," his mother said, speech slurred, staring down at Carrie. He saw a few drops from his mother's mug sprinkle the top of Carrie's head.

"What!? You weren't a virgin and you goddamn well know it. And I didn't find out about it until our wedding night!" His father sounded exasperated, a little bit bitter, even after all that time. Andrew thought how amazing it was that some feelings didn't die out. Maybe even got stronger.

"Well, you wouldn't have been able to tell the difference anyway," his mother said. "I wasn't going to die guessing."

Andrew looked at Carrie, and his heart went out to her. Virginity was still an ideal in the Midwest—among everyone, including parents who obviously hadn't practiced what they preached.

"Wow, and in the 1940s, no less . . . I guess you could say you were ahead of your time," Jules had laughed—trying to lighten the mood, Andrew thought. He had always thought she had a freakish grin, like someone in pain. He wondered if she knew what her face looked like when she was around their mother. Come to think of it, what did his own face look like? he wondered.

Carrie had looked down at her lap. Her eyes grew shiny, and seconds later two tears, barely detectible, slid down the inner corner of her right eye. She looked up at him, waiting to be rescued or at least supported. Given a smile, perhaps. But he offered nothing.

"You're absolutely gross," Jules had said to their mother quietly, shuddering.

Andrew watched as their father stood up quietly, walked over, and tapped Carrie gently on the shoulder before marching stiffly back to his seat.

Andrew had felt embarrassed for her, but not moved to action. Jules, though—she seemed to feel a sisterhood, a solidarity, with Carrie that he couldn't imagine. She had guts—perhaps to the point of reckless-ness—and knew her mother's dark side as well as any of them.

Their mother looked alternatively oblivious and defensive, trium-phant and chastened. He was no match for her. He wanted to be, but he hated making things worse. He just wanted to be more like his father.

No one ever saw Carrie again after that night. After their breakup, Andrew didn't mention her anymore, although he tried to Google her for years after his marriage to Abigail and the birth of his boys. All four of them.

"Oh, Aida," Abigail said, interrupting Andrew's reverie. He blinked. It surprised him that he was thinking of Carrie after all this time. His wife was a different story: a Carrie killer. He had met her on the rebound, six months after Carrie broke up with him. At a dental conference in Cleveland. As in almost everything, Abigail won out.

She was the only daughter of the dean of humanities at the University of Denver, and every humanities professor on campus dreaded having her as a student, because they knew her opinion counted far more than peer reviews or lists of publications. She was an "opinion leader." And in Andrew's mother's defense, she did look like she would rather plant squash and fava bean seeds than look at a copy of *Vogue*. Her hair was untamed. She didn't toss her head and try to make her hair swing. His mother said it was because her hair was dirty and she didn't care. But Andrew liked that about her.

She made no exceptions for Andrew's mother, no matter how aggres-sive she became. Despite continuous protestations to call her "Mom" or "Mother," Andrew had never heard his wife address her mother-in-law as anything but Aida. Jules couldn't—or wouldn't—call their mother "Mom" either. She also wore overalls—but that was where the similarity between the two women ended.

"Maybe I was a bit hasty with Carrie," Andrew's mother had said to him when the twins were babies. "She was stunning, the way I was at her age. She was no match for me, you understand—but she was pretty. Still, Abigail is certainly a small price to pay for being with my one and only son and my twin grandsons."

And now they had a third child—Ethan, an angelic, Raphael-like cupid with blond hair, blue eyes, and very fair skin. Their newest little blessing from heaven; another Whitman to add to the burgeoning family tree.

"Don't you want a little girl, so you could have one of each flavor?" his mother had asked before the baby was born.

"Whatever God wills is always welcomed," Abigail had replied sweetly. Andrew envied her seemingly effortless ability to render their mother speechless. Abigail would not shed a tear over anything his mother said. She was the only one who would never react to her criticism. How he wanted to learn that!

"But surely after the fatigue and demands of twin boys, in your heart you want a baby girl," his mother had pressed on, her voice rising at the end of her sentence.

But Abigail had been unruffled, unblinking. "My heart matches God's—only he knows what will truly make us happy," she said.

His mother, as in most of her conversations with Abigail—was finally silenced. She had confessed to Andrew once that Abigail seemed like some other species, but she didn't quite know why. So unrelated— like she'd come from a gene pool of unknown provenance.

Now, his mother moved in for a closer look at her grandbaby, and Abigail pulled the infant towards her breast. Arms outstretched, his mother's jowls drooped, and she shivered a bit as she let her arms sink down to her side, deflating.

"Oh my, he's different," she observed, staring into the baby's ice-blue eyes. "He *is* a cute little guy, so freshly baked." She lip-printed his soft cheek while Abigail still cradled him.

"If you want to touch him, wash your hands," Abigail instructed, elbowing her mother-in-law away. "I usually don't let smokers touch Ethan, you know. But you two are exceptions, of course."

Andrew's mother sneezed. *Does she think Abigail smells feral?* he wondered. Maybe his mother was allergic to his wife.

Abigail reached into her pants' pocket and offered his mother some Altoid breath mints. "Here, take two of these. So Ethan's not offended. Babies are very sensitive, you know. They have a superb sense of smell."

His mother was the one offended. Her shoulders hunched, her thin lips in a tightly pinched line. "What else should I do before kissing my own grandson?"

Andrew heard the ice in her voice, but Abigail didn't crack.

"Oh, that's it for now . . . I guess. It's really a privilege to be trusted with someone else's baby, as I'm sure you're aware."

Andrew could hear his mother's words inside his skull: *"I've held more babies than you have."* But that's what she would say to her own daughters. Abigail was not family. She was the lucky one. Andrew took satisfaction in the fact Abigail wasn't afraid of his mother, not like everyone else. That was her most admirable quality.

He loved staring into baby Ethan's sweet little face: a few fine blond strands, a very pink bald scalp, blue eyes staring up at him. He was a beautiful infant—so different looking from the twins. After his mother finished washing her hands at the kitchen sink, he watched as she took the baby from Abigail. After a few seconds, she frowned and passed Ethan to him.

"This is no grandson of mine," she said. "Both sides of our family have only black or chestnut-brown hair, and either black or brown eyes. This is *not* my son's child. If he had blond hair and brown eyes, or dark hair and blue eyes, it's *possible* he could be my grandchild. But this baby . . . not a chance!"

Abigail smiled. "Oh, Aida, can't you be happy for us? That we have another little boy? God didn't want to give us a baby girl this time. Don't be disappointed."

It was late. Midnight. They all went their separate ways to bed.

The house seemed quiet, but not at peace. His parents had left very early—in a cab this time, Andrew had an oral surgery to prepare for. He had heard the door click as they left, but he hadn't risen to say goodbye to them.

It was still dark when he downed his muddy coffee and went to strip the bed in the guest room, making it tight with new sheets, GWMA-style. He wanted to rid his house of his parents' smell. Thank God, life could now go on as usual. He backed the car out of their one-car garage, grateful that he hadn't had to leave his car outside that night. He and Abigail always fought over whose turn it was. The loser had to allow a good ten to fifteen minutes to wipe all the snow off the windshield and warm up the engine after the car had been out all night. In the pitch dark.

Later that night, as they sat on the couch watching a talk show on TV, Abigail scrunched up next to him, trying to cuddle. But Andrew wasn't in the mood.

"What's wrong, hon?" she asked.

"Nothing," Andrew muttered. "My mother just puts me in a bad mood, that's all."

"Is this about Ethan? What she said about how he couldn't be your son because of his blond hair and blue eyes?"

"Nah. What does my mom know about genetics? She was just shooting her mouth off. Never liked blonds for some reason. Always called them 'pasty faced.' "

"Hmm. Don't pay attention to the old bat. I don't like to speak ill of people, but your mom's the biggest bitch I know."

Tell me something I don't already know, Andrew thought. Still, he didn't like it when Abigail called his mom a bitch. Carrie and Grissim had both been kinder.

When Ethan was sixteen months old—his big boy—Andrew remembered his mother's words again.

He had walked into the kitchen to start a big pot of water boiling. He loved their old-fashioned stove, how it had a folding metal top to hide the burners, converting to a work surface for cutting boards and mixing. He relished how much cleaner and more aesthetically pleasing it was with its metal top flattened down. The kitchen in general was soothing to him, just as Ethan's breathing had been when he was an infant. The gentle, trusting sound of his inhalations and exhalations, like the back-and-forth petting of a kitten, had always put Andrew at ease.

Andrew enjoyed being a father. The pleasure of knowing you could love and be loved. Like his love for his father and his father's love for him. All sons loved their fathers and vice versa, right? The only

difference was, Andrew felt comfortable showing his love for his sons—
and his need for theirs.

Abigail had just closed the books for the day. He knew he could trust
her with money—with everything. Besides, she was better than he was
with accounting.

"Oh, darling, our books are worse and worse," Abigail said, looking
over his shoulder into the pot of water on the stove. "We have to talk."

"Does it have to be right now?" he asked. "I'd like to get the show on
the road. The twins are going to be famished when they get back from
baseball practice."

As if they had been eavesdropping from the sandlot, Adam and Jake
rushed into the kitchen, occupying all the space in the room.

"What's for dinner? We're starving," Adam asked, giving his mother
a big kiss on the cheek while Jake waited his turn to do the same. They
knew how to manage her.

"Guys, we need some alone time. Can you go do something—like
take a shower? You have that guy smell, stinky and sweaty. Go clean up
while we talk," Abigail said as she reached for the box of spaghetti in
the pantry, not making eye contact.

Andrew thought that was strange. His wife always got twinkly eyes
whenever one of their sons kissed her. Just like his mother had. *What's
going on?*

"That's gross, Mom. You've been married too long to have alone time.
But hey, we don't want to know." He shook his head and threw up his
hands. "Let's get out of here, Jake, before they embarrass us. Geez."

Andrew heard the thud of baseball cleats through the house as they
escaped upstairs.

"Hon, can you give Ethan a meatball while we talk?" Abigail asked.

He spooned out a meatball, cut it into tiny pieces, and put it into a
plastic *Toy Story* bowl for his little boy. He picked up Ethan and after
a wet, sticky kiss—*Why do kids always have sticky mouths, even when
they haven't been eating anything sugary?*—he placed the toddler on his
food-encrusted booster seat.

"Okay, what's so important?" he asked as he reached for salad greens
and a bottle of salad dressing from the refrigerator.

Abigail looked on edge. Burdened. She had never been that way before. Not even when Ethan fell down after trying to run on his still-unsteady feet, hit his head, and had to be taken to the hospital.

"We have to talk about Ethan. There's something I have to explain."

"Must we now? I know his tantrums are nerve racking. It's just a stage. I'm so tired. I just want to eat with you and the boys. I need some downtime."

But no, something was wrong. Andrew could feel it.

"No, no. It's not his tantrums." Abigail paused. "I know you love Ethan as much as I do, sweetheart." She smiled and came over to where he was sitting. Feeding Ethan.

"Remember, darling, the Christmas before last, when your parents came to visit?"

He couldn't remember what she was trying to have him remember. What was one Christmas from another? They all blurred together in his mind. His parents staying, Abigail getting irritable, the boys getting overexcited by all the lavish gifts, and then his parents leaving without saying good-bye.

"Don't you?" Abigail pressed. "It was the Christmas before last. Ethan was no longer so wobbly headed, was beginning to look around, trying to understand his world. Your parents told us about their money problems getting more and more serious. Asked for help. Now do you remember?"

"Yeah, yeah, sure," Andrew said. "So, what's the big deal?"

"Don't you remember your mother's hissy fit? She said, as she held Ethan, that he was 'no grandchild of hers.' "

And then Abigail said it, in an almost joyful way: "Andrew. Ethan is not yours."

Andrew stared at her.

"I wanted to tell you so many nights. But I was afraid of what you would do. You were always in a world of your own. No place for me. Not even during sex. Maybe especially during sex. I wanted to hurt you."

He was silent. It was as if his wife were speaking a language he didn't understand. As if he needed subtitles. He folded into himself, curled up like a sow bug concealing and protecting its vulnerable parts. His soft underbelly. Abigail yanked at her wiry hair, loosening and then tightening it in its gnarled leather band, one with a stick that pokes through. Then she took Ethan and left Andrew and their twins.

~

Following Abigail's confession, Andrew found out she and God had decided that baby Ethan was a gift for Abigail and his best friend, Jonathan, not for Andrew. Jonathan—the friend he had weekly target practice with, reliving his days at George Washington Military Academy. He had thought his best friend was like Grissim—trustworthy. Maybe his mother had understood genetics and Mendel's theories better than the rest of them after all.

Abruptly moving out with Ethan, Abigail had asked Jonathan to start a new life with them. Jonathan declined; he had decided God wanted him to stay with his wife, not with Abigail and Ethan. They still met at evening Bible meetings, however. God forgives.

After the loss of his wife and son, Andrew had felt very lucky to find Ashley. A recent transplant to Shrewsbury, Ashley had a similar style to Abigail's. When she leaned way over the patients to clean their teeth, her cleavage flashed before his eyes, just as Abigail's once had. No Bible reading, though. No more of that, thank you very much.

Six months after he and Ashley started dating, Andrew casually mentioned to his parents that his "new friend" was pregnant. (Sometimes he called her Abigail. They seemed almost identical at times.) This fourth grandchild—technically the third, Andrew reminded himself—Jason, was offered to his mother as a gift, but not the kind arranged under the Christmas tree. He was barely a month old that Christmas—a scant two years after his mother's discourse on Mendel. Chestnut-brown hair, black eyes.

He and Ashley organized the presents in six piles that year: one for each of them, one each for the twins, one for Jason, of course, and also one for Ethan, a little boy Andrew could never give up. Ethan would stop by for a glass of milk and Christmas cookies and pick up his gift-wrapped surprises. Abigail would wait for her son by the front door. *What more could I possibly want for Christmas?* Andrew thought bitterly.

Abigail still demanded and received monthly alimony checks. Andrew had two families to support now. But it was never going to be three—in his mind, his parents were no longer family. If his sisters could come up with the money that would leave his parents some breathing room to recover from their debts and prevent eviction, good for them. But he couldn't afford to contribute.

The last time he saw his parents was more than five years ago now—Jason's first Christmas. After that trip, their visits had stopped. And Andrew hadn't traveled to Washington since their move. Birthday celebrations for his parents, family matters at SafeHarbour, those things were not part of his life anymore. And never would be again. He had problems of his own. *Five years,* he thought, shaking his head. It seemed like just yesterday.

BRAIN DRAIN

Almost two weeks after her mother's eightieth birthday, the pain had changed. Something added to it. She wasn't quite sure what. But she felt an increased pain, and a sensation that her skull was expanding. The falling down and searing headaches had puzzled her at first. But she hadn't worried much yet, no great concern. Everyone had headaches. Hers were just more intense, that's all. And that was to be expected. No doubt it was from stress—over her ongoing separation from her feckless husband and her concerns about attracting another man to hunker down with.

But then her ears had filled up, pooling with liquid in the canals, blocking her eustachian tubes. Joanne had had the sensation of the car lifting into the air, vortexlike, spinning so fast she blacked out. Ménière's disease. It was a near-fatal traffic accident; she'd wrapped her Subaru around a telephone pole. But somehow she escaped unscathed. Thank God there had been no damage to her face! She was lucky.

So now Joanne was calling her dad, because she needed medical advice she could trust.

"Hi. Oh. Mom. Can I talk to Daddy right away? We can talk later, okay?" she asked when her mother answered.

"Darling, darling. No time for your own mother? You always talk to me first. Leftover time is for him. I don't like secrets kept from me, you know that. So, you're not going to talk to him until you tell me first."

Joanne exhaled loudly, then held her breath, worried her mother could hear her. Nagging was going to be attached to what she had to say next. She was sure of it. She pinch rubbed the bridge of her nose with her right thumb and index finger, an acupressure move. The light pouring in through the window made her clamp her eyelids shut. She started in again blindly, with clenched teeth. Fighting nausea.

"I've been having severe migraines, Mom. I've been having them since right before my boob job. Don't know if I should see a doctor. That's why I need to talk to Daddy."

"No sense in talking to him, Joey." Her mother always called her "Joey" when she wanted to treat her like a baby. "I was a nurse, you know. A very good one, I might add. And there's nothing to worry about. You hear me? Just relax. A mother of two teenage girls has no peace of mind. I should know better than anyone about that. More rest. That's what you need. Perhaps a facial or two—that wouldn't hurt either. Then you'll be as good as new. We can have a mother-daughter spa visit, if you want. My treat."

"Mom, you better not let Jules hear you making offers like that. She's bailing you out. She wouldn't like it if she heard you talking about going to the spa."

"What she doesn't know won't hurt us." Her mother's voice sounded almost gleeful, the way it had when she had talked to Andrew about *her* topaz ring. *"What Joanne doesn't know won't hurt her."* That's what her mother had said. About the ring. The one promised to Joanne when she was a little girl.

How could she? Joanne could hardly believe it—wouldn't believe it, if she hadn't heard the conversation herself. It had been recorded by the surveillance system before the cleaner discovered it and they'd had to get rid of it.

"Now, there's no need to talk with your father anymore, is there? It's all taken care of."

"Please, Mom. Just this once. I really need to talk with him . . . now."

"Geez, sweetheart, if you insist. No need to become a nervous wreck over this. Everyone gets headaches. Maybe it's just your time of the month."

"Nope, I have . . . these goddamn . . . headaches almost every day . . . several times a day." She had to get to her bed to lie down, before she passed out. She pulled the curtains shut, darkening the room. Stumbled to bed, not sure if she could make it. She grabbed her stomach. Her hand tightened its grip on the phone.

"No need to be so snappy," her mother retorted.

Joanne just lay on her back, waiting. Finally, she heard the shuffling of her father's footsteps on the other end of the receiver. Slippered feet—probably those same old leather slippers the three of them had given him as a Father's Day present when they were all living under the same roof. Worn, torn, like he seemed to her.

"Joanne?"

"Daddy, oh, I'm so worried . . . don't tell Mom." She was almost panting. Gasping. Behind her eyelids, her vitreous humor—her eyeball juice—seemed to pulsate and boil: up and down, up and down. She felt a relentless throbbing—in her eye sockets, temples, neck, even her stomach. In and out, in and out. "My headaches—they're blinding. Unbearable." *Like kicks to the skull,* she thought, but her words halted as spit filled her mouth, the way it did when she was about to throw up. Pause. "My balance is off."

Her father sometimes took a staggeringly long time to answer even the simplest questions. It unnerved her. She couldn't hear what he was saying on the other end.

"Daddy, please. I feel an attack coming on."

"Go to a neurologist immediately. By ambulance. Go to the ER," he said, his voice suddenly strong. "Call now."

She felt herself drifting backwards to the operating room at the University of Washington Hospital in downtown Seattle. Rolling and rolling—like meat on a conveyor belt. Then she had the mask on, was breathing deeply, counting backwards from one hundred. At eighty-eight she thought about guardians for her two girls. She didn't remember counting after that.

The presurgery prep had been awful. Two ham-fisted med-techs had jammed a tube down her throat after pushing her head back, chin up, as she lay there on the gurney. First a rigid, thick metal rod—like a steel penis—had been shoved down her trachea to prop open her throat, like a pipe brush used to first trap and then clean a shower grate. Or like a plunger, but with nails sticking out on all sides, for unclogging a toilet. Then had come a narrower polymer tube. The taller dude had stubbornly avoided her eyes, ignoring her muffled screams. Her eyes squeezed tight, her body torqued, sweaty, gagging, arms held down by the other medic.

The supervising surgeon had stood over her, his mask tight, the magnifying light in her face as she peeked up at him. "Your airway anatomy is unusual, crooked, so be patient," he'd explained. "We weren't expecting this." He had patted her hand, or at least the part not covered by the med-tech, with his blue nonlatex glove.

Be patient!? she thought, tears stinging. *Why don't you see what it's like with a pair of huge male bodies towering over you!* But she was powerless, and finally submitted. Her throat had been penetrated, the pain had subsided. The gagging had stopped. A local IV and then the general anesthesia had taken effect. She had faded out.

She remembered all this as the sound of Jules's voice pulled her awake. Her sister was there for her! Joanne was groggy; she closed her eyes again. *So sleepy.* Then came the feel of wet, soft young lips on each of her cheeks. Sarah and Megan. She opened her eyes and looked up into their healthy, worried faces, and was wounded by their fear.

"God, Jo, how are you doing?" Jules had dry eyes as she patted her shoulder tentatively, but her voice sounded tight, pulled, strained like a wire contracting behind a picture frame. "We were all paralyzed with fear." She could always count on Jules to cut right through, the way she always had, with a minimum of emotion. "Great news, though. The surgeon said they got everything—the meningioma that caused this."

Joanne studied her sister's face: it looked wounded, too. Jules's eyes misted, pooling. "When you told us we were your kids' guardians, in case you didn't pull through, I felt . . ." The quaver in her sister's voice hit her hard. Jules looked down at her cell phone.

Joanne opened her mouth but shut it immediately, wincing and gagging. She tried again to talk. Cautiously, very slowly.

"No, no, dear." That was her mother's voice, cracking. Joanne looked over at her. Her black mascara in rivulets, streaking her cheeks.

"Joanne, you absolutely cannot say a word for at least twenty-four hours," her father said, sounding clinical. "Doctor's orders."

Which doctor? she wondered. *You or my surgeon?*

"The endotracheal intubation to prop open your airway severely irritates the trachea and can cause post-op complications, especially infection. An intracranial meningioma is complicated, so you must follow doctor's orders."

There he goes again—hiding behind medical mumbo jumbo. Joanne thought she detected a sniffle, though. And watery, amphibious eyes.

Joanne watched as her sister guided their so-called family out. Guiding them. Jules had that way about her. Always there when their parents called. She saw her check her cell phone yet again on her way out the door. Probably just checking in with Mike and Zoë.

Five days passed. Each day better than the last. Everyone except Andrew—he was never there—waiting for her release, standing by 24/7. At one point, as the sedative was taking effect, oozing from the IV hanging above her left arm, and her head nodded in its headrest, she thought she noticed her mother placing something on the side stand next to her bed. But then she drifted into sleep.

Today, at last, it was time for Joanne to get back to her own apartment, to be with her girls. For days she had felt that her release date couldn't come fast enough, but now it was here.

"You're ready to go, Mrs. Grant," the attending nurse said to her, getting the wheelchair ready for wheeling her out of the room she hoped she'd never see again.

"It was a bit rough, I have to admit," Joanne said to her in a voice barely above a whisper, like that time she had severe laryngitis and could hardly swallow her own spit. "But I'm happy I survived. I'm still living and breathing. So I feel pretty darn lucky. Not everyone survives, I've been told. And now my girls don't have to be stuck living with Al and no mom." Joanne reflected on how circumstances could have been radically different. Her parents, daughters, and Jules were huddled around her, silent.

A nurse's aide handed off the post-op instructions for treating her head wound, carried her small duffel to her bed, and brought her a Styrofoam cup of ice chips. Joanne jammed the handouts into her bag. *Soon I'll be back to the old routine,* she thought as she sucked on a few ice chips. *I should check for messages on my cell phone.*

And then Joanne saw it. A beautiful, ornate, gem-encrusted hand mirror sitting on the table next to her bed—was it a present from her mother? Joanne picked it up. At first she only peeked from the corner of her eyes. Then she looked more resolutely, more intently. She gazed at herself. *Hmm, not as bad as I thought it would be.* She touched the bald spot near her right temple. Sutures: small and neat, a hole about ten millimeters in width. She stared at the small divot. No scar would be visible once her hair had grown back. It would soon be the same old face staring back at her in the mirror. The nurse's aide wheeled her out to the exit door while her parents and daughters walked behind. No one said a word. Jules carried the duffel bag.

Joanne's first night's sleep in her own bed was mostly uneventful. Bathed in sweat, reliving the ramming of that tube down her throat, she woke up every two hours. At midnight, her throat seemed swollen. At about two o'clock, after the same nightmare, she lightly stroked her neck, feeling for swelling, as if there were abrasions deep down her throat all over again. At four she touched and played with the soft depression at the front of her neck. No more sleeping after that. With all the OxyContin in her system, she couldn't feel her head wound. She tapped at the divot. What harm could there be, with the gauze padding the wound? She lay there, staring at the ceiling, counting the beams. She could just make out their outlines in the soft glow of her nightlight. She also counted her breaths. Reassuring. Confirmation of life.

By six the sun was up.

She must have dozed back to sleep at some point, because when she next opened her eyes, she was startled to see her parents and her sister eating breakfast around her bed. She glanced at the clock: seven. Both her throat and her head felt achy, so she just pointed to her neck. Her parents rose in unison from her bed and Jules from the chair nearby to look for her meds. Jules was the first out the door and the only one to come back into the room—with the OxyContin, and also a cup of ice chips and a Popsicle to chase it down. Megan and Sarah must have already left for school.

"I feel like I might break, Jules. I feel anxious. Didn't get much sleep with all of my nightmares and all." She didn't have to look in a mirror to know that she looked awful. Her eyes felt swollen. All of her seemed puffed up. She looked around. Where had her parents gone?

Jules handed her the cup, listening.

"You know, right after the surgery I felt like a clogged toilet—something wrong with my plumbing, shit backing up. That's how my saliva felt to me. Viscous and lumpy." She sipped and made as if to continue.

"Save your voice," Jules said. "Look, here's a pad of notepaper."

Joanne had already spotted the notebook tied to the post of her bed. She picked it up.

"I didn't realized just how complicated your surgery was until I started learning more about it," Jules said. "Two surgeons were required. You see, the meninges are a one-way valve system between the water system of the brain and the veins that drain from the brain to the heart. It will take weeks, maybe months, before you feel like your old self."

Joanne smiled as she listened to her sister, knowing she must have read for hours about meningiomas online. Jules rarely disappointed her.

"So not so much talking, Jo. Did you know meningiomas begin to grow in the embryo? In other words, when Mother was pregnant she already had this brain tumor inside her. Your meningioma. Here, look on top of your dresser. It's so cool." Joanne watched as her sister reached for something on top. The dresser was tall, so she couldn't see the contents right away. Jules carried it closer. In the bell jar was what looked like a pickle of some kind, floating in formaldehyde. Jules laid it on the nightstand, next to Joanne's new hand mirror.

"Just like Andrew's formaldehyde cats in the attic. Do you remember?" Jules asked. "Your brain tumor affected the communication system, which protects the integrity of brain-to-heart flow. In other words, your brain and your heart don't seem to have much to do with each other."

Joanne attempted a laugh, but stopped. *Not a malignant event, though,* she wrote.

"Good. Here, suck on this," Jules said, passing Joanne the cherry Popsicle. Joanne had always loved cherry Popsicles when she was little. They turned her lips red, like her mother's—"Popsicle lipstick," she had called it. She swallowed and smiled, loving the coolness on her throat.

"I had to change my health insurance plan after leaving Al," Joanne began, but her voice was whiskey sounding, like her mother's. So she wrote instead: *My medical costs are too high. There is a large deductible and a cap. I'm maxed out.*

She didn't write anything else; she didn't feel anything else was necessary. Jules would help her. She'd been bailing out their parents for years. She wouldn't fail Joanne either.

Joanne tried to read her sister's face to calibrate her reaction. Jules gazed back steadily.

"We'll talk about your doctor bills when you're stronger, Jo. Not now." Her sister's voice sounded warm and caring, but weary, too. "We'll get through this together. This sort of thing must happen all the time. Hospitals understand, I'm sure. They must."

Joanne wrote on the pad: "I want to visit you. To recover." She had thought about going out there all week. How they could hang out together the way they had as kids. Sometimes her sister drove her crazy, but she could use the change in routine.

I'm so lucky to have a sister like you, she thought. She wanted to say that aloud, but all her meds were confusing her. So she wrote it down, but she wasn't sure how Jules received what she'd written. She'd expected at least a smile, but Jules's face looked grim.

"Now's not a good time for a visit," Jules mumbled.

"Thanksgiving is around the corner, and now is a better time for cheap tickets," their mother said, appearing at the foot of the bed. "Right before the Thanksgiving holiday frenzy. Jules, how can you be so selfish?"

How could their mother call Jules selfish?

"Why don't we talk about all of this later?" Jules said, and Joanne could tell she was relenting.

I really am *looking forward to visiting you,* Joanne wrote in the note-pad. To getting away from everyone and everything, she thought to herself. To unloading the details of her ordeal onto her sister. No one else bothered to listen, and she couldn't tell her friends—they would worry too much. But their mother was wrong about Jules—she wasn't selfish. Their mother was.

A CORPSE IN THE CLOSET

Jules slept fitfully. Her sister's operation had drained her. Dreaming of her toddler self. Bump, bump, bump on her tummy, going backwards, feeling free and fast.

"Can you be Mommy's helper right now? Take this milk bottle downstairs, hon, and put it in the box. You know, near the front door. Outside." Her mother's words sounded furry, like her lovey—her Velveteen Rabbit. The bottle was so heavy and slippery to hold, even with both hands. Lying on her tummy, cradling the bottle in her arms like her rabbit, she started down. That was all—she only made it down the first two steps. Then, looking up, there was Andrew falling, sliding, his feet in her face. Then she didn't see anything at all.

Silver flecks on the ceiling. Stretched out on the red Formica dinette table in the kitchen.

"Now, little darling. Don't cry, you hear me? You are a big girl now. Mommy's big girl. This isn't going to hurt," her mother said as she stuffed a red-and-white-checkered kitchen towel—one that matched the color of the table—into her mouth. It tasted like old spaghetti sauce.

Her father stood over her with shiny steel rods and thread. Eight stitches. Jules peed herself. But she shed no tears.

"What in God's name was she doing going down the stairs with a milk bottle?" her father asked, turning towards her mother so stiffly Jules wondered if his body had become steel, like the legs on the dinette table.

"Turned my back for a split second, that's all. I don't have eyes in the back of my head," she answered back, quickly hiding her pretty

149

glass, the one Jules saw her with every day. Her mother then teeter-tottered—or was that her own head wobbling from being held down so she couldn't move?—out of the room.

The next day she had to be x-rayed. All that pushing down on her in the kitchen, she supposed. Two protruding bones jutted out below her neck, below her throat. She got to wear a cross-your-heart bra—or so she called it—at bedtime until her collarbone healed. She felt really grown up wearing it. It was like a mommy bra.

Her mother was right about stairs: they could be dangerous.

Jules woke up. She had had that dream too many times to count. But this time she wasn't covered in sweat. Her fear was concentrated somewhere else. On Zoë. On wondering where she was, and whether she was okay. It was clear now that Mike no longer knew where their daughter was. And the only contact Jules had had with her recently was a text Zoë had sent asking her to send her money to a Palo Alto post office box. Jules had texted back, pleading with Zoë to give her a real address where she could stop by to see her, but she had heard nothing else.

I'll go to Palo Alto tomorrow and look for her, Jules decided. What else could she do?

Jules's eyes hurt from the glare of the monitor. Too bright in stark contrast to the darkness outside her study. Her cursor went right for her sister's e-mail.

> Hi Big Sis:
> It's 4:00 a.m. I can't sleep. Worry, alcohol, and meds keep me up. I don't know why—they're supposed to make me sleep. My bank balance is minus $9.30. I asked Al for money. He says: "What am I supposed to do? I have to pay a mortgage." But I had to pay for all the child care, food, and children's clothing out of my meager paycheck. As if Megan and Sarah belong only to me! But that is the past. That can't be undone. I'm your only sister, and you've always been there for me. You never

disappoint! My loan's coming due now. And my store rent's going up.

I know you don't want to hear this, but tough. Neither you nor Mike know what severe depression is like, or bipolar disorder. Yesterday I slept most of the day since I had been cleaning all day Saturday. Went to bed again in the afternoon, got up four hours later. I couldn't cook dinner. I eat saltines with cheese most of the time. I have lost the desire to cook or eat. And I used to love to do both. Now nothing makes me happy. I just cry and cry. Sometimes I go to sleep just to reset my mind, so the crying will stop.

Depressed means unable to move. It takes me all day to do the simplest task—like make the bed—and then I get more anxious and the crying starts all over again. After a couple of days, I stay up all night to get something done. And the cycle repeats itself. My happy pill doesn't help anymore. The world is closing in on me. I feel I could fit into an urn—one that matches one of my favorite dresses in color and pattern. Try not to throw this in the garbage with "what does she expect from me." I will not be hospitalized, period.

Love you,
Your little sis

Jules's heart raced as she read the e-mail over and over again. The computer glow was the bluish-green color of the Magritte painting she had viewed with Zoë a few months before. That same *Ghostbusters* color Uncle Wilson's check had been. A bad-luck color to her, associated with death.

How she missed them. Her family.

She remembered that gallery visit to the San Francisco Museum of Modern Art. Zoë still had that girl-boy quality: beautiful with her dark chocolate–brown eyes, girlish but athletic and frenetic. And such beautiful, curly, jet-black hair. Like most teenagers, she had concealed her feelings as best she could from her parents. But she'd exposed herself anyway. Wandering through the rooms, hesitating and weaving through the crowds, not saying much, her daughter had eyes only for paintings done by Magritte, the artist who had created the man in the bowler hat, apple perched on top—the piece of art she'd seen and fallen in love with in the movie *The Thomas Crown Affair.*

Magritte's most famous paintings were happy, whimsical fantasies— clouds floating across living rooms, fruits in the sky, floating doorways. A crowd gathered around *Homage to Mack Sennett*—a woman's headless corpse, transparent nightgown draped over the hanger, in a closet. Her nightgown was *Ghostbusters*-colored. A radical departure from the joyful images that Magritte created thirty years later: bowler hats in the sky, birds cut out of clouds.

"Something very bad must have happened to Magritte when he was very young, before he painted this," was all Zoë had said.

They read the accompanying placard. Magritte had been thirteen years old when his mother committed suicide, and in his early twenties when he painted *Homage to Mack Sennett*. It wasn't until his fifties and sixties that he blossomed, literally painting blossoms and fruits floating in the sky.

"If you can't forgive or forget, you're a corpse in the closet. Magritte wanted to live again," Zoë said in that offhand fashion a teenage girl sometimes has with her mother. Then her daughter came over to give her a powerful hug. "I love you so much," she purred, knowing exactly what her mother needed. And the cells in Jules's body softened in return. *Where is my daughter now?*

The rain clouds were clearing. Still sleepy, Jules sped down Highway 101—on her way to search for her daughter for the fourth time that week. Palo Alto was a two-hour drive from Carmel. Jules yearned to clear out the toxins, the insane anxiety she was feeling. She had read about a glymphatic system of mental mine sweeping, dumping the brain's waste products so the mind could function more efficiently. She could use something like that.

No more bailouts. She had to make it up to her husband and daughter somehow, some way. Were those tears in her eyes, or floaters from being groggy? Maybe it was both. She clutched the steering wheel, staring straight ahead, slugging back Starbucks. Blinking. Spots before her eyes.

Jules pushed the visor down and pulled her baseball cap lower; the sun was starting to peek through. She fumbled for her sunglasses in the side compartment and unzipped her rain jacket.

Please, Buddha, Kuan Yin, the deities of the universe, let Zoë be safe and not come to harm, Jules prayed. Her little girl—now a phenomenal young woman—was still her sunshine. But did she know it? There was so much Jules wanted to say but never had. Only when Zoë was very little, more a sweet little pet, had Jules felt entirely free to share her feelings with her. Not when she had to really be there, when Zoë needed answers and a mother's love.

Please, Zoë, don't give up on me. She chanted the mantra to herself. *This time I am going to find you. No more turning back.* Her daughter had needed someone to watch over her. How could she have let this happen? What was she thinking? Maybe she needed to hire a private investigator if she didn't find Zoë this time. If the police did nothing. How had she let her family come to this?

All those months they had talked about colleges—Berkeley, San Jose State, other UCs where Zoë could get in-state tuition. She had such good grades. She had been accepted at Stanford, so she certainly would be accepted at some of the other California universities. Just for a while. Until they developed a plan for how to pay for Stanford. Then she could transfer, and be where she really wanted to be.

I failed, Jules thought. An epic failure, Zoë would call it.

What had she been thinking? To leave her daughter swinging in the breeze, abandoned by her own mother? The road blurred. She rubbed her eyes and squinted until it came back into focus. *Just a few miles to go.* She was almost to campus.

She called Zoë for what must be the twentieth time that morning. Zoë picked up. *Oh my God, she picked up!*

"Hi, sweetheart."

No response. Jules felt the silence. Loud and clear. The kind of silence she didn't want to interpret.

"Oh, it's you," Zoë finally said.

Jules glossed over that. "Just wanted to check back with you." She waited for some kind of response. More silence. "You know, you haven't responded to any of my texts."

Zoë was silent again. Then, "I've been busy." Her daughter's voice sounded slurred and amorphous. Wounded.

"Honey, are you all right?" Jules could hear voices in the background. Rough voices. Male. Tough. "I'm on my way. Driving as fast as I can to see you."

"Don't bother. Gotta go." Pause. "Sorry about Grandpa. Grandma told me he's been strange. Stranger than usual." Pause. "I'll let you know where I am. Could use some money, though." Jules would have to check online. What could her daughter be spending so much money on? "Sorry about Uncle Wilson, too. Didn't know his inheritance was a secret from Grandma."

Jules heard shouts in the background, but couldn't understand the words. Laughing. Fuzzy speech like her daughter's. "But, wait . . ."

Click. That was the end of her contact with the light of her life. But Jules was not leaving her now. That light was not going out. She pulled off the freeway and dialed a second number.

"Officer Hyde speaking. Division of Missing Persons and Runaways."

"Hello, Sergeant Hyde. You asked me to contact you within two weeks if there has been no contact with my daughter. But I still would like a 'voluntary missing adult' investigation report filed. The City of Palo Alto or East Palo Alto has got to help me."

"I need to have the specifics, ma'am. We have so many inquiries a day."

"Yes, I'm so sorry but I'm extremely worried and upset, Sergeant Hyde. I'm Julia Foster and we talked last week about my eighteen-year-old daughter, Zoë, who is somewhere in Palo Alto or East Palo Alto. She does not want to communicate with me. I have no forwarding address and only a bank account for wiring funds to her. The bank refuses to give me her address. But, as I said last week, she is almost certainly in danger. We just finished talking and she sounded inebriated or under the influence of drugs. You must help me. I don't know what else to do."

Jules remembered her first trip to the East Palo Alto Police Department. Sergeant Hyde had explained that Zoë was not considered a runaway because she was no longer a minor. Plus, since she'd left of her own free will, she was a "voluntary missing adult." He had taken the information and the photo from her, but Jules knew he was just being patient.

"I have a file number . . ."

"There is nothing more I can do for you, Mrs. Foster. Your daughter left of her own free will, after a domestic dispute with you, and your husband has had contact with her. She seems to be unharmed. If she is taking drugs, as you're suggesting, we can search the premises, since that would be considered suspicious circumstances and a criminal act endangering the individual."

"Yes, I want you to search for her." Jules didn't want a criminal record for her daughter, but what else could she do?

"Do you have an address?"

"But Officer Hyde, that's the point. I don't have any knowledge of her whereabouts."

"Until you do, Mrs. Foster, we cannot proceed with an investigation. I am very sorry."

The skies were as gray and moist as the underbelly of a fish. Jules grabbed her handbag, still open, and caught sight of Mike's note, a stark white rectangle, like a small dead white thing against the darkness of the paisley interior lining. She reached for her keys and buckled it closed. She put the top of her copper-colored Le Mans Sunset Nissan 350Z down before pulling back onto the road. The wind cooled off her sweat, but it couldn't blow away her panic.

No more bailouts. She had to make everything up to her husband and daughter somehow, some way. If only Zoë hadn't told her mother about Uncle Wilson's money.

Jules drove around and around down the main street, University Avenue, which joined Palo Alto with East Palo Alto. Where could her daughter be? She'd keep on driving in the hope against hope that she might find her. Young people liked to hang out. Maybe she was walking with friends window-shopping, hanging out near local coffee shops.

Jules squeezed her car into a very tight parking spot—the kind of spot her Chilean friend called *un suppositorio.* Zoë always had advised her to make a circuit around her Nissan to remember the little scratches and the keyed scar some brat had made when she last parked the car. Some kind of class warfare, Zoë had told her. Young people who couldn't afford nice cars deeply resented those who could, perhaps. *Is that really true?* Jules asked herself. *Do people resent others' happiness?* She hoped not. She had felt a little foolish liking her car so much. Maybe it was some residue of growing up in Akron. Why hadn't she realized what was really important in her life until now?

Jules thought of their credit cards, their line of credit, the past-due notices for their mortgage payments, the fines and penalty fees. This had to stop, and fast. She had been generous to the point of being ridiculous: taking out a second mortgage, using their daughter's college fund for her parents' recklessness. And now Mike and Zoë had left her. Jules couldn't blame them. How had she been so blind, so stuck? Her parents didn't seem to care what they were doing to her. *I'm a good person. But this? Really?* Did her parents even care about her? And if her actions were making Zoë and Mike suffer, how good could they possibly be? Was it dementia?

Joanne had benefited most from their mother's addictive shopping and love of beautiful, expensive things. She'd helped support her when she wanted to open her store, A Real Gem. And then there were all those luxurious teenage treats for Sarah and Megan: the latest shoes, hats, cosmetics. For Zoë, though, only a birthday card with a crisp ten-dollar bill inside. Still, Zoë was always excited to receive these tokens, and never failed to call her grandparents immediately and thank them. And all of Uncle Wilson's inheritance now gone. For nothing and everything. More baubles for her mother, exorbitant medical bills to pay for her sister, and her parents' care at SafeHarbour. And now no funds left for Zoë.

She pulled out her phone. She had called five, six, seven times—during the day, night, middle of the night, twilight—but until now, Mike hadn't answered. Sometimes it was hard to interpret his silence. But this time the meaning was unmistakable.

Still, Jules hoped he would answer—and he did. There was the sound of his familiar voice on the other end of the line. Maybe he was ready to talk to her now, to forgive.

"Do you care about your own family?" Mike began without preamble. "Are we even in the picture? Our daughter has saved every summer to help pay for some of her Stanford tuition. How do you think she feels about this? Huh? What kind of mother chooses her sister and parents over her own daughter? Tell me that!"

"I never *wanted* to do this—to you, to us—don't you see? I just wanted to meet my obligations since I knew my father hadn't met his. I thought I had no other choice, but I was *so* wrong. I should have listened to you. I don't know why I didn't. I really don't."

"I told you over and over again. Unbelievable! Debts are debts. And now, because of you, we have them. Giant ones. A second mortgage. Tuition coming up next fall. Aren't we allowed to have dreams, too? They blew their chance to have theirs come true. Now you've turned your back on us, just like your mother always turned her back on you. There isn't always love in a family. You know that. Open your eyes, goddamn it. You chose us last." Pause. "I have nothing more to say to you."

"Mike—" Jules began. But he had already hung up.

"You'll see," Mike had been telling her for months now. *"You'll see. There's no happy ending to any of this. You're just enabling them and screwing us over."*

That was exactly what she had done. She had thought she had to choose her mother first. How could she have known that this would happen if she did?

COLLECTIVE KARMA

"Have hired a private investigator. Hope I can do better finding Zoë."

Mike's text was small comfort. Jules had driven in the pouring rain around East Palo Alto from midnight until four a.m. before finally giving up and coming home. No luck finding Zoë. She was losing her mind. *I've lost her.*

Jules hadn't heard from Zoë, except for texts asking her to send money to different East Palo Alto addresses. Thank God for those; at the very least they let her know that Zoë was alive and nearby. And she was still getting text messages from Mike, in spite of everything.

How could she have fooled herself into thinking she was doing the right thing? Jules hadn't been there for her daughter or her husband. Now Zoë had left, and Mike as well. There was no one to call family.

She needed oxygen—lots of it—for what she had to do now. Zoë was nowhere to be found in East Palo Alto, so she had driven back to Carmel. She needed desperately to take a long walk to meditate, clear her head. Give herself a chance to think straight before she took further action. Breathing in the sweet marine air, Jules recalled how some of her foreign patients had become so used to the polluted air in their own countries that the coastal air in Northern California sickened them. It made them nauseous, they said. It was too fresh. She hoped in every cell of her being that life would be fresh again for her family. Safe. Loving. But the air was rotten.

Her parents were on their way out. Eviction was a possibility. Perhaps they would move in with Joanne, even though their cognitive faculties might soon decline further, which would make things difficult on Joanne. If they refused that option, and if Andrew wouldn't help, maybe they would go into some kind of government-subsidized public housing. And her sister—Joanne would have to figure out for herself how to get her health costs covered. Jules had her own family to think about. Her *real* family, and her karma, the consequences of her actions. Why had it taken her so long to see how wrong she had been?

Jules slowly slipped into her jeans and pulled on her old gray T-shirt. The material was silky, like Zoë's cheeks when she was a baby. She walked briskly up the canyon road behind her house, then sat down near a stunning waterfall, wildflowers in neon purples and oranges laid out on the hills like slabs of gigantic mosaic tiles. Jules looked past the hills to houses with spectacular ocean views—postcard perfect. She had always loved this spot. But nothing was as it had once been.

Sitting near the curb was a small, squat, cement-gray figure—misshapen and deformed, obviously abandoned. Like Gollum of *The Lord of the Rings*. A cracked five-inch gargoyle. Jules thought about taking him home—using him as a garden gnome. She picked it up—it was heavy, as if filled with someone's ashes—and read the sticker on the bottom: *Stone Boy. Made in China.* As she carried him down the hill towards her driveway, going so fast she almost tripped, she hid him in the crook of her arm. He seemed forbidden, somehow.

She entered the house with her abandoned nebbish. She wanted to share it with Mike and Zoë. Jules loved getting their reactions to things. Zoë was very observant. Saw what others didn't. And she had imbued objects with spiritual values ever since she could say her first words. Like almost every small child Jules met, the world, for her daughter, was a magical place where everything was alive, warm, compassionate, and caring. The difference: Zoë had never lost the feeling that the sky listened to her wishes . . . until now, that is.

Placing the nebbish near the tree outside her daughter's bedroom window, Jules imagined the backstory behind it. Someone else's castoff. In some Asian cultures there was a belief that merely possessing something that once belonged to another was highly risky. The previous owner's past karma lived in the discarded object. Usually a bad omen, but not always. The concept was *bachi*—punishment or retribution for past deeds.

Jules was superstitious. *He won't bring bad karma to my family,* she reassured herself. *Mike and Zoë will be safe. We will be together again. Someday soon. No external threats. Nothing alien threatening us. Collective karma.*

She looked out at the sunset—startlingly red, a surreal cinnabar sphere dropping molten lava into the ocean's horizon, melting, a red-lacquered soup bowl with a lid on it. Dissolving into a funnel-shaped vortex that drained into the sea.

Mike and Zoë were at risk, and Jules was the cause of it. But she had a plan.

Every tiny creak in the walls, every rustle under the windows of the living room, every sound seemed magnified in the house, both inside and out. Funny how even her five senses had changed since Mike and Zoë had left. Everything about this room seemed too big now. She sat down on the oversized, four-cushioned red Italian leather couch and picked at spoonfuls of a defrosted Trader Joe's *chana masala*. She and Mike had a routine: half the time they watched a movie or something they had TiVoed while eating on TV trays, and the other half they spent at the dining room table, with candlelight and fresh flowers arranged, ikebana-style, in a centerpiece. Routines were wonderful. Pleasurable and reassuring.

There were lessons to be learned from her family's buildup of unspoken truths, promises broken, obligations obliterated. *Bachi. Karma.*

Letting go. Disposing of parts of the family. How could she do that?

Family and dysfunction went together—like peanut butter and jelly. Family sagas. Everything would be okay. But how? She needed to find Zoë and Mike. Now.

REHAB

Five o'clock: still pitch black outside. Jules listened, nerves splitting apart, blackness in her peripheral vision. Jules was stalking her own daughter—living in this cheap motel in East Palo Alto, studying Google Maps, and leaving countless messages, both voice mails and texts. Zoë was living God knew where.

She had gotten a brief "Happy Thanksgiving" from Zoë, with a strange man's voice echoing hers. But she'd missed the call; she received it only as a voice mail on her cell phone. Who was that, anyway? His voice wasn't a young voice. Had her daughter met someone? A ne'er-do-well, perhaps, as Mike liked to call slackers?

Mike had moved into a tiny apartment in Palo Alto. What kind of mother had Jules become? Why weren't the police doing anything? Where the hell was her daughter?

Stanford's campus was unusually quiet over Thanksgiving break. Very few cars in the parking lots. The place looked deserted. Not the typical stream of bodies with backpacks heading towards the student union. Or bikes zipping in and out of the Inner Quad, almost running down any students and other pedestrians trying to cross over to another building. Even dormitory row seemed unusually still. As far as Jules knew, Zoë was still somewhere near campus. Mike said the private eye suspected Zoë was living in East Palo Alto, though.

Maybe a cup of chamomile tea would calm her nerves. Jules felt wired, as if amped up on amphetamines. But she needed, above all, to think clearly. Driving into the visitor parking lot behind Tresidder student union—usually an impossible place to find a spot—Jules pulled into a parking place no more than twenty feet from the back patio of the café. She walked inside, eyes adjusting to the dark.

A young student, piercings in her left nostril and upper lip, smiled unenthusiastically, as if she were in pain, at Jules when she ordered her tea. Jules watched as the young woman steeped the tea bag for her, rubbing at her nose and then touching part of the rim of the mug. She made a note to avoid touching that side of the cup with her lips.

Tea in hand, Jules sat down outside, under a large sun umbrella, at a small round café table cluttered with old copies of *Stanford Daily* and crumpled-up napkins. Two students, dressed in beautiful saris, sat at the next table. No one else was outside on the sunny, cheerful patio. Jules soaked in the sunshine and picked up the *Daily*.

A grainy photograph on the front page, captioned with "Another beautiful day on the world's most beautiful campus," caught her eye. Was that Zoë in the photo? Who was the old man with her? Grungy, at least middle-aged, with his arm around her? Her jeans were torn at both knees—was that the style nowadays? Zoë's body was draped on his, as if she had collapsed, but her face was turned up, tilted to the sun. What photographer would want to take a photo of that? The two were identified: "Zoë Foster and Carl Nagy." There were several other photos: students playing Frisbee, reading on the grass, and sunning. But Jules wasn't interested in the other photos.

Her phone beeped. She looked down. Another text from Zoë asking for money—but this time with an address in East Palo Alto. An actual address, not a post office box. *She wants me to find her!* Jules thought, heart lifting. She jammed the newspaper page with the photo into her purse. *I'm out of here. Now. Today is not tomorrow. I will not leave here without my daughter!*

She looked up the address on Google Maps. She wished she could give her daughter a heads-up that she was coming, but she feared Zoë wouldn't be there when she arrived if she did. Oh, she hoped she would be there.

She slowly drove by the busiest Starbucks on University Avenue in the direction of the apartment complex matching her daughter's address. She was looking for a place to park when she spotted Zoë and that Nagy guy from the picture walking into the building. What an unbelievable coincidence! Maybe she had earned some good karma after all to give to Mike and Zoë.

She leaned on her horn. "Zoë! Zoë, it's me! Your mother!" she called out the window.

Zoë didn't turn. Hadn't she heard her yell out her name?

Dragging her index finger down the list of metal mailboxes and across each line, Jules found her last name. Small, inked-in letters: *Foster.* Above it was another name: *Nagy.* She tried to stay calm; she buzzed apartment 470 and waited. She was relieved to find the apartment was in a well-kept building, at least. Impatiens and azaleas had been planted in front and were carefully maintained. Nurtured the way she had wanted to nurture Zoë.

A male voice came through the intercom. "Who is it?" His voice sounded sleepy. Or worse.

"I'm Julia Foster. Does Zoë Foster live here?" She waited. Whispering came through the screen of the intercom. A female whispering and others, both male and female.

The buzzer was earsplittingly loud, but brief. She couldn't open the door in time. She rang again. This time the buzz to open the door was sustained, dragged out, as if the person pushing the button was annoyed.

No elevator, but the hallway up the stairs was brushed clean. It even sparkled—there was some kind of mica or other metallic element in the white paint. Down near the fire escape, the last door on the right was open. She could smell something cooking—it smelled bad, like skunk or rotting waste. Reminded her of the smell of rotten carrion, those small animal carcasses their cat Neko dragged into her bedroom closet in Carmel from Mal Paso canyon.

The curtains were half drawn, so Jules couldn't see in right away. She had to adjust.

Then she saw: a circle of men and women, half sitting, half lying down on the floor. No furniture. No light. Some only in underwear. Lots of smoke and pungent body odor like raw, overripe onions. Jules looked at each face. The first one her eyes landed on was a beautiful very young woman, dark hair pulled tight into a ponytail, leaning on a guy much older, her eyes half closed, mouth gaping open. The guy's hand was between her legs, under the seam of the crotch in her jeans. Nagy. Maybe forty-five years old, he looked alert like a frog on a lily pad, ready to catch whatever flew by.

It was Zoë. Almost unrecognizable. So skinny and frail, shirt stained a grayish brown.

Jules recognized the shirt, a birthday present. Very expensive, but Zoë had wanted it so much that she had bought it for her. Zoë's hair was cut very short in the front. Bald patches revealed her pale scalp—*Maybe from malnutrition or drugs?* Jules speculated. And then there was the guy—flabby, sporting a Rasputin-type goatee. He could have been Schlepp's clone, except for the flab. Jules felt she had flown backwards through time, to that day when she had to endure his touch while carrying Zoë in her baby carrier.

No one seemed to notice her. Zoë looked half asleep. The guys— except for Nagy—just stared, eyes glazed over, pupils probably dilated, although she couldn't see them in the dim light. Who had pushed the buzzer if they were all so comatose? Nagy? Was he the dealer? Jules couldn't breathe in all that smoke. She was claustrophobic.

Walking over to Zoë, carefully avoiding stepping on anyone else sprawled out on the floor, Jules almost lost her balance. She had to grab on to what seemed like someone's head—sparsely hairy—in order to keep from going down. But she steadied herself and focused on her daughter. It was all about Zoë.

Just before she got to her dazed daughter, she tripped and fell against her shoulder. Her tears dropped, but she didn't know where. Hugging Zoë, shoving Nagy aside, she whispered in her ear, "Come on, sweetie, we have to get out of this place. Now. I'll help, but you have to wake up. You can do it, sunshine. Just lean on me." She shook her. No response. She tried again, harder this time. "Now, darling. Now. Before it's too late!"

Zoë, eyes half open, just stared. Her gaze was flat. Like that vole Neko had left in Jules's closet that one time. Her daughter's pupils seemed too huge as Jules examined her closely. Her own eyes had adjusted enough to the dark to get a good look.

"Hey, lady, she's not going anywhere," Nagy said, shoving her hard. Jules fell backwards and landed in some man's lap on the floor. Without hesitating, she struggled to right herself, kneeled close to her daughter, and put her arm around her. "It's now or never, sweetheart. You can't be in this place. You hear me? I'll call the police if you don't come with me."

"Mom?" Zoë mumbled.

"Goddamn it, lady, if you don't leave now, I'm going to make you."

"Please, Zoë. Please. You're breaking my heart."

Nagy got up, yanking Jules's arm, and dragged her to the door. Then he shoved her out into the hallway and slammed the door.

"I'm calling to report illegal drug use—perhaps marijuana, heroin, God only knows—in an apartment in East Palo Alto. I think my daughter, Zoë Foster, eighteen—almost nineteen—years old, is under the control of perpetrators of a drug ring, Officer. You must help. Go there. Raid the apartment and get my daughter out." Jules was sitting in her car outside Zoë's apartment building. Her cell phone battery was almost dead.

Jules was connected to Sergeant Savage, East Palo Alto Police Department. She had wanted to talk to the other police officer, Sergeant Hyde, who at least had some knowledge of her situation. Or so she assumed.

"We'll look into it," Savage said, and he gave her a case number before hanging up. Yet another case number. How many case numbers would it take before her daughter was safe?

Her phone vibrated next to her. She answered on the second ring. "Zoë?"

"Nope, sorry," a male voice responded.

Jules couldn't place the voice. "Hi," she said warily.

"Don't you recognize your own brother's voice?" Andrew sounded hurt. Jules hadn't seen him for almost ten years.

"Geez, Andrew. It's midnight."

And then he told her. He didn't know exactly when it had happened.

That evening around eight o'clock perhaps. The ambulance had arrived almost immediately. It was gusty, windy out, but the storm had calmed down by that point. Their father had suddenly stopped talking and then slumped over, motionless, his face in his food—his favorite, sushi takeout, a rare treat. He was the last one still eating. His right arm had raised momentarily, his chopsticks no longer in his hand, then fallen.

"Paramedics carried him out on a stretcher, hooked him up to ventilators and other monitoring devices, and started to work on him with defibrillating paddles as they whisked him away. Mother said she went with him and Joanne. In one of those high-tech American Medical Response ambulances with all the latest equipment. But I don't know if Dad can pull through."

Jules slouched in her car. She was so tired.

"Dad called me on the telephone before dinner, yammering on and on, and seemed fine. Sometimes I walk away from the phone to rest from all the preaching, and when I pick up the receiver again he's still delivering a sermon. Mostly gloom and doom about his stock portfolio. That he hopes things will get better. I feel so bad now," Andrew confessed. "Maybe he won't ever be able to talk to us again." Jules could hear him trying to clear guilt from his throat.

Jules thought about how she did the same thing almost every time her parents had called—but she had never told anyone that, not even Mike. It seemed so depersonalizing and disrespectful. *But some simmering resentments and lurking grievances,* she thought, *are best left unspoken. And sometimes that means walking away from the phone.*

She could hear Andrew closing down as he said good-bye. Jules would have to fly to Seattle before her father died. But first she would tend to Zoë. She prayed her daughter was safe.

Jules was about to unlock her car door when she spotted a police cruiser pulling up in front of the building. She froze. No searching for a flight out to Seattle. Not now. She would fly to Seattle later.

She looked at her phone. Dead.

Another police car arrived, siren blaring. Jules jumped out of her car and, walking over, got the attention of the officer closest to her.

"I'm the one who called. Jules Foster."

"Mrs. Foster," the officer said. "I'm Sergeant Savage. We spoke on the phone. I'm going to need you to wait in your car, ma'am. Or, better yet, at the police station."

"But I have to be there when you arrest Zoë. She'll be so scared and confused."

"It could be dangerous here, ma'am. I know you want to help your daughter, but the best thing you can do right now is wait for her at the station, where the booking procedure starts. You have the right to hire counsel for your daughter, and you can talk to her after we question her. But she is now an adult, and she will be treated as such."

Before Jules could find her voice, Sergeant Savage was gone. Along with six or seven other officers, he rushed the front door and broke it down.

Jules collapsed in her car and sobbed. Fighting paroxysms of tears, she started her car so she could recharge her cell phone and call Mike.

The second the phone came back on, she called him.

"Hi," Mike said. He sounded cautious. And why shouldn't he be? But that was good. She and Zoë were going to need his circumspect counsel.

"This is such bad news, Mike. But . . . Zoë is probably going to be arrested on a drug charge. I need you . . ." Jules couldn't finish the sentence.

"I'll meet you at the station," was all Mike said.

Joe Santini, a rotund, tanned attorney, slapped Mike on the back.

"Good to see you, fella. You never call me . . . until you need me, apparently!"

Mike attempted a smile as he shook his friend's hand.

"I know, I know . . . you don't want to see my handsome face under such unhappy circumstances," he said, jocular, "but don't you worry. Me and Sergeant Savage go way back. Don't we, Joe?" He winked at Savage.

Jules tried not to look annoyed and impatient. She was relieved, though, that Mike had some connection to the attorney.

"Now, Joe, these are good folks, you hear me? I can vouch for them. Can't find better parents. And teenagers sometimes just feel like going astray. So, what can we do for Miss Zoë Foster? This would be a first-time offender. Straight A student. Ready for Stanford. All those good things. Can't get much better. Not like the repeat offenders you usually have to book. And you've been trying to get Nagy for years now, haven't you?"

Jules relaxed, just a little, for the first time since she couldn't quite remember. Santini was a good choice—friendly, easy to talk with, and he knew how to navigate the system for their daughter.

"Well, yeah," the sergeant admitted. "The guy moves around so much he is more difficult to apprehend than a conger eel, I'll tell you that much. And we are booking him on multiple charges."

"Enough about that giant asshole," Santini said. "For my client here"—he turned to Zoë, who had said nothing since she arrived at the police station—"I'm sure we can work something out, right?"

Zoë had been looking at her feet for so long that Jules thought she might be sleeping standing up. She reached out and rubbed Zoë's back. *We'll get through this.*

At the hearing, Judge Fielding, serious in a Hollywood-casting sort of way but with a kind face, looked down at Zoë and Santini from the bench.

"I can see that Miss Foster is not a career criminal, but there are booking procedures and standard charges for drug possession, even for a first-time offense," the judge said as she twiddled her pen over the forms before her.

Jules chanted her mantra, trying to stop her quiet crying.

"I have a daughter, too, and I know that sometimes young people get confused when they are in pain. Mr. Santini, if you speak with your client and she agrees to rehabilitation for at least three weeks, I will suspend the charges until I receive certification from a licensed facility that Miss Foster has successfully completed therapy. If she does not undergo therapy and finish rehab to the standards required by the facility, Miss Foster will be charged with drug possession. That is the best I can do."

Mike and Jules hugged, the first hug she'd had in almost a month. Zoë stared at them in wide-eyed disbelief. Then they group hugged. Mike let go before Jules wanted him to. But Zoë continued to hug her. Like a small child, not an eighteen-year-old young woman.

Sergeant Savage and Santini filed their signatures and gave Jules and Mike a list of the approved rehabilitation facilities for the drug program. And they walked out together. *Still a lot of healing ahead*, Jules thought, but she was smiling.

Palo Alto Addiction Recovery Services accepted Zoë immediately, thanks to Joe Santini, who had represented many of their patients. He confided to Jules that many Silicon Valley executives and Stanford faculty and students were alums. Palo Alto prided itself on its low crime rate—except for drugs, that is. The "recreational" crime of the privileged.

The grounds of the rehab facility reminded Jules of SafeHarbour— the facade of an up-market hotel, faux–Cape Cod and resortlike. There was even a doorman.

In the vestibule by the front door, Zoë was the first to speak. "Mom, I don't want to be here. It's scary." There was no affect in her voice, as if she were still in an OxyContin haze. Was she? Jules didn't know.

"I'm planning to stay nearby, sweetheart," Jules said. "I've booked a weekly rental nearby until I can take you back home."

"But how long do I have to stay here?" Zoë's voice sounded plaintive.

Santini interrupted Jules's response and smiled, choosing his words carefully. "I'm afraid, as I've already told Mike"—he glanced at her husband as if for his approval—"there can be no outside contact with Zoë for three weeks. Until she successfully completes the initial stage of therapy."

Jules said nothing; she watched as Zoë crumpled, her eyes shiny and pooling.

"Does that mean I can't visit? Even though I'm right next door?" Jules asked.

"Rules are rules, and I have to insist. Zoë will be thrown out of rehab here and instantly booked on drug charges if she fails to complete the treatments. Now, no one wants that, do they?" Santini asked. It didn't seem like a question.

Jules texted her brother and sister: *"I'll check to see when the next available flight is. After I take care of Zoë. She is very sick and I'm not the only one in our family who can be there for Daddy. I'll be there as soon as I possibly can."*

Zoë had to come first. Once she knew she was okay, then she'd go to Tahoma. She shut down her phone.

"I promise. I promise, Zoë. You may not be able to see me, but I'll be here. Nothing, absolutely nothing, can tear me away from you. Not ever again," she whispered, as much for her own sake as for her daughter's. She would miss being at her father's side if and when he passed. But she needed to be there for Zoë.

LIGHTNING IN A BOTTLE

Aida stared at the medical devices strapped to her husband—the latest generation of equipment, not the vintage machines she had trained on many years ago at Montefiore Hospital—with clinical eyes. Bob lay there in intensive care.

Their relationship had somehow been defanged: they had reached a truce. Twenty hours after his heart attack, her husband had asked her in shallow breaths, "Where are we? Who's in our bedroom?"

Aida had answered softly, taking his hand: "That's Joanne, darling. Jules will fly out later, when you're all better. Zoë is sick."

Bob was delirious. He wouldn't know about his number one daughter's disgraceful behavior, not being there. Aida's lips were pinched, calm eyes dry. Her body seemed reduced somehow, desiccated, starved. After twenty years of talking about Bob's death, it was finally happening. She was quiet. She could hear Joanne sobbing, choking. Bob had fallen asleep, so she quietly bent over and kissed his hair. It smelled sweet and clean.

"Don't worry, dear," Aida whispered, still holding her husband's hand. She wondered why her heart was racing. A symphony of cymbals and percussions in her head, almost shattering her eardrums. Where was she? She didn't belong there. Neither did this man.

"Where's Andrew? Is he going to make me some chicken kebabs?" Bob had asked her earlier, delirious. How could she forget that story? About raising chickens. And eating them. His memory loss. Their world together had started to spin apart years ago, and rapidly. Bob seemed in a trance.

Aida still could hear her husband slipping off his belt and chasing Andrew around and around the house, running upstairs until he caught him in his room. She remembered how he just kept beating him and beating him until he couldn't lift his arm anymore. How she had wished her son were not too old for her to kiss his owies. He'd wanted so badly to be like his father. She shuddered at the memory.

Horrible stories kept filling her head like dead fish surfacing in a polluted pond. This was the time to conjure nostalgic, Norman Rockwell–esque images of family life in Ohio. When the head of their family was near death. Instead, Aida thought of family photo albums. Photos of her grandson Adam at his Marine boot camp. Like Andrew, hardened, forged in a furnace of shared hardship and tough training. But she had survived her own form of boot camp. She hoped her kids had, too. Aida would endorse the check from Bob's life insurance policy to Andrew once she received it; Bob would certainly want their only son to have the money, wouldn't he? As a sign of approval? He owed Andrew that much. After all he had to bear. No one would be the wiser, least of all her two daughters. Jules and Mike had steady jobs and only one child to care for. Soon they would be empty nesters. Zoë—such a talented girl. Wished she could see more of her, but Jules kept her away. Why did she do that?

She looked up at the machine, at the two slightly undulating horizontal lines that were slowly flattening. Going still. Bob's ordinariness had been heartbreaking. She knew her husband had been a shadow father to Jules, who had told her—when was that? Jules was only a little girl then. She had told her that she wanted a star for a Daddy. Aida's heart had stopped pumping as she listened to the words coming from that sweet little face. How she'd loved that pure, gentle first child of hers. Now there were only good-byes.

Maybe food would make her feel better. Seeing someone die was horrifying. She had had to take a break, get away from the hospital for just a few hours. Aida sat stiffly, gnomelike, at the small bistro table on Joanne's patio. Her younger daughter should really get a larger apartment. She wished she had more space—to lounge on soft pillows, for one, so she wouldn't have to scrunch up her face on that narrow futon couch. Beauty enhancement was essential to the soul—the key to preserving your younger self, the one that had dreams.

Joanne set out dishes and utensils buffet-style, along with a tray of condiments—cilantro she had diced, guacamole from Mexicali avocados, and two kinds of salsa. Aida didn't like anything spicy, so Joanne always made two of everything—one spicy, one not. *Probably begrudgingly,* she thought. She wondered if Joanne knew anything about what was going on with Jules and Mike. Where was Mike these days, anyhow?

"Mom, you have to eat something."

"Okay, but only if we sit down and talk about your sister. Surely you must know something? Julia would never miss seeing her father when asked to come immediately. I told her he was dying. And I haven't talked to Mike or Zoë for what seems like forever. Something is definitely not right!"

"No one ever seems to be home when I call. You know she is deferring college, Mother, right? Because of Mike and Jules's financial situation. Zoë's going to take some classes at a local community college near Palo Alto and then reapply in a year or so, I hear."

Well, perhaps no one was keeping anything from her. Family was family. And she loved them all, even Julia.

"I didn't get a good night's sleep," she said moving the entire plate of food in front of her. "I'm too old, you know. See—aging is no fun for me either."

Joanne dropped a spoon, and Aida repressed a smile. Seeing her groggy daughter fumbling in her bathrobe fixing Mexican food made her want to laugh.

She'd told herself she was satisfied with Joanne's answer, but she wasn't. She tried again. "Where is Mike these days, anyway?" she asked, trying to make her voice light. "I miss my son-in-law. He came through for us, too. With a check, I mean."

She watched Joanne playing with her napkin, and saw her feet jittering through the holes of the wrought-iron bistro table. Joanne was hiding something. She just knew it.

"Mom, I was thinking of trying to help Jules so Zoë wouldn't have to give up Stanford. When you give me that topaz ring you promised, that is. I can sell it and give the money to Zoë. After all they have done for us, it seems like the right thing to do," Joanne said.

Aida's lips thinned. "Can we talk about this later, dear? God, if I didn't know better, I swear we're in for a thunderstorm." She wasn't going to say anything about that ring. "I think I just saw a lightning flash, like a silver-white bolt shooting down the sky, or an illuminated vein in a CT scan. Must be some kind of heat lightning . . . it's still so damn hot." Aida could imagine Jules straining her neck to look high over the roof ridge at rain clouds, using a literary allusion or an art reference to describe them. "Julia would say, 'Wow! That was scary . . . let's see. One hundred fifty miles, I think. Ten miles for each second between.' " Julia had loved to solve math problems no one else could. Counting, always counting to see when the lightning would strike. She could almost see the ciphers Julia would add in her head. Almost the way she herself liked to conjure up new lyrics—word by word—for tunes she would have liked to have sung, if only she had had the chance. If luck had ever struck.

Joanne's apartment garage had a storage attic: raw wood beams with some nails curled over, others' brutal jagged edges aiming straight down, ready to gouge out a person's eyes. Aida peered up at the beams from the landing below the trapdoor as Joanne stooped over boxes, yanking at the untaped flaps crossed over each other.

Joanne dragged six boxes over towards the ladder and handed them down, one at a time, to Aida. Then she gingerly climbed down to look at their past with her mother.

Gently Aida coaxed open the ancient blue cover of what looked like a very old album, perhaps the oldest one they had. Memories. Tongue pressing into her teeth, opening the album and turning to the first page, Aida stared at an old black-and-white photo—at least four decades old. The five of them on a boat on Lake Tamsin, circa 1968 or 1969. Joanne was barely in her teens. Bob looked content or smug, hard to tell . . .

he never could smile naturally. Aida smiled at her own image—holding her white straw hat, her white, Audrey Hepburn–style sunglasses masklike, obscuring half her face. The photo was terribly faded, sepia with gray tones.

"What're you going to do with all this anyway?" she asked Joanne.

"Oh, just hobbling down memory lane, trying to recapture what happened to us when we were so young," Joanne said. "What photo are you looking at?"

Aida surrendered the album willingly. "Didn't I look like a movie star? I was so glamorous! No wonder your father was so taken by me," she said, reaching over and stroking the photo.

"Hmm, the sunglasses certainly are theatrical." Joanne seemed subdued. But as she continued to flip through the photos, most of them taken at Lake Tamsin, her mood changed visibly. "It would be so fun to spend a whole day reminiscing over them. That would be so much fun, wouldn't it, Mother?"

Aida sniffed. "Suit yourself. I threw away all of our movies from years ago. All of that old 16mm film. Your memories are only what you have made of them . . . all in your mind. Who wants to relive the past?"

CLOSETS AND DRAWERS

On the way to the Tahoma National Cemetery in Kent, two hours south of Mukilteo, Aida saw Mount Rainier when she looked southward. It was the end of turning-of-the-leaves time, but a few still remained scattered on the maples and oaks, autumn colored, reminding her of the Bronx botanical gardens of her youth. November weather. Just the way she liked it: sunny, crisp, and cold. She stuck her hand out the window to grab at the invigoration she felt.

Aida didn't feel like talking with her kids, or even her two grand-daughters. Perhaps she was preoccupied, thinking of the memorial service and buffet scheduled after Bob's urn had been placed in its mausoleum drawer. The five of them—Julia wasn't there—rode together in a limousine. It was the first time her son and daughter and two grand-daughters had been together for more than a day. But no Julia—how could she do such a thing! Telling her that Zoë was sick. *Zoë's a big girl now—she can be by herself for a day,* Aida thought.

Her husband had a reserved spot—actually a his-and-hers spot—because he had received military honors as a Korean War vet. The paperwork had taken some time, however. Bob's discharge papers had been lost years ago. An airplane carrying thousands of documents on Korean War veterans had crashed in the Appalachian Mountains and nothing was ever retrieved.

Now their small one-room efficiency at SafeHarbour was hers alone. She could do what she wanted with it. More room. She hoped that Joanne wouldn't pressure her once again to move in with her. For Christmas.

Along the sides of the national cemetery were rows of committal shelters, structures that looked like places to picnic in areas of the country with lots of snow. Sturdy roofs and pillars, but open on all sides to let the fresh air in. Set up on the side of the long cemetery park. Rows of committal shelters for newly deceased veterans. A handsome Air Force officer, tall and straight like her son had been in his military school days, escorted them to a row of chairs in a committal shelter near where their his-and-hers spot was located. Aida knew her son would like the military funeral, all the pomp and circumstance. It would remind him of his son's military training at Parris Island and his time at George Washington Military Academy. Forged in steel, taught to live in service to others. Her own life had been spent in service to others, too, and what had she gotten for it?

The band played "Taps." She looked around her. No one cried. She didn't cry either, even though "Taps" always made her sad. She hummed along. Five servicemen marched in front, two carrying and then folding the American flag into a compact triangle. Saluting, then bowing towards her, one of them offered the red, white, and blue triangle to her in both hands. She smiled and nodded, and rifles shot into the air, four bullets in all. They would make nice souvenirs. Aida would pass hers on to her son, so he could have two.

One of the military guides escorted them to the mausoleum "niche" where Bob's ashes would be placed in an urn designed specifically for Korean War vets. Instead of a tombstone, there was an engraving on a drawer set into a marble wall filled with hundreds of identical drawers. Twenty-six letters, including spaces, were allocated for summing up his life. Aida would be allowed only nineteen letters—seven less than Bob—when her own time came. Who knew why.

Aida had thought of having "Ladies aren't fat," the title Bob had proposed for another book he never wrote. It would be about losing weight, he had explained to her—about how obese women weren't ladies because they preferred food to looking attractive for men. That fantasy book would be written after his first one, *Beat the Wife and Save the Marriage,* a title that seemed inappropriate for an epitaph. She had heard him mutter the title in his sleep once. So much for secrets from her. How Julia had been embarrassed by her father's views as a teenager! But she supposed "Ladies aren't fat" wasn't particularly appropriate either. The marble drawer would proclaim: "To a beloved dad and gramp." Joanne had looked up epitaphs online to get that one. The original sentiment had actually read, "To our beloved father and grandpa." No one called Bob "Gramp." But they would have needed seven more letters for that.

An MIA-POW flag was prominently waving in the northeast corridor. Megan and Sarah walked together down the lanes, if you could call them that, where the marble walls were lined up like bunkers in the beautiful 160-acre park. Aida never liked having her granddaughters around her older daughter. Not quite sure why. Julia could influence Megan and Sarah too much, if left to her own devices. Perhaps say something not so nice about her. Although she couldn't imagine what that might be. Still, Julia could concoct something. That was just like her—always imagining. Why couldn't she just let memories be? Maybe it was better that Julia couldn't attend. Though it bothered Aida that she didn't know the real reason why. Her daughter, gone AWOL.

It would have been a nice park for her friends to take their afternoon walks, for exercise in a spirit of recreation—you know, if it weren't so formal and somber. All that carrying on. *Completely unnecessary,* she thought. She'd stick with the shopping malls for her walking exercise.

Aida patted her younger daughter on the back as they headed in the same direction as Andrew and the girls. Joanne was always blubbering about something. *That's probably why she needs me so much,* Aida said to herself. She held Joanne's hand as they walked closer behind her granddaughters, trying to overhear their conversation. Megan asked her Uncle Andrew, "Do you think if you had a partner who was gay, you'd be allowed to have the partner's name on the other side of the tombstone?"

"I don't think the military's that open minded—yet. Not even after death. Forgiving the already dead," Andrew answered. "What do you think?"

Megan hesitated, thoughtful. Aida watched her closely. Sometimes this granddaughter reminded her of her older daughter's soulful, way-too serious demeanor. Could become a wallflower if she wasn't careful. Then Aida would have to step in and help out. Just like she had for Julia.

Her younger daughter was her happy girl, just like Aida had been all those decades ago as a nightclub singer. She must mention to Joanne that it was okay to entertain Megan's boyfriends and put them at ease. A little glamour and flirtatiousness on the part of the mother always appealed to a teenage boy with raging hormones. It certainly helped her daughter Julia, on many occasions, to smooth things over.

Megan smiled at her Uncle Andrew—*Even her smile is like Julia's,* Aida thought—and said, "I'd be insulted if my tombstone had the same thing that everyone else had. 'Gone fishing' or 'Gone home' is even worse. As if those left behind don't matter."

Aida said nothing. Of course family mattered. She had always warned Megan and Sarah that their Aunt Julia had an "active imagination"—unreliable, dark, and not to be trusted. Fickle. They continued to walk along the rows of mausoleum drawers in the sun, and Joanne let go of her hand and caught up with her girls. Aida didn't mind that they were all walking ahead, leaving her behind. Sarah noticed, though, and waited for her to catch up. *So atypical for a teenage girl,* Aida thought. *And such a beauty.* Sarah held her hand.

"If Auntie Jules were here, she wouldn't make the sign of the cross or mumble the prayers at Grandpa's service," Megan said. "I'm more Buddhist now than Catholic. I believe that the body's karmic ashes recycle, becoming compost. Your time on earth's like writing with a stick in water—brief, washed away in a moment. The transitoriness of life. That's what Aunt Jules told me. I think it makes sense."

Aida listened closely.

"And I can't wait to read her book! I've never known a real author. And you know I love reading, too," Megan said, jumping up and down gleefully, hair flying up around her. *Oh no,* thought Aida, *both granddaughters may turn out to be like their aunt, despite all I've done to prevent that.*

Buddhism. And that book. Julia was always talking about it. Something about motherhood. What did Julia know about motherhood? She hadn't exactly been an exemplary daughter, so what made her think she could be a good mother? Aida reached out for Megan and took her hand, cutting in front of Joanne, as they went to the mausoleum. Three bouquets had been placed at the base of the block. One of the military personnel carefully pulled out the drawer, placed the small urn into the center, and carefully pushed it closed, looking down all the while to avoid stepping on the flowers.

The five of them walked in silence towards the limousine that was waiting to take them back to the funeral home. Her husband was gone. Andrew seemed a lot more like him than she had felt before. Like his shadow. She'd almost forgotten he had attended the service, too. Whatever it was that was missing remained missing.

SafeHarbour's conference room, neatly arranged folding chairs lined up in ten rows or so, felt bone cold. Aida hated these "Celebration of Life" ceremonies. A lot of fuss over nothing. She knew her husband's memorial service would be a very small, quiet affair. Only two of her children and her two granddaughters—and a few SafeHarbour residents who could barely remember who he was—would be there. A ghastly photo of her husband was suspended from the stage. His photo was like the portrait of Dorian Gray: it made him look older than he'd looked in real life. Looking down at her like a preacher, like she was a lost sheep in his flock. How could she sing "Someone to Watch Over Me" now, with that image imprinted in her skull?

She sat there in the front row, turned around to see who would show up. Two gigantic floral wreaths blocked her view of attendees unless she twisted herself completely around, pretzel-like. There was Linda Higgins—slowly pushing her three-pronged cane before her, concentrating on the ten inches in front of it. *What would happen if she fell?* Aida wondered, feeling a stab of excitement at the idea. Many of the octogenarians at SafeHarbour were no longer ambulatory, or were suffering from dementia or Alzheimer's, or both. There was Pam Taylor, who had secretly had a crush on her now dearly departed, always bringing cookies and even the occasional sushi tray. The nerve of her! Had a face like a horse. A few of the other residents she didn't know by name. There was Tom Stephens, shuffling in. He was more her type—not too senile, and didn't smell like an old man. Yet. Had some possibilities.

A smorgasbord of tasteless, incompatible foods was laid out on a side table: Chinese takeout, soggy Japanese sushi, and Taco Bell Mexican tacos, along with her own mother's favorite comfort food—spaghettini with giant meatballs—and an antipasto of Italian processed meats. Her mother would have loved stuffing her diabetic face with it all. Aida thought how the leftovers of her family—Julia, Joanne, and Andrew— were just as incompatible and mismatched as the food, and she frowned.

The director rang a little bell. The hard of hearing didn't look up. Walking up and down the aisles, Ann Pike put her index finger to her lips, hushing the residents in a type of sign language, and motioned for Aida to walk to the stage. The microphone had been lowered down as far as it would go to accommodate her height.

"I would like to thank all of you for coming this evening." *All fifteen of you, that is.* "Please make yourselves comfortable and help yourself to the buffet"—*You're just here for the food*—"before we have some testimonials and speeches from family and friends."

"Hey, could you speak up? Use the microphone or something. Can't hear a word you said," Tom Stephens shouted, hand megaphoned to the front of his gaping mouth. She could usually throw her voice—her singing voice—even in a crowded room like this one. Reaching for the microphone at the podium again, clearing her throat, she spoke louder: "I would like to thank all of you—"

"Still can't hear you," Tom interrupted. "What's happened to your voice?"

Aida felt that in the space of just a few days, her gigantic personality had somehow shrunk. She left the stage and sat back down in the widow's seat of honor. She reconsidered Tom Stephens. She hadn't noticed before, but he was an annoying man. At least Bob hadn't been that hard of hearing. He could still hear her sing, up until the end.

This was it. She was finished.

Their—now her—apartment smelled empty. Like death. Like loneliness. Aida pulled off her widow's dress. Black still looked great on her. Dressed in one of her Valentine's Day–pink nightgowns, her faced wiped clear of her pancake foundation, eyeliner, red lipstick, and mascara with Pond's cold cream, she looked naked to herself in the mirror. As if she had wiped off her personality. Her identity. She pulled and stretched the skin around her cheeks, then her neck, then her arms. Bob always had commented on her beauty. Even the day of his death. An endearing habit of his.

Aida turned off the light and crawled into her side of the bed, which seemed to have expanded overnight.

In the morning Joanne rang the doorbell, then inserted the key, letting herself in before Aida could reach the door. Her daughter's habit of unlocking the door for herself, often without announcing herself first, used to be comforting. It didn't now. Aida felt scared.

"Hi Mom, brought you coffee and bagels. Before we go out and shop. Christmas season is starting. Maybe we can even drive into Seattle and take a walk around the botanical gardens—if you feel up for it, that is."

"Sweetie, the memorial service just exhausted me. Do you think we could just have quiet time?"

"Anything you want, you know that." Joanne kissed her. "We could freshen up your apartment a bit." Her daughter reached over the couch to draw the curtains open, letting in fresh air. Aida inhaled deeply.

"The closets are still full of your father's stuff. Lots of old golf clubs, doctor's white coats, shoes he never wore. Debris. Garbage. We could bag it up for Salvation Army."

"If it's too difficult for you, I can come over and bag it up with my girls when you're working at Yellow Brick Road or out with a friend, if you'd like."

"Nah, I'm fine. I just want to get it over with and make room for some more clothes for me." She was already yanking his clothes off the hangers, dropping them in heaps on the floor.

Joanne immediately started to pick them up off the floor, separating the slacks from the shirts, setting the shoes to the side. Miscellaneous specialty items—golf equipment, medical paraphernalia, formal wear— she bagged together in gigantic white garbage bags. In thirty minutes, Aida and her daughter had emptied her husband from her walk-in closet. All that was left were eight bags of junk.

When Joanne had finished loading the bags into her car out front, she came back in and sat down on the couch, her eyes clouded over. The visual reminded Aida of her own cataracts.

"Mom, I don't want you to be alone now. Without Dad."

Here it comes, Aida thought to herself.

"We'd love to have you move in with us. Christmas will be here before you know it. Sarah and Megan will be leaving for college soon, and without Al, there's so much room. Plus, it would help Jules if you didn't live at SafeHarbour anymore—make it easier for her to take care of your debts. I think she could use our support now."

"Oh darling, darling. You worry so much. Julia didn't even bother to be here. Abandoned her own family! And for what? So she can focus on that damn book of hers?"

"Actually . . ." Joanne hesitated. "I think she may be having some problems back home. With Mike and Zoë. I kinda feel bad for her."

"What makes you say that?" Aida perked up. She wouldn't mind some juicy bit of gossip about her oh-so-perfect daughter right now.

"Nothing, Mom. Nothing. Just think about moving in with me, okay? Down the road. When you have more time to plan."

Before Aida could press for more details, Joanne left to dump off the bags at Salvation Army.

Aida steeled herself to clear out the computer desk. Bob had been such a mess. Stacks of papers had toppled onto the floor. Overdue bills. The notice about updated information needed for his Air Force insurance policy. Had to sign that off to Andrew so he could have the funds right away. The 1967 *Encyclopaedia Britannica,* still on its original bookshelf, had an inch of dust coating the top of each volume, right where the stitches of the leather spine met the pages. Bob had spent hours looking up minutiae about nothing—a certain type of seaweed, for example, or marine flagella. How many times had she screamed at him and stormed out? Running to Yellow Brick Road, seeking refuge?

The desk drawers were full of business-size check registers, the kind Bob had used at his office over twenty years ago. How she had hated working there. She knew it upset him that she couldn't keep the messages straight, or the phone numbers. But who cared?

Aida moved slowly, back and forth, pushing empty boxes into the middle of the room and emptying shelves and desk drawers. She rested on the desk chair, swiveling and looking at the clutter all around her. Then she pulled out the top drawer—but something all the way in the back, way, way back, was stuck. The drawer resisted as she tried to pull it out completely. She heard paper crunch. She reached back behind the drawer, her skinny arm lying flat on top, and her index and middle finger tweezered the thick paper causing the jam. She pulled hard, and it came loose. An envelope.

Aida slipped open the flap and saw two brittle sepia photographs. The kind their old Brownie camera took. The first was their wedding photo; the second showed the two of them holding their firstborn child. Both were crumpled. She smoothed out the photo of Julia and turned it over. On the back Bob had written the lyrics—the first stanza—to "Someone to Watch Over Me." Tears dropped on first one photo, then the other, smearing the emulsion.

HAPPY PILLS

What was going on? No response yet from Jules, either by e-mail or snail mail. Zoë was a healthy girl—she'd never had any medical issues before. Had she gotten in some sort of accident? Why did her sister always keep things to herself? And what could be more important than their father's passing and his funeral? Jules had changed. Dramatically. Suddenly. Wasn't even there when their parents needed her most. She seemed to have dropped off the face of the earth. What was wrong with her?

Joanne had to get out of her own head or she'd go stark, raving mad. She shook her head hard, feeling her ears beginning to fill up: vertigo. Another episode of Ménière's disease, perhaps. If only she could shake the clutter out of her mind, she thought as she walked down Main Street to open her shop, A Real Gem. Business was so slow around Edmonds, in the deepest recession in the Seattle area since the Great Depression. Joanne liked to call it the Great Recession. She was in her own Great Depression.

She didn't like going to work when there were no customers, those days when she spent the whole time organizing the inventory and dusting. But her shop was an escape, a clearing of her mind, her own little haven, her sanctuary. There she could be herself and not think of her daughters, soon-to-be ex-husband, or any of the other shit that pressed down on her as soon as she woke up.

Opening the front door to her shop, Joanne sighed heavily. All around her, stores were closing, even though Edmonds was a tourist town with quaint historic architecture from its glory days as a silver mining center. Joanne worried her dwindling savings foreshadowed doom. She could usually count on selling a few trinkets each week, enough to cover rent, if not take-home pay for her. But her AmEx bills were piled up on the kitchen counter, unopened. She hoped she could continue to make the minimum payment. Until Jules came through. Then life would get better for her. Sometimes her sister seemed like superwoman, Joanne thought to herself resentfully. Like she was so superior. But she could count on her sense of obligation. Maybe even more so now that their father had died, and his gambling on stocks had died along with him.

Joanne dusted off the head, a dead ringer for Cleopatra, resting in the papier-mâché tomb in the front window. She had bought the faux mummy in Seattle from a costume shop that was closing. The majority of its business, the girl at the register had told her, was at Halloween and for the hospital costume ball—no wonder the store hadn't survived. But Joanne loved her mummy—it was a real eye-catcher, perfect for showcasing all her fossils from the Jurassic and other prehistoric periods. Then again, maybe she just identified with its bandaged face.

His office was minimalist, located in a four-story building, tall by Edmonds standards. The tallest in town, in fact. Soft, russet-orange leather couches, colorful abstract prints, tall dracaena plants. Joanne felt she was going to be paying for some of that decor. Or, rather, her sister would. Divorce lawyers were expensive, almost $300 per hour. But well worth it, according to her friends who should know.

She waited in the reception area as the attractive, silver-haired receptionist answered what seemed like nonstop incoming calls. Divorce must be big business.

Joanne had bought a burrito from the greasy takeout place, Maya's, across from her store. Comfort food. She had only one hour to consult with Seligman. The message she had left on Al's answering machine was probably garbled, and she hated the thought of having to repeat herself at the end of her workday, explaining what was obvious. That it was over.

Seligman entered the waiting room straightening his tie—probably an Italian Zegna silk one. Impeccably dressed. Handsome, early forties. Joanne tugged at her skirt and pulled down her Indian peasant blouse, one of her favorite ones: black cotton with embroidered flowers of red, yellow, and aqua. The drawstring around the neckline could be loosened with one finger. Joanne extended her hand and flashed a smile. Seligman zoomed in on her décolletage, introducing himself to her breasts before looking up.

"Why don't we step into my office?" he said, waving her ahead of him.

Joanne obeyed, and soon found herself sitting across from Seligman, a cup of tea in hand.

Seligman leaned forward in his chair. "And what can I do for you this lovely noon hour?"

That sounded a bit sleazy, but Joanne decided to give him the benefit of the doubt. "You are a divorce lawyer, aren't you? So you probably don't have to read my mind to figure it out."

"Well, I'm good. Don't you worry. We'll get you what you want."

"I know this is old hat for you, Mr. Seligman. But this is my first—and hopefully, my only—divorce." She steadied her voice. When she felt it was safe, she went on. "My heart and mind are backed up. Screwed up, I know. But. I've got to stop poisoning myself—and Sarah and Megan, my daughters, too. I really do, but I don't know where to begin. I've been living apart from my husband for years."

"Then you can start by actually divorcing him. Not just thinking about it. That's my job." Seligman touched her hand. "We'll try for an amicable divorce settlement without a lowered standard of living for you."

Joanne nodded. That sounded good. She needed some breathing space.

"You shouldn't consider it a disgrace or anything," he said in a lighter tone.

Before Joanne could respond, her cell phone lit up. "Mom," bright and white, on the screen. One too many calls from Mom. This time she was going through with it. Enough of Mom's advice that a woman without a man was nothing.

Joanne placed her and her husband's joint tax returns on the attorney's desk, fluffing her hair and pulling her peasant blouse down as she did. Maybe he could reduce the fees. She was almost sure he was single—or at least that he wished he were.

"You can see from my tax returns that my income by itself wouldn't be enough to live on. And my mom wouldn't be comfortable if I had to lower my standard of living. She couldn't bear seeing me that way. I'd be a failure in her eyes. And besides, I can't move Sarah and Megan out of our neighborhood—it has the best school system here! They have to have the very best, no matter how lousy my marriage is."

Joanne thought again of the conversation her mother had had with Andrew about her topaz ring. Was she as concerned with Joanne's well-being as Joanne was with that of her own daughters? She wasn't so sure now.

She heard her mother's voice again: *"What Joanne doesn't know won't hurt her, now will it?"* Listening to the recording, Joanne had been able to hear her own breath stop, and her eyes had clouded up so she couldn't see clearly anymore.

Why would her mother do that to her? Break her promise to give her the topaz ring she had wanted as a little girl?

After Joanne returned to her shop from the attorney's office, she saw two young photographers, dressed in jeans and sweatshirts, hurrying down the street, heaving equipment—cameras, tripods, and lights—as a van followed slowly behind them. A pretty young redhead dressed too stylishly for Edmonds was setting their pace. In a snug black-and-white-striped knit dress—the kind so formfitting that only a young woman who worked out every single day could pull off—she led them single file down Main Street, carefully avoiding divots with her stiletto heels. Joanne watched the three of them walk into the Wine Sip, the wine bar that had opened two months ago across the street. A huge wooden placard with purple-colored globe grapes hung outside; at night, it was lit up neon. Joanne liked their happy-hour wine tastings because some of the local guys were hot. So was one of those two photographers.

Wonder what that's all about? Joanne thought as she dusted, peeking out the storefront window. Back from Seligman's just in time for some action, perhaps.

She was in the back of the store making herself a cup of Tibetan white tea—hoping for good karma—when she heard the ringing of her sleigh bells slapping against the front door on their leather strap. Her friend, Stacy, had bought the bells as a Christmas present for her. She loved old things—they reminded her of happier circumstances, childhood. And Christmas was fast approaching.

The two photographers came into the store, followed by the tall, slender redhead. "Good morning. Welcome to A Real Gem," she beamed, trying to look busy, dusting more frantically. Her happy pill always could be called upon, kicking in in sixty seconds, fast and furious.

Thank God for her happy pills. Celexa—a lifesaver. Not quite literally a Life Saver; they were more oval, without the hole, and a paler red than the candy she'd liked to suck on when she was little.

Joanne couldn't quite remember what had first propelled her to call her shrink. She thought it had something to do with crying at the movies—crying so hard she couldn't stop, even after the closing credits. Someone in the theater had gotten up out of his seat and yelled at her to stop all that racket one hour in.

It had to have been a Friday evening—her weekly movie date with Mom, after she closed the cash register and locked up. Just the two of them, mother-daughter quality time. Sometimes Megan and Sarah, or just one of them, would tag along. But not usually. At the last movie they went to see—*My Sister's Keeper*—Joanne had run out of Kleenex. Her mother kept needling her, impatient and annoyed.

"Why can't you stop all that crybaby stuff? Do you have a bladder for tear ducts, like my mother had? Sobbing at nothing," she scolded, passing a tissue like a small white flag to her.

Joanne had surrendered. After her visit with her psychiatrist, Dr. von Simson, she'd watched the same movie, Kleenex box within reach, by herself—and she was fine. No tears.

"I had gone from cable TV with one lousy channel before I had my appointment with my shrink. But now I'm back to the entire two hundred channels, more alive," she remembered telling Jules.

"Happy pills may help," her sister had said. "But you should seek counseling when you get back to Seattle. Not just medication."

Joanne wanted her sister to give her free counseling. Jules had refused.

"It's never a good idea to treat your own family," Jules said. "You need some distance to see the dynamics. Besides, I do learning disabilities, not depression. And since I deal with kids—and don't approve of medicating them—I just don't keep up on such things."

"Well, I have a new, brighter personality. Don't you know I don't want the old me—the one no one likes? I donated that one to charity."

Where was her sister's exuberance about her new self? Had she left her capacity for joy by the curb for the garbage collectors to pick up? She was no fun anymore.

"Well, hello," the older camera guy said, cutting off her thoughts about her sister. He was about forty, maybe forty-five. Looked cute in his baseball cap and dark blue sweatshirt, which was emblazoned with "Seattle Mariners"—probably bought at the Sea-Tac airport. He was lean, clean, athletic.

"You must be new in town." Joanne grinned and stared straight at his camera, admiring her own reflection in the large lens. Surprising reflection, mirrorlike. Her face looked like it should.

"Yeah," the younger man interjected. About thirty years old, Joanne guessed. Thinning blond hair, a friendly face, kind of soft in the gut. A bit taller than the other guy. Someone you would feel comfortable with. *But definitely not my type,* she thought. She liked the older one. The twenty-something, freckle-faced redhead now stepped forward, reaching for her business card in her expensive-looking woven-leather tote as she did.

"Hi, I'm Gwyneth Chambers, a reporter for *Sunset* magazine," she said, carefully handing off her card as if it were a Tiffany diamond ring.

Joanne could feel her heart pounding. *Sunset* magazine! Did they want to feature her store? *What a stroke of good luck, and I badly need it,* she thought. Maybe it was the Tibetan white tea she drank every day—or maybe those Buddhist chants her sister recommended worked after all.

"These are my photographers, Brett Ashcroft and Keith Cherkoff.

They take all the photos after I decide who we interview. Then there's a follow-up e-mail requesting any information we may need before publishing the issue."

Joanne's nervousness was almost freezing her insides.

"We're doing a piece on downtown Edmonds and thought we would feature a few stores, no more than four," Gwyneth continued. "Brett liked the looks of the mummy in the front window as a photo-op." Brett smiled and looked right at Joanne with his steel-black eyes. *That sweatshirt probably hides quite the body, from lifting heavy camera equipment all day,* she reflected.

Joanne could feel the two photographers' eyes checking her out. She'd always liked that. She slowly unlocked the drawers that held her most interesting minerals and semiprecious stones.

"Let me explain a little bit about what makes A Real Gem stand out from other jewelry stores. Then, why don't you take a look around?" Joanne suggested, leaning over the counter to display herself. "Would you like to see a piece? For someone special in your life?" Joanne asked shamelessly. All the guys she had dated in the past had been losers. But her luck was going to change. She just knew it.

Brett looked for a long time at one case that held some of her favorite amethyst geodes. He flashed his perfect white teeth at her—a smile that she hadn't seen or felt, even on her own face, for so long—and said, "There's no one in my life right now. Don't know how to get back in the game." He smiled and slowly took shots of different parts of the store before landing the camera lens directly on her. "I'd like to take you home and place you around my coffee table," he said, his voice low.

Joanne sighed to herself. He probably was a player after all.

"Well," Gwyneth interjected. "We could linger here all day, but we do have to find two other stores besides this one. The Wine Sip's a good choice as a showcase for some of the burgeoning wineries around this area. So, why don't you"—she turned towards Brett—"get some background info on Joanne while Keith and I go off to take some wide-angle shots of the street and the harbor."

As Gwyneth and Keith walked out, Brett awkwardly shifted his weight from one foot to the other, looking down at Joanne's high-heeled shoes—or maybe it was her bust he was focused on. She could never tell about those things. Didn't matter, though. Her cleavage was deep, and she was proud of her newly reconstructed breasts. Perhaps they would turn out to be a better investment than even she had first imagined.

"Guess I should just take photos of the merchandise . . . and you. You'll be an eye-catcher on the page," he said, gulping, his Adam's apple moving up and down. That always endeared a guy to her. Had a vague phallic connotation. Sexy.

She was busy plotting a night's fun with Brett—tonight's happy pill—when the bells on the front door clanged, and her friend Pamela strode in.

"Hey, how're you doing?" Pamela asked, not looking at Joanne but zooming in on Brett, curious, trying to figure out the connection.

"Hey yourself, Pamela," Joanne grinned. "Want you to meet someone from *Sunset* magazine—Brett Ashcroft."

"Hi. Would love to take some photos of customer-owner interaction. Always good for our magazine. Doesn't look so staged." He aimed his telephoto lens at Joanne, focusing and refocusing.

I'll light aromatherapy candles to capture the right mood tonight, she thought.

The next morning, Brett left very early—without even leaving a phone number or e-mail address. Joanne, uninterested in getting out of bed, phoned her sister. She was surprised when Jules actually picked up.

"Hey, Jules, what's up?" she said. "I miss you. And I've been waiting for your response to my e-mail. Did you get it?"

Silence.

Uh-oh, what does that mean? "And I went to see a lawyer. Followed your advice about that. Of course, good advice—besides yours—is expensive. Seligman—that's my hotshot divorce attorney—charges $300 per hour. So freedom won't come cheap."

"Well, I need to talk to you about that, actually," Jules began. Her voice didn't sound welcoming. "I can't talk long. Have to be someplace." She continued, her voice sounding tight. "I've been thinking how to respond to the e-mail you sent. You know, Mike and I are not a money tree. This is just too much. Have you thought about asking your health-care providers for relief from some of your medical expenses? A payment plan?"

"You know I haven't been able to make much money on my own. But I just found out that I'm going to be featured in *Sunset* magazine, so that will certainly help business. Maybe help me pay back some of what I owe you, too."

"That's great! I mean it. Congratulations on *Sunset,* Jo. But still, you're going to have to find another way out of debt. Sell some jewelry Mother has given you, for example. Right now, Mike and I have to think of our own daughter. Try to understand. We'll try to help, but we can't do it all by ourselves. We're in serious trouble ourselves." Jules began to cry.

"Sis, don't cry. It will be okay. But the money stuff . . . you've got to help me out there. I feel trapped." Joanne cradled the receiver. "I still feel like ending everything sometimes. Maybe it would be easier on everyone if I did."

"It's okay, Joanne. It's okay," Jules said. "We'll work something out. Got to go."

Joanne promised herself she wouldn't refuse to see what lay ahead and make matters worse by spending more . . . on her face, her clothes, and jewelry. She would not be like their mother. But she did want a way out of the mess she was in. Nothing but bills, bills, bills. She was on her way to give them all to Seligman for the asset disclosure review.

The settlement conference was happening tomorrow. Al would be present with his lawyers to negotiate the settlement over the house. Since they lived in a community-property state, she was confident she should get 50 percent. Still, this year was not exactly the best for real estate. She'd be lucky to get $300,000. They had had the house a long time, at least, so there was some equity built up.

Joanne could imagine the relief on her sister's face when Joanne told her she was getting that kind of money from the settlement. And maybe she could help Jules out later. When she got back on her feet.

"Keep your emotions out of it," Jules had advised her when she first told her she was looking into hiring a divorce attorney. "Try to settle without destroying your family or bankrupting yourself. Don't fight for petty things. It could cost you $1,500 in attorney fees to get $200 more—that's what my divorced girlfriends told me. And remember, don't let Al's lawyer inflame the situation. You've waited the required ninety days for cooling off. Remember this is a 'good faith' settlement, not an adversarial one. Not hostile. Do not polarize things. Soon it will all be over. I know this is tough for you, little sis."

Easy for Jules to say, Joanne thought as she left the box of past-due bills at Seligman's front desk.

~

Seligman was there waiting when Joanne arrived the next morning, wearing a very conservative, serious black suit. He smelled like an overdose of aftershave.

"Hi, Mrs. Grant. Your husband and his attorney will be here shortly. Are you ready?" he asked, peering too closely into her eyes. "This may be difficult for you—an intense discussion over financial affairs."

Then Al and his attorney walked into the room. Her husband avoided making eye contact. Rusty Weisbroth, his attorney, made with the niceties and then started negotiations. Joanne liked that—the meter was running. The less time they spent there, the better.

"Both parties seem to be in agreement over everything except the house," Seligman said after the preliminary rundown of assets.

"My client feels that the house shouldn't be split down the middle, 50/50, because of the work he has done to repair and remodel. Here are the receipts, although you've received these disclosure documents previously," Weisbroth said.

It just isn't fair, Joanne fumed. She had lost the lottery. She actually preferred her small loft apartment—beautiful, open, and airy—to the house she'd shared with Al. Her new place was spare and minimalist, the opposite of the home she had moved out of, the one her parents had bought for her. She could see the harbor, where the ferry carried commuters and tourists, and the Cascades from her porch—that was the reason for her exorbitant rent. But she had downsized significantly. And most of the time, she had the girls with her.

"You asshole," Joanne blurted before she could stop herself. "Do you want to destroy any shred of dignity I have left? Bankrupt me and our daughters? I need half the proceeds from the sale of our house."

"Bitch. I'm not the one who wanted this divorce," Al said.

She wanted to chew the smugness right off his face. "And I suppose your living in that house while I had to pay rent somewhere else doesn't count in the housing settlement?" She wanted to listen to Jules's advice: *"Don't fight over petty things. It will cost more."* But she couldn't help herself. This wasn't petty.

"If we don't come to an agreement, we'll be forced to go to litigation," was all that Seligman said.

Papers were signed, subtracting the amount of the home repairs but not Al's estimated labor. No consideration was given to the rent she paid for her tiny apartment. The net sum that would go to her after attorney fees would be enough to pay off her loan, but not all of her surgery and therapy. It would leave her nothing to live on but what Jules could provide. A Real Gem still had no value.

Where was Jules when she needed her?

RECOVERY

"**M**other's suffered a stroke."
Jules had received the same message every day for three days from both Joanne and Andrew. Joanne had enlisted Sarah and Megan into the mix, too—Jules had gotten a *"Grandma is dying"* text from each of them.

"I know," she texted back.

Jules was walking while reading their texts. It was two blocks from Bayview Apartments to the Palo Alto Addiction Recovery Services. That was her routine now. Her morning began by standing below the window of Zoë's room and waving. The front desk receptionist, Trudy Wang, had given her Zoë's daily schedule—against all rules and regulations, but Trudy seemed to feel her pain, so much so that she was willing to risk her own employment by giving Jules that information. Did she have a family member going through the same thing? Jules wondered. Her actions made more sense if that were the case.

So Jules waited in the perimeter of the outside courtyard and never veered off from staring at the corner room on the third floor. She would love to throw a pebble up at the window, Romeo and Juliet–style, to try to get her daughter's attention. But she was afraid of drawing the attention of the center's staff.

She felt her phone vibrate. More text messages from Joanne or Andrew. They were supposed to keep her posted about her mother's condition, but not at ten o'clock and two o'clock. She had instructed them not to. They kept texting anyway, but she never read them or texted back until bedtime, and then she shut down her cell phone for the night.

Jules had read that spouses often can't bear the loss of their partner. But her father's loss was an ambiguous loss, wasn't it? For their mother? Perhaps for all of them? Less than a month since he had died.

Her phone buzzed yet again. Jules caved and looked at the e-mail from Joanne: *"I'm at the hospital with her—University of Washington Hospital in Seattle. They're still doing tests. To see how extensive the damage is. A clot in her brain, they suspect. Can you come as soon as you can?"*

Jules's mouth went dry. Teetering, grabbing at one of the bushes on the grounds to steady herself, she wiped the sweat from her hands onto the denim. Left a dark stain.

Jules's knuckles turned white. Her other hand clenched into a fist. She could picture her sister crying, bent over, as she composed that e-mail. She kept reading: *"Mom was so upset, Jules. That you didn't come to the memorial service at Tahoma—for the military honors and everything. I think it was just too much for her."*

Earlier that week, their mother had been in the SafeHarbour walk-athon to raise funds for breast cancer. All the little old ladies had dressed up like the Seahawks. There was newspaper and television coverage and everything. Their mother placed third. She had thought they might want a photo of her, the best-looking woman in the seniors group, so she'd had her hair done the day before in anticipation and had heavily sprayed it so her bangs wouldn't curl with her sweat. Always ready. In her fanny pack were her favorite cosmetics. An audience cheered her as she crossed the finish line.

Joanne and the girls had taken her to Fuki Sushi afterwards. She said it was to remind her of their father, even though she refused to step into the place when he was alive. But she picked at the food. Didn't really eat much. And by the time they got her back to Joanne's apartment, Joanne said, they knew something was wrong.

"She kept taking her compact out," Joanne had told Jules later that night when she called to tell her the news. "Wiping her forehead, which was sweaty. Said she felt clammy. Oh, around ten o'clock she started really complaining that she wasn't feeling so hot." Joanne's voice cracked.

"But you know how Mom can be an unhappy camper. I thought the music and alcohol might have given her a bitch of a headache. So I was getting the futon made up for her to spend the night when I heard a crash. There's Mom—lying on the kitchen floor, still conscious but she was having trouble speaking. The right side of her face looked like an awful Halloween mask. Droopy, lips all twisted—like a Munch."

"Oh God."

"I called 911. But, Jules, I was shaking so hard I could hardly push the buttons on the phone. Wanted to get Mom to a hospital as fast as I could, but I was too afraid to drive. I think this is it. It's serious. A stroke. Massive."

Poor Joanne! Jules had almost been able to hear her sister's heart pounding.

"Oh—" Joanne's voice had broken off. There was a pause. "When can you come out here? I can't do this all by myself."

That was the last time Jules had spoken with Joanne on the phone. She hadn't answered her calls since.

Jules looked up at the window again. She had memorized her daughter's schedule—every meal, every group and private session. Even her exercise and art classes. Zoë had exactly thirty minutes at ten fifteen in the morning to either shower or read. Her free time. Like a postal carrier, even in the rain, Jules stood there under her umbrella promptly at ten fifteen. To wait. To hope. And again at two fifteen she stood there. And waited. And hoped. Another thirty minutes for Zoë to be by herself. What did Zoë do at those times? Did she read? She knew her daughter loved novels about family sagas. No vampire fiction for her. Just family curses. But then again, Zoë had changed. Maybe her taste in books had, too.

How she wished she were allowed to leave books for her. She had tried once, but Trudy warned her that the security guard would be called if she dropped by the waiting room again.

Jules texted Mike to let him know about her mother's condition. And that she was with Zoë. She would not fly to Seattle yet. She just couldn't.

Almost at the end of the week, Jules saw Zoë for the first time since she was admitted to rehab. December 18, 2:22 p.m. What a smile! Her moment with Zoë. And Mike had been there that day with her. Luckily, Zoë had not taken the OxyContin for long, and had only taken it in small dosages. She was resilient. Her doctors were very pleased. And so was she. Ecstatic. A miracle. Recovery.

"Rehab will soon be a thing of the past," Zoë declared proudly. "My doctors say I can go home soon."

To be a family again, Jules hoped.

She reached out and touched her daughter's hair. Zoë had never liked her touching her hair—not since she had become a teenager. She'd say her hair needed to be washed. Or that Jules was messing it up. But Jules couldn't resist touching it now. Her daughter's hair was lovely again. Long and lush. Not falling out in patches, as it had been before rehab.

"I'm sorry. I'm so sorry." Pause. "I know you don't like me touching it, but I just love your hair." She cried into her daughter's hair, kissing the top of her head the way she had when Zoë was a toddler.

"It's okay, Mom. I know what you've done for me." Jules was surprised to hear her daughter's voice break as she said that. Zoë didn't like anyone to see her cry. "Quiet crying," she had called it when she was in kindergarten. So Jules pretended not to notice now.

She cleared her throat. "We'll talk about college options later. I've been doing a lot of research on psychology programs for you, sweetie. And your dad is on board, too. We'll work this out together." She willed herself not to tremble.

They kissed, a mother-daughter, shy sort of kiss.

"You chose me after all," Zoë whispered.

Waiting standby at the SFO airport for a flight to Seattle on Alaska Airlines, Jules curled up under her jacket on a vinyl-and-steel chair. She was bone tired. The waiting area was as dreary and depressing as her mood. Going to see her dying mother. Beige dominated the curtains, walls, linoleum.

When they brought Zoë home, Mike hadn't said anything before but now volunteered to stay at her apartment while she flew out to see her dying mother. She had loved how he used to crawl into bed with her and they fell asleep curled up, warm and safe, in a spooning position. The silence had been reassuring.

Now, turning, curled up fetal-style, alone in a plastic chair at the airport terminal, she thought of her mother and her Zoë and reached inside her purse for her travel pillbox. She knew she would have to nibble on some Ambien if she was going to sleep on the plane.

LETTING GO

The University of Washington hospital room machinery was all shiny stainless steel. Jules shuddered involuntarily. Merely looking at her mother was painful, even alarming. She seemed shrunken—an unbelievably small homunculus, spine twisted. The turquoise hospital clothes seemed draped over a cadaver that was getting smaller and smaller before her eyes. It both was and was not her mother's face. But she had waited for her after all. Was Andrew coming?

She hugged Joanne, whose eyes were all glassy, lids tear swollen, and her sister seemed filled with water—insubstantial and vulnerable.

"Hello, Mother. How are you?" Jules bent over her mother's bones to give her a kiss on her cheek. Joanne walked over to the other side of the bed and patted their mother's hand, and Jules robotically copied her. The hand she touched was cold, like their grandpa's hands had been in his open casket, Jules remembered. Like Italian marble. The only dead body she had ever touched.

"It takes . . . a lot of . . . to talk," her mother rasped.

Jules and Joanne looked at each other in silence. Sarah and Megan sat there, quietly watching.

"Why don't you two go downstairs and get something to eat?" Jules suggested.

"We don't want to leave Grandma," Megan said, her large doe eyes turned downward.

Even Sarah's eye shadow seemed to have lost its glitter.

～

"Hello. How are you doing, Mrs. Whitman?" the attending nurse, clipboard in hand, asked brusquely, walking over to look at the machine readings. "She'll be here when you come back," Joanne whispered to her two daughters. "Go on. It'll be good for you to get a little fresh air."

Sarah and Megan left the room. "It won't be long now," the nurse said to Jules and Joanne, smiling gently. "I take it you're family."

Jules cleared her throat and nodded.

"Well, I'll tell you . . . she has a very strong will to live, in spite of her vital signs. She doesn't want to let go." Still smiling, the nurse left, dimming the light as she went.

"She's mumbling," Joanne said, bending over their mother's mouth. "Mom's saying what a hateful man Dad was!"

"No! You're kidding, right?" Jules leaned in and put her left ear closer to their mother's mouth. It was hard to get close to her; it always had been.

Her mother picked at the hospital sheets—agitated, jerky—as if she were having a small seizure. Her pressure was dropping. Her pulse was decreasing rapidly. But her eyes still seemed to give off heat.

"Your father's such a . . . selfish man," she now gasped into Jules's ear. *She doesn't remember that Dad is already dead.* Jules felt disconnected, like she was looking at some exotic animal in a zoo. All she needed was to take out a notepad and write field notes. "But . . . I was selfish, too. Didn't know how not to be." Her mother's voice gathered force, compelling and apologetic all at once. "Mother . . . mother . . ." Jules thought that's what she heard her mother saying. She was probably delirious.

Her mother tried again: "I wanted to be a good mother. I tried, but I don't think . . . I don't think I knew how."

Her eyes closed, but she kept talking in her sleep. Her skin was a purplish-blue, her legs a network of green veins. *She would be mortified to see her diva appearance had vanished,* Jules thought. To see what she looked like in the end.

Jules took both of her mother's hands in hers: cold, almost unbearably so. Their mother had always been self-conscious about those hands, thinking that the curves of her fingernails were too rounded, like claws. Now her nail beds were aquamarine. She breathed in short little pants, stopped and started again. Her hands were folded in on themselves like clams. Jules had always been afraid of those hands, but now she kissed them gently.

She wanted her mother to leave this world now. In a moment when she seemed more at peace—not in a rage. Jules stroked her hand, then gently glided her fingers up her arm. She heard rattling, the sound of dying, deep in her mother's lungs and upper throat. But it was almost rhythmic—musical, even.

"Mother? Why don't I ask the nurse for something to help you sleep?" Jules whispered, as if she were talking to Zoë when she was a baby. She stiffly bent down to kiss her mother. The air seemed to puff out, a blowing of the lips with every exhalation. Her mother's lips, once so beautiful, ruby red and vital, looked defeated. Jules looked away.

Andrew blew into the room, throwing off his heavy overcoat before sitting down to snack on potato chips and pretzels. Joanne and Jules both looked at him, and then down at the coat he had thrown on the floor. Stepping around it like it was the outline of a murder victim at a crime scene, Joanne took a few steps towards him and tried to hug him. He leaned back, jaw dropping, as he saw their mother. He remembered her lecturing on what his and Abigail's son should look like, a cram course on Mendel's theory of genetics, so many years ago. Almost ten.

Even with Andrew sitting down, the room suddenly felt too crowded. Too confining and claustrophobic. The space seemed to be shrinking, closing in on them. Like their mother.

"You know, I hear her voice inside my head," Andrew said, choking on the words. "And Dad's." He rose and went to their mother, bent down to kiss her forehead. She doubled over coughing, but nothing came up.

"Would you like something to drink, Mom?" Joanne asked as she tried to fluff the pillow beneath her head.

"No!" she panted. "Everything... tastes... bitter. I want... I want... to die. I never thought it would be like this." And with that, their mother's mouth collapsed. She exhaled once, very loudly and harshly, a fish out of water. Two long shudders followed. Her eyes snapped wide open, unblinking, looking less lifelike than her Sarah doll. Then they fluttered shut like a moth too close to the light. Fluid, perhaps a single tear, leaked out. Jules dabbed it with a Kleenex.

Jules ran down the hall. She spotted the attending nurse at the on-call station, chatting with one of the doctors. Jules waited until the nurse noticed her before stepping closer. The doctor, glancing at Jules, left.

"I think our mother has died. Can you please come quickly? Tell us what's happening? If she's still alive?"

The nurse reached out to touch Jules's hand. Ordinarily she didn't like to be touched by strangers, but the nurse's touch soothed her.

"Let's go," the nurse said as they walked together to room 583.

When they entered the room, the nurse checked the machines. "She's not gone yet," she said gently. "Almost, but not yet."

As if sleepwalking, Jules went to her mother and bent over her hands again. She held one of them as she reached into her tote bag. She had read someplace that talking to the dying was a comfort to their departing soul. That hearing was the last sense to go.

"Mother, it's just us here: Joanne, Andrew, and me," she said, She pulled out her copy of *The Tibetan Book of the Dead*.

Somewhere deep in her mother's throat, gurgling bubbled up. "Don't leave," her mother rasped—or so Jules thought. Her voice was so faint now. Hard to hear.

"Are you ready now?" Jules whispered softly, feeling nauseous, though she didn't know why.

Her mother's eyelids were still, but her hand tightened like a vise on Jules's.

There's still time, Jules thought, *to be the good daughter.* So she opened her book—a book for the dying, for transitioning from one rebirth to another, for change—to the page that was folded over. The words she read throbbed, pressing up, behind her collarbone. She remembered how little Max, her student, had described words as having power, the power to surprise. "Words move," he'd told her.

Jules read: "If we cannot stop struggling to hold on to our old life, all our fear and yearning will drag us into yet another painful reality. Let go into the clear light, trust it, merge with it. It is your own true nature, it is home."

Andrew blew his nose. Joanne sobbed.

"At death, we lose everything we thought was real. Unless we can let go of all the things we cherish in our life, we are terrified." Her throat tightened. The words became blurry on the page. She stopped reading.

Then Jules began to sing—"Someone to Watch Over Me," her mother's torch song.

Joanne and Andrew hummed along, halting frequently, choking, quietly patting Jules on the back.

Her mother's memorial service was only the second one Jules had been to. The first was the open-casket affair of her Sicilian grandfather, who'd died over forty-five years ago, the day before Father's Day.

"That's the last thing I want to think of. All those family members and friends gawking down at me in a box. I want to leave this world knowing no one will ever see me again. No makeup mask, prettified to make the gawkers feel more comfortable," their mother had written about her preferences. So the funeral director at Soleil Funeral Home in Seattle complied with her wishes. There were lots of flowers—yellow roses were her favorite, so they were in abundance—and purple drapes over every surface that could be covered. Lots of purple bows, too, with gold sparkles—the school colors of Sarah's middle school. Jules guessed her mother had been thinking of her death for some time, since Sarah was now almost finished with high school.

Jules had been in middle school when she went to her grandpa's funeral. He'd been a fake Catholic, like a lot of Italian men in those days—so, since he had lived with no close relationship to any parish, his requiem Mass had turned out to be quick and conventional, as if the priest just wanted the payment for his effort. She could still remember looking at her grandfather, so nice and powdery—as if he were sleeping in full makeup and costume. She had dug her index fingernail into his folded hands, the one on top, to see what it felt like. His skin was too cold—rubbery like baby doll skin, but stonelike underneath. Like a Stone Boy. That was almost forty years ago, but she still remembered.

Now, as she prepared to bury her mother, Jules understood. *It's not the dead we cry for,* she thought. *We cry for ourselves.*

Their mother had specifically requested a cremation. When Mike's mother had passed away, she had also requested a cremation but his oldest sister, Suzy, had refused. So everyone had been forced to look at the cadaver, the corpse in its open closet. No one had liked it much.

There would be no Catholic requiem for their mother, just as there had been none for their father. Catholics did not "condone" cremations, and their mother did not condone open caskets. A Catholic lay deacon who wore the vestments of a priest—also in purple and gold—would preside over the service, however.

Andrew sat with his two sisters in the front pew on the left, reserved for their mourning family. He fidgeted with his tie as if it were a subway strap that he had to hang on to so he wouldn't stumble and fall. Joanne looked tranquillized, eyes inflamed, and she kept sobbing softly when she thought no one was looking. Jules stared straight ahead at all the purple.

After the brief Lord's Prayer, led by the deacon, their mother's seventy-one-year-old baby brother, Uncle Sal, was the first to speak. Rasping and rattling—just like their mother right before she expired, Jules thought—Sal soldiered on bravely, his voice straining up and down the scale several times. When he was done speaking, elegant in his dark suit and yellow tie, Uncle Sal approached the podium near the low table with the urn of ashes, carved with ornate yellow Romanesque roses and grapes. Joanne had selected the gold and purple pattern from a catalog provided by Soleil's director because, she told Jules, it looked like a skirt that their mother had always loved. The skirt they dressed her in the day she was slipped into the crematorium furnace. A diva to the end.

The ceremony in the committal shelter was simple; no military honors for the veteran's spouse. As their mother's remains were made ready for deposit where their father's ashes lay waiting, Jules thought about the inscription they'd decided upon. Jules had wanted "I'm not chopped liver" for their mother's mausoleum drawer, but Joanne hadn't approved, even though that had always been one of their mother's favorite expressions. "I'm not chopped liver, you know," she would say when she felt she was being ignored—which was often. Her voice still reverberated in Jules's eardrums. But that was one letter too many, anyway. Only seventeen were allowed for the veteran's spouse, empty spaces not counted. The epitaph would have been cut off at "I'm not chopped live." So instead the epitaph read, "To our beloved mom." Two spaces more were allowed, but that wasn't enough to allow them to spell out the word "mother."

Jules left a rose in front of her mother's drawer, a yellow one similar to the Romanesque ones on the urn. Beautiful, without a crease or wrinkle on any of its petals. Her mother would have loved it. Jules's shoulders felt numb. Frozen. Her grief was a subtle one. Like a marinade on some meat. Her parents' ashes were now deposited safely in a drawer in a cemetery she would probably never visit again.

THANKSGIVING

They were approaching the anniversary of her parents' deaths. Nearly one year.

Almost eighteen boxes in total, in three piles, each towering almost seven feet. Jules arched her back, rubbing her aching lumbar, and bent back over the box she was packing. The Mayflower moving van was coming for a nine o'clock pickup the next morning. Sunday. She had been taking trips to Salvation Army all day, cleaning out a life's worth of throwaways. Photos and family memorabilia were nonnegotiable— worth keeping. But everything else . . .

Jules had thought it would be traumatic to discard all the schlock she had accumulated over the years. But it wasn't—not in the least. After boxing up so many cartons, she couldn't even imagine what the contents were. What a relief. An evacuation. A cleansing.

She and Mike had to sell the house in Carmel to recover from all the loans they'd taken out. Jules was moving into a caretaker's cottage in Pebble Beach. In exchange for some light gardening and cat-sitting, Jules would pay below-market rent and have time to write. And she would buy some bright pillows for the futon couch for Zoë, who would stay with her in her new place until her plans for college were finalized.

Jules watched as her daughter picked up a photo album and flipped through it half-heartedly.

Jules walked over and looked over Zoë's shoulder. Photos from Lake Tamsin. Strange. The time and place seemed so distant now; the photos were like memories of someone else's life.

"Geez, Mom, these are seriously old. Retro. You guys all looked like hipsters before hipsters even existed!"

Jules remembered how Zoë had looked on the Internet for photos of old people to represent her great-grandparents for a family tree project in high school. She had had to make up names for ancestors no one knew. She wanted Zoë to have some connection to her roots—to have a sense of control over her life through knowing her ancestors, her old family. Even though her parents and siblings had not been all she had hoped for. But her parents had done nothing to preserve their own past. Her mother had hated photo albums.

Carefully, with a thick-tipped black Sharpie, Jules labeled each box of photos by year. Almost forty years' worth there. She breathed in deeply, feeling grateful for Zoë's big heart. Unlike her mother, Zoë liked exhuming old memories. Her daughter loved going over ancient history—which, for her, was anything that had happened before she was born. Seeing her parents as kids and teenagers was like a sci-fi trip for Zoë, a blast from some strangers' past. Two young people not even remotely connected to who her parents were. That was to be expected.

Jules wiped away a tear.

Zoë laughed and kissed her on the cheek. "Mom, you've always been such a sucker for this stuff. No need to cry!"

It seemed like years since Zoë had had that smile. Jules kept on packing, feeling her daughter's sunshine.

Zoë had been on a mission lately, planning her independence, her future. Now she sat cross-legged on the floor of the almost-empty house and tapped rapid fire on her laptop—applying for financial aid. For next semester's work-study program. Jules's eyes lingered over her daughter's face, and she smiled as she watched her daughter sort through a big stack of college brochures, attaching Post-its with scribbled notes on them to some. Zoë was with her again. And Mike had decided to move closer to be nearby, too. They were all that mattered. Why was he so generous to her after all that had happened?

On her own, Zoë had decided to look at other psychology programs besides Stanford's, particularly the one at the University of Colorado Boulder. Palo Alto had bad memories for her, ones she didn't want to revisit, she had confessed to Jules when she told her she was consider-ing Colorado.

Sergeant Savage had reassured them that Nagy would be in prison a long time. Only two months of Zoë's life had been lost to her crisis. Her daughter was lucky. So was Jules. Thank God for Mike and Joe Santini.

"Mom, did you say you called Financial Aid at the University of Colorado? What did they say?" Zoë asked, fidgeting with flyers and envelopes. Jules caught the enthusiasm in her daughter's voice.

"Oh, honey, I kept careful notes . . . If you can find them in the clutter. The bottom line is that with your grades and a work-study program, you can cover all costs for their psych program. But Stanford is also very open to working with you . . ."

"That's okay, Mom. Not interested in them anymore," was all her daughter said.

Jules gave her shoulder a squeeze. "It's so good to have you here with me. You and your dad. To have him close by, I mean."

Zoë smiled, but squirmed a bit. "I know, Mom. No need to get emo-tional about it."

"I'm going to go box up some stuff in the study," Jules said, walking away before her daughter could see the tears in her eyes.

No more procrastination. No more distractions. Jules reached for some of Mike's books that had been boxed for about a year now, ever since he had moved out. She frowned. His copy of the SEC's Investment Company Act of 1940—Mike's bible for mutual fund legal code—was there. That was odd. Why hadn't he taken it with him? Then again, he never asked about it.

Jules struggled to pull the volume out of the box. When she finally managed to yank it free, a yellowed, handwritten note fell out. She picked it up.

It was a page from Mike's appointment calendar: January 9, 1998, 5:30. T. Schlepp. "For my Jules," Mike had written in pencil in the margin. Another page fell out. From Schlepp's desk calendar—same date, noting a meeting with Mike. *What is this?*

Jules boxed up the Investment Company Act of 1940, then carefully folded the note and two ripped pages, slipped them into her bathrobe, and crawled into her bed. The digital clock flashed 12:45. The Hour of the Mouse in the Buddhist zodiac: the Hour of Secrets. Not so late. Jules was wired from all that packing. Maybe Mike was still up. She had to know. She picked up the phone and called.

Mike answered on the second ring. "Jules? Why are you up?"

She hesitated. She thought of how much she loved waking up in his arms, shaking off the effects of a nightmare. She burrowed her face in the neck of her old nightgown, the one Zoë had given her as a birthday present years ago. After all this time, it was still her favorite. Mike loved it, too.

She willed herself to be direct. "I found your copy of the SEC volume. While I was packing."

"Oh yeah, that. Donate it. I'll pick up the rest of my junk tomorrow, along with anything you'd like me to store for you."

"I know. But . . . something fell out. A torn-out page from your appointment book. Hidden in the space between the leather binding and the sewn pages in the spine. January 9, 1998. Remember now?"

Silence on the other end. Then, finally, "If you had found it before all this, maybe we would still be together."

"I never knew. Never. That you had visited him. In his office that day. For me."

"There's nothing left to say, Jules."

"There's always something more."

"Not now."

"This is our secret, sweetheart. I promise never to tell." Pause. "You just talked, right?"

"More like rage. Spit out lots of words that had been bottled up inside me for way too long. But nothing more."

He was crying now. Their being a couple was no longer realistic, even though she wanted it. Mike had been generous—too generous— for a long, long time. They were done.

"Zoë and I are going to cook up a storm for Thanksgiving. Make silly orange-and-brown turkey cookies, too, like we did when Zoë was little. I'd *really* love to have you there with us. Can you come over? Zoë would love to see us together—carrying on the 'Rockwell' version of the family Thanksgiving. For old times' sake. It will also be close to the one-year anniversary of my parents' deaths." Jules mentally scanned for the most benign topics she could think of to talk to Mike about, but came up blank. So instead she said, "And I miss you . . . so much."

"I can't make any promises," Mike said, his voice thick. "But you know, you *are* the very best mama."

Jules couldn't speak. She knew he knew she was crying now, too. Her quiet crying. Flicking tears, like fleas, from her eyes, she fluffed up her pillow in the dark and pressed her face into it.

Mike had been right all along. About the old battlegrounds. She had thought she was so self-sacrificing—meeting obligations to her parents, bailing them out. But she had been thinking only of them. Not of her own family. She understood that now.

"I do still love you, Mike." She swallowed hard. "Did I tell you I'm psyched about a new book idea? A children's book for dyslexic children. Like Max. He's always made me laugh. What do you think?"

Mike laughed—that strong belly laugh of his that was so contagious. "That's great. It really is. Zoë told me. I'm so happy you didn't give up. Can't wait till the movie comes out."

That had always been their standing joke—that her book would be made into a Hollywood movie and all the women who were afraid they would turn into their mothers would buy tickets and see it over and over again. Mike still knew how to relax her; his voice was like a shiatsu massage for her mind.

"I'll be there for Thanksgiving," Mike said before hanging up, and she heard his kiss on the phone—the kind reserved for family.

BONFIRE

The air was brisk. Winter air. Energizingly cold. The kind only experienced in New England, especially in Vermont. The kind of chill that warmed Andrew, that made him feel good to be alive. He double counted the chairs and place settings for Thanksgiving dinner. Never could keep straight how many were coming. Ashley was an only child of a single mom, so she liked large family gatherings. He guessed she was trying to make up for something she thought she had missed in her childhood. Who wasn't?

There were six dining room chairs that matched the table. Adam, Jake, Ethan, and Abigail made four. Then there was Jason, his son by Ashley. Five. Grissim, his military classmate who had looked him up on Facebook after all these years, made six. Jake's friend, Kyle, was number seven. And he and Ashley, the two of them made nine. Nine people and enough side dishes for at least a dozen—insurance that they wouldn't run out of food. Ashley would be exhausted after all the preparation. Andrew's job was easier. He was just in charge of making the pies and grilling vegetables. And locating extra chairs.

He was in the garage getting out three folding chairs when the door-bell rang. It was four o'clock. Abigail. Damn her. She was always at least an hour early.

"Hi Andy," she said. He cringed at the nickname, as he always had. She gave him a peck on the cheek. It felt like a pinprick, still annoying minutes after it happened. "We brought pumpkin pie." Andrew thought Ashley had told her to bring mashed potatoes. Now they would have two pumpkin pies. "Ethan here made the pie himself. Just for his dad."

She knew Andrew melted at being called Ethan's dad. And Ethan had no one else to call Dad since Jonathan would have nothing to do with his biological son. "With love and gratitude."

He picked Ethan up and raised him high in the air, smiling at the lanky boy.

"Put me down, Dad. I'm too big to be picked up."

Andrew still felt Ethan was his son. He always had loved boys.

Adam, removing chestnut-and-corn stuffing from the turkey, looked up when Andrew entered the kitchen and grinned. Andrew loved the Early American kitchen, the knotty-pine counter and copper-hooded stove. With the food laid out on the counter, it could be a picture-perfect, vintage *Saturday Evening Post* cover.

Adam's cheeks were stuffed with nuts, just like the huge bird he was tenting with foil. It was strange that he was doing this without his brother; the twins always did everything together, to the point that Andrew sometimes felt like he had double vision. It could be disorienting.

"H-h-hey, Dad, what's up? Do y-y-you like the size of this fella?" Adam stuttered. All that money on speech therapy, and he still stuttered like that. Just like Andrew had as a teenager, before GWMA. His father had often mimicked him. How he'd hated that! He would never do that to Adam. He patted himself on the back for having saved for family expenses like speech therapy, braces, things like that. For following his father's advice, but doing it one better.

"Looks great!" Andrew said. "But where's your brother? Shouldn't he be helping you?"

Adam shrugged. "Dunno."

The turkey was enormous, a least twenty pounds, and the aroma was overpowering, seeping out from underneath the aluminum foil. A reminder of family gatherings—of chicken. Andrew assumed it was roasted all the way through, but didn't check; he didn't want to mess with Adam's work. Ashley could deal with it. Anyway, he needed to go out to the woods in back and gather firewood for the great big bonfire they would have later, the kind you could only have in Vermont. It would be at least six or seven feet high. He knew it was illegal to have open fires burning in California, and somehow that made him want to build his own bonfire even more. Do something that Jules couldn't.

His feet crunched on the pathway he had cleared around Halloween time—some of the yellow and red leaves crispy, others limp. He always had his heavy work boots on when he went back there for the soft places in the mud, the puddles that never seemed to dry up—even in the heat of the summer. When it was hot like that, they were habitats for new families of mosquitoes—or, as he liked to call them, the "Vermont state bird." At least during the winter the puddles froze, keeping the mosquitoes at bay until the next thaw.

He walked farther in, towards the creek, which would be frozen by Christmas. He was heading to his usual firewood-gathering place, where fallen tree trunks downed from previous thunderstorms made for good scavenging. But as he approached, he heard whispering. Who could that be? He stopped in his tracks and peered around the bend.

Jake was bundled up in his familiar navy-blue Patagonia and huddled over someone sitting on a log. Andrew couldn't see the guy's face, but he recognized his voice. Kyle. He almost called out his son's name, but something made him stop. He moved behind an old maple tree, and stayed just long enough to see that Kyle was unzipping Jake's jeans. Then quietly, very quietly, Andrew turned around. He crept away, hoping the leaves didn't betray him.

"Hey, why aren't you working on the bonfire?" Ashley shouted through the kitchen window as Andrew stomped the leaves off his boots on the porch and then swiped them along the porcupine boot mud-catcher near the backdoor. She looked at his empty, leather-gloved hands. "Where's the firewood? You haven't even brushed the area to clear a spot!"

Unsure how to respond, Andrew stared back at her.

"Come on. People will be here any second now. Don't you want a bonfire?" Abigail was standing right there next to her, beside the kitchen island, but Ashley always acted like she didn't even exist. "Have Jake and Kyle help you, if you can find them. They seem to have run off. Then go get the box of Roman candles—we can shoot them off after dinner if the weather stays this mild."

Andrew walked inside and his wife smiled and looked into his eyes. "Hey, you look weird. Is something wrong?" she asked, twisting the topaz ring his mother had given her. Andrew still wasn't sure why his mother had insisted Ashley have it, and not Joanne.

Andrew shrugged and said nothing as his wife touched his forehead, eyes curious. He said nothing about what he'd seen.

"Anyway, guess who has already come for dinner?"

"I know," he mumbled, trying to rid himself of the view he had just stumbled upon. A remembrance of things past. Of his own father and secrets he had kept from him. Of wanting his dad's approval so badly.

"I don't mean Abigail and Ethan, silly," Ashley said. "Guess again. It's the one you always talk about. The one friend I have always wanted to meet. Now, after all these years . . ." Her voice trailed off, because there he was, standing before them, filling the entryway.

"Grissim," Andrew said. "My God! You haven't changed in all this time!" He looked so handsome, the way he had always remembered him. Tall, athletic, an attention getter. His Facebook page had no photos. But they had exchanged e-mail and Christmas e-cards over the years. Andrew's pulse drummed inside his head.

"Hey, old bud," Grissim greeted him as he walked into the kitchen. He placed an empty beer stein down on the island and patted him solidly on each shoulder, the way they had always touched in the dorm. But Andrew thought the touch lasted a bit longer than necessary. Ashley had her back to them, mashing potatoes.

"Why, you old fart," Andrew laughed, opening the refrigerator door to get two cans of beer. "Let's catch up on what's going on in your life. You've got to fill me in. I still need to build a bonfire—why don't we go outside and build it together? Male bonding."

Grissim laughed and gestured for Andrew to lead the way.

Outside, the sun was dropping quickly. The skies were burnished, aflame like the bonfire soon would be. A reminder that autumn had grown up. Grissim started for the woods. "No, no, not in there. Too dark now." Andrew hesitated, then touched Grissim's sleeve. "We should be able to find enough scrub wood right around here if we both look."

"Remember the old days, Andrew? When we'd go out into the woods, just to have a blast?" Grissim asked as he bent over and gathered kindling into his arms. His arms reminded Andrew of how Grissim had comforted him in the shower.

Before Andrew could respond, he heard the rustling of leaves. Cracking of twigs. Then Jake briskly walked out of the impending darkness and straight over to Grissim. He hugged him, resting his head on his shoulder. His signature hug. "Grissim. You're Grissim. You must be! I didn't think you really existed."

Grissim grinned until his face looked overstretched. "Jake, right? I never thought your dad would get married. Didn't think any woman would have him. And then he hit the jackpot with first Abigail and now Ashley. To say nothing of four great boys. Twins, no less. I'm so jealous. I always wanted to be a father."

Then Grissim noticed Kyle, who was hanging back, and his eyes met and held Kyle's. *The way they used to hold mine,* Andrew thought.

"And who is this handsome devil?" Grissim said, that rakish voice of his ringing out. Kyle was slightly built, and barely average height. Grissim's type. Like Andrew had been before he had grown his paunch. They had both shamelessly flirted with each other, but only on campus.

"We've set a place for you, Kyle, if you don't have other plans. Probably should have cleared it first with your family. Sorry, should have thought about that ahead of time." Kyle didn't have a good relationship with his father, so Andrew had assumed that another chair and place setting would be in order. "You can call them, if you like. Or even have two dinners," he said, winking.

Kyle didn't laugh. The kid had never felt comfortable around him. Andrew didn't know why. He'd have to change that. Kyle was a good kid, and he was good for his son. *Did my dad know about Grissim?* he wondered. He didn't think so. Suspected, maybe.

"Say, why don't we all sit down and I'll show you how your dad and I used to compete over tequila shots," Grissim said. "Would you like to see if he can still hold his booze like he used to? Back in the day?" He seemed wound up, so much younger than Andrew felt.

Bonfire assembled, they headed inside, and Andrew saw that both Kyle and Jake had taken to Grissim right away. They were slapping each other on the back and laughing like old friends.

Soon they were all seated at the table, food overflowing on the plates before them. Andrew tossed back the shot Grissim handed him and thought of the old, faded photo of the two of them at George Washington Military Academy, and of Grissim's message on the back. Where was that photo, anyway?

"So, old man, what have you been doing in your spare time? When you're not frightening patients with that damn drill, that is?" Grissim asked. He was good natured as ever.

"Well, I've been asked to volunteer in the local AIDS clinic because they need a dentist and apparently no one wants to touch an AIDS patient's mouth." Andrew looked down at his boots and spied a bit of mud clumped on the bottom cleats. He leaned down to pick at it.

"So you're helping your brothers, man. That's good. Feels good. We all need to stick together." Grissim leaned down and kissed him on the mouth—in front of everyone. Andrew kissed him back.

Ashley looked a bit surprised, but she recovered quickly. "More mashed potatoes?" she asked, passing the dish.

ANOTHER LEAGUE

Joanne's business loan had covered a portion of her parents' debts—the part Jules hadn't been able to cover. And now that her divorce was finalized, her finances were going to be better, much better. The sale of her and Al's house would pay off both her first and second mortgages and repay the loan she'd taken out for her plastic surgery. Thank God there had been equity in her house in Edmonds.

"Seligman's fees are exorbitant," Joanne had complained to Jules the last time she had called her asking for money. "In the old days, I would have just gone to bed with him. But I can't do that anymore"

"So, what's your plan then? To get out of debt?" Jules had said, unmoved. "I can't pay your debts anymore, Jo. No way. I have my own debts and our daughter to think about."

"You never used to be so bitchy!" Joanne had said, growing teary. "What's going on?"

"I'm sorry, Jo," Jules had said, "but I'm not doing you any favors by continuing to bail you out."

And then she'd hung up.

Joanne had felt panic welling up, but then she'd pulled herself together. *Fine,* she'd told herself. *I can do this on my own. For once. I won't need my sister.*

Joanne reminded herself of this as her new sign—a neon aqua and orange orb—came into view. She had moved A Real Gem; it was now right next to Yellow Brick Road, the store where her mother used to volunteer. Cheaper rent, more foot traffic. And just in time for the biggest holiday shopping season. New beginnings. This would be a new year for her business for sure.

Her sleigh bells rang, and someone she vaguely recognized came through the door. Perhaps one of her mother's friends.

"Why hello, Joanne. I don't think you remember me. I'm Francine. I used to work with your mother at Yellow Brick Road, before I broke my foot and moved into SafeHarbour."

Now Joanne remembered her, but she didn't recall Francine dressing so fashionably. Perhaps it was her mother's influence on her.

"We missed your mother so much at the store after she passed."

Joanne hated the word "passed." What was that supposed to mean? Passed by? Passed into oblivion? Still, she needed to be friendly. Good for business. And she was hoping to generate enough income to meet her current expenses soon. She hoped she could help Jules now for having carried their parents' debts. At least she would try. After all that Jules had gone through. Her sister—was it because she was the oldest?—had always wanted to be in control, but what had it gotten her?

Joanne's new boyfriend, Matt, was a moron—he loved to play the violin at funerals and secretly still nurtured sexual fantasies for his ex-girlfriend, who had never officially divorced her husband, supposedly because of his comprehensive medical and dental insurance. Joanne hoped to find a less self-absorbed boyfriend in the near future, but so far she hadn't had much luck. And without her mother as a witness, nothing seemed as meaningful. Still, she was thinking of dumping Matt, who liked to run his hand down each of her cheeks before they had sex. "Let the fingers do the walking," he liked to tease her. Called it foreplay.

Matt also liked to take a flashlight and stare behind her ears first, then her hairline above her forehead, and finally the nape of her neck—where her surgery scars were. At first she hadn't minded it when Matt had insisted on slathering her scar gel ointment on for her. But now it bothered her how obsessed he was with her imperfections. "Maybe they'll go away eventually," he often said. "Or at least fade." He sometimes compared her skin to her daughters' silky complexions, too, which definitely worried her.

"Honey," Francine said, breaking into her thoughts, "ever since your mother died, you haven't been wearing as much makeup. Is that because you're still mourning, almost a year now, you know—or are you just relaxing a bit?"

Joanne ignored her comment and flashed her a smile. Francine, looking vaguely disappointed, bent over the glass counter to admire her display.

"Would you like to look at our new merchandise? A bracelet perhaps?"

"Well, you know, I do have a male admirer at SafeHarbour now," Francine said.

Now Joanne remembered. Her mother always had said that Francine would die a lonely spinster. *Guess she got that one wrong.*

After the sale, Joanne looked in the mirror she had installed in the back office, a magnified one that allowed her to apply her eyeliner, red lipstick, and two foundations—one for wrinkles and one for powder—flawlessly. She always did it exactly the same way—starting at the neck and then working up, massaging with a light touch, making sure not to pull the skin—but it had been a long time since she'd gone through the routine. Her mother's death had sapped her of her vanity; it had taken her almost a year to get back to feeling enthusiastic about all the effort required to primp. *I haven't taken this stuff out for so long, it's probably rancid by now,* she thought.

She stared more deeply at the mirror, to the point where her reflection seemed to dissolve. She zoomed in on her pores, her eyelids, her neck. Joanne thought about Matt, Stephen before him, Gus, and then Dean before him. Four in the past two years. All losers.

She abandoned her mirror and, sitting down at her computer, she called up Alan Fox, the consultant who had installed her Microsoft Office software the day she moved the store. He had been helpful.

"Hey you," she started as she heard him pick up. "This is Joanne. Remember me? You made an office call to set up my computer so I could start using Excel for my business ledger?" Not exactly her type, her mother would say. Ten years older, by no means handsome. Kind of geeky. But considerate. Patient. Respectful. Alan had walked her through the rudimentary bookkeeping using Excel and hadn't charged her for the entire time he spent with her. He'd explained things well, too. No question was too stupid. He wasn't a know-it-all like Al. Maybe her mom was wrong about guys like him. Just as she was wrong about giving that ring to Ashley. Her mother had broken her promises.

"I'm still setting up my books and want to create some simple formulas for tax purposes. So I can do things by myself." She thought of her sister. "I'd like to get my income statements entered as soon as possible, since the holiday shopping season's just starting. What would you say to making a house call tonight? I could fix you dinner—if you're interested, that is."

What would her mother say? That he definitely wasn't in her league. That's what she would have said. But maybe it was time to try another league—one in which Alan Fox could be a major player. She felt comfortable around him. He wouldn't take out a flashlight and the scar gel.

MOMMY'S LITTLE HELPER

Piles of sketches surrounded the bed, covered all the surfaces in the room: Jules's small desk, the chair and end table, and the floor of her caretaker's cottage. She thought about little Max as she tapped rapidly on her laptop. *In the Night Kitchen*. But the scene would be different: A little girl carrying a milk bottle for her mommy—this time a plastic, unbreakable jug. Her mommy sitting on each step with her, holding her hand and helping her hold the bottle. Both of them laughing and pretending they were on a roller coaster—delighted, happy. Bump, bump—safely bouncing down the stairs. Bump, bump.

Her ability to draw and sketch had never gone much beyond doodling. Joanne was the serious artist. But Jules sketched line figures with ease, almost subconsciously, as she daydreamed about those stairs from her own early years. When she looked down, she saw the doodles and realized that Zoë was the little girl, and she was the mommy. They were wild, gleeful, carefree. She continued with her charcoal until her fingers were so covered with carbon, some of the lines started smearing.

She had shown some of her earlier charcoal drawings to her students, and the kids had loved them. They'd made them laugh—especially the black-and-white sketches of kids getting dressed and undressed in their pajamas. Drawings of their bare bottoms and genitals. Like little Mickey in *In the Night Kitchen*. But maybe she would play with watercolors for the final version. The compositions needed to feel more organic, flow easily, not be bound by the lines. They should be spontaneous and unexpected. The colors should come to life and then dissolve, float away into pools of beautiful pastels, shimmering prisms of light.

Mommy's Little Helper would soon be in its final rewrite, she promised herself—imposing her own deadline. The publisher she had spoken to had admired her initial sketches and hoped to create a toy line based upon the story. Mommy-daughter dolls dressed alike, holding hands. Computerized games based on the story that could be played on mobile devices, or maybe a chip embedded inside the dolls that would allow them to talk, quote from the story. They wanted to do a publicity blitz next year in time for Christmas.

She should call Mike to invite him over for a drink, to toast to her book. Joke about movie rights for *Mommy's Little Helper.* Who knew— maybe it would actually happen. An animated movie from Pixar about a little girl who wanted to help her mommy and felt joy in being a child. Bouncing, bouncing down the stairs, riding a roller coaster to the clouds. The mother blissed out by the sound of her daughter's laughter.

Break time, she thought. She set aside her colored pencils and charcoal crayons and looked at the ten pages of illustrations she had outlined. A good beginning for a storyboard. Her story would avoid the troublesome letters that dyslexic children struggled with most, like *b* and *d.* *S* and *z* were troublesome letters, too. But exciting ones. Letters that move.

ACKNOWLEDGMENTS

M any people helped make this novel a reality. The tenacity required to be a writer can only be sustained through the generous support and encouragement offered by many others who wish to see a story told. My deepest gratitude extends to all who expressed an interest in *Things Unsaid*.

I would like to express my appreciation to authors who offered their guidance and expertise with humor, efficiency, and insightfulness: Caroline Leavitt, Phyllis Theroux, and Nora Cavin.

Thank you to my first readers who critiqued my work and urged me to keep on writing: Maryann Bartram, Susie Berteaux, Evelyn Klein, Tobi Ludwig, Sunny Scott, David Spiselman, and Patty Thompson.

My publisher, She Writes Press, particularly Brooke Warner, Caitlyn Levin, Krissa Lagos, and Paula Brisco guided me every step of the way to make this novel the best it could be. And a special thanks to Matilda Butler for recommending She Writes Press in the first place!

Most of all, thanks to my family, whose faith in me and my love of storytelling has not only made my writing blissful but also has made my life an adventure with them.

ABOUT THE AUTHOR

© Douglas A. Paul

Diana Y. Paul was born in Akron, Ohio and is a graduate of Northwestern University, with a degree in both psychology and philosophy, and of the University of Wisconsin–Madison, with a PhD in Buddhist studies. She is the author of three books on Buddhism, one of which has been translated into Japanese and German (*Women in Buddhism*, University of California Press), and her short stories have appeared in a number of literary journals. She lives in Carmel, CA with her husband and two cats, Neko and Mao. Visit her website at dianaypaul.com to learn more.

SELECTED TITLES FROM SHE WRITES PRESS

She Writes Press is an independent publishing company
founded to serve women writers everywhere.
Visit us at www.shewritespress.com.

Play for Me by Céline Keating
$16.95, 978-1-63152-972-6
Middle-aged Lily impulsively joins a touring folk-rock band, leaving
her job and marriage behind in an attempt to find a second chance at
life, passion, and art.

Shelter Us by Laura Diamond
$16.95, 978-1-63152-970-2
Lawyer-turned-stay-at-home-mom Sarah Shaw is still struggling to
find a steady happiness after the death of her infant daughter when she
meets a young homeless mother and toddler she can't get out of her
mind—and becomes determined to rescue them.

A Cup of Redemption by Carole Bumpus
$16.95, 978-1-938314-90-2
Three women, each with their own secrets and shames, seek to make
peace with their pasts and carve out new identities for themselves.

Duck Pond Epiphany by Tracey Barnes Priestley
$16.95, 978-1-938314-24-7
When a mother of four delivers her last child to college, she has to
decide what to do next—and her life takes a surprising turn.

Clear Lake by Nan Fink Gefen
$16.95, 978-1-938314-40-7
When psychotherapist Rebecca Lev's father dies under suspicious circumstances, she becomes obsessed with discovering what happened to him.

*A Tight Grip: A Novel about Golf, Love Affairs, and Women of a Certain
Age* by Kay Rae Chomic $16.95, 978-1-938314-76-6
As forty-six-year-old golfer Jane "Par" Parker prepares for her next
tournament, she experiences a chain of events that force her to reevalu-
ate her life.